SECRETS OF THE VOL´AERAI

SECRETS

OF THE

VOL'AERAI

SETH MYHRE

ISBN: 979-8-9911507-0-5 (paperback)
ISBN: 979-8-9911507-1-2 (hardback)

Book Cover by Sadia Shahid
Edited by Michelle Gean
Illustrations by Seth Myhre
First edition 2024

To the Author and Sustainer of Life

Two sides are warring over the control of our souls. One reminds us of our past and sucks life away; the other promises a future and breathes life into us. Regardless of our past, it only takes one decision to begin a new future.

CONTENTS

Prologue 1
1: Choice 7
2: Opportunity...21
3: Journey..31
4: Instinct..45
5: Coalesce 55
6: Ascension..67
7: Reunion...81
8: Preparation 95
9: Conflict 111
10: Skirmish 125
11: Face-off...141
12: Alliance 157
13: Defiance 169
14: Migration 181
15: Relieved...197
16: Promise 211
17: Voyage 223
18: Portent..237
19: Candor 247
20: Anguish 261
21: Rebirth 273
Epilogue 287

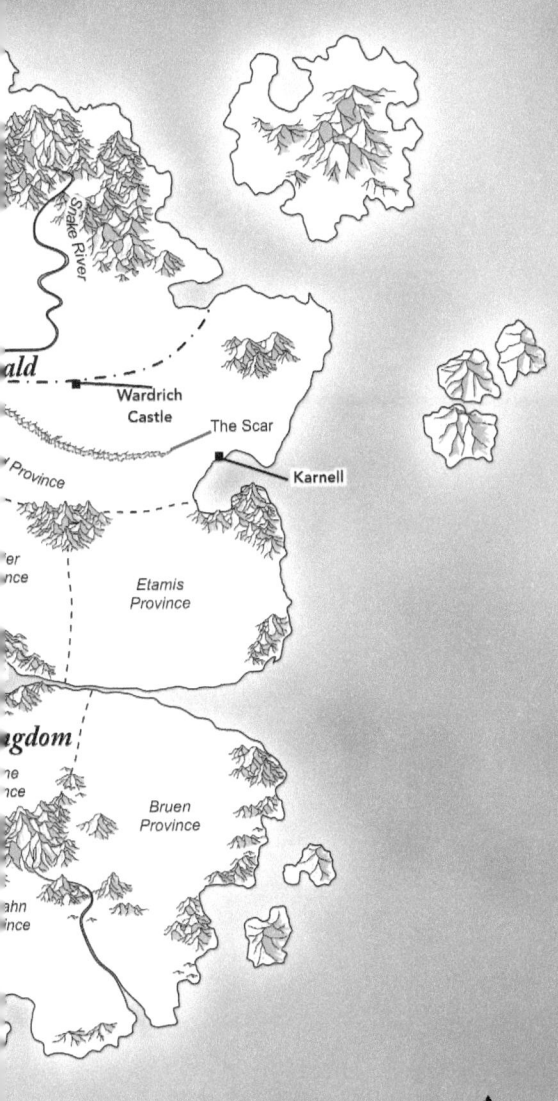

Snake River

ald

Wardrich
Castle

The Scar

Karnell

Province

Etamis
Province

er
nce

gdom

ne
nce

Bruen
Province

ahn
nce

Sardus Sea

Dashran

Tashtari
Islands

PROLOGUE

"BY THE TIME THIS LETTER ARRIVES, the celebration of your sixty-third year will have passed," King Dhar dictated while pacing in a ponderous manner as Sargon wrote every word; the only noise was the sound of a scratching quill. "I hope it has been a good year and that many more come your way." Dhar stopped pacing and turned toward Sargon. "Do you have that?"

"Yes, Sire."

"Good. End it in the usual manner."

Sargon dipped the quill into the ink and rapped it on the lip of the jar, making a slight tinking sound. He scratched out the final words before holding the letter in the light shining through the window and read the letter back to the king to ensure he hadn't made a mistake.

"Impeccable as always, Sargon."

Sargon folded the letter and wrapped it in a ribbon before dripping wax upon it for the king to press his signet ring into.

"Summon a courier to take this small package and letter to Lord Darrick in Wardrich Castle."

"Right away, Your Majesty."

Relvin sat on the edge of his assigned bed on the barracks' second floor, pulling his dagger blades over a whetstone when his captain called for him from the door.

"Relvin, get ready. A courier is waiting for an escort in the courtyard," Erdon said.

"Why so soon? I returned last night," Relvin said.

"You are the only guard of the lot that isn't sick, drunk, or assigned."

"Health and sobriety have their downsides," Relvin said as he put his daggers away and gathered his things.

"Don't pretend you aren't happy to be back on the road. You'll be going to Wardrich."

"To the north? That's a first."

Relvin grabbed his belongings and walked through the doorway. He exited the barracks as Captain Erdon's voice thundered from the windows, "Get up, you drunkards! Think your hangover is bad? Wait until you see what I have planned for you…"

Relvin was almost to the courtyard when he heard the voice of his least favorite courier.

"What is taking so long?" Morgon asked while sitting on his horse in the keep's courtyard.

"I don't know, my lord," the stable boy said, but it would've been better if he kept silent.

"Of course you don't. You are as competent as whomever they sent to guard me," Morgon said before seeing Relvin approach with his saddle bag and rolled bedding. "It would be you, Relvin. Where's Jorde?"

"My apologies for the delay, but Jorde came down with a fever last night," Relvin said.

The stable boy took the guard's belongings from him and secured them to the horse's saddle as Relvin greeted the mare while stroking its neck.

"What about Daxis?" Morgon asked.

"Daxis was assigned to another courier, and before you ask, the rest of the guards were up until the wee hours of the morning and are too drunk to stay in the saddle. I'm your only option unless you wish to journey alone."

Morgon responded with a low growl. The stable boy finished working with the belongings and reclaimed the reins from the guard. Relvin wandered to the greenery at the courtyard's edge and cupped one of the white roses in his hand while stooping to take in the sweet aroma through his nose. He closed his eyes and exhaled for several seconds before letting go of the flower and returning to the courier.

"It baffles me that you insist on smelling the roses each time you leave," Morgon said. "They always smell the same."

"While pleasant, the smell is of little importance to my reason for the tradition, but a curmudgeon like you wouldn't appreciate the reason even if I told you."

Relvin took the reins from the stable boy, thanked him for his help while mounting his horse, and guided the mare past the guards at the gate. Morgon rode his horse close behind.

Karah crawled on the ground in the alley as she gathered the coins thrown around her. Picking up the last coin, she discovered that the man had paid her half of what he had promised.

Karah looked to the sky, crying as something inside said, *"Kaden would be ashamed...worthless whore."*

"I'm sorry, Kaden," Karah said. "I don't know what else to do. We haven't eaten for two days. Please don't be angry."

Karah sniffed and wiped her tears before rising from her knees. She adjusted her dress and walked from the alley through a side street leading to the main road out of eastern Islatria. The capital city had seemed like a dream come true when she and her late husband Kaden were married. The main streets were kept clean, buildings were well-maintained, lawfulness was enforced, and commerce was booming. Although the events leading to Kaden's death weren't under her control, she was beginning to think her in-laws were right to throw her to the streets for being cursed. Karah and her son now huddled with the other poor and homeless in hidden nooks and crannies away from the abuse and judgmental gazes. They watched the unscrupulous prey upon others while dodging the guards. If they were lucky, the rich and powerful gave to the poor to appear generous, but their wealth was gained by treating people as chattels bought and sold on a whim.

"Let's get something to eat," Karah said, helping her six-year-old son, Shadir, stand from where he had waited for her return.

"The man gave you money?" Shadir asked.

"Yes," Karah said, glad her son didn't know what she had to do to get the coins.

"Can we get apples?"

"Of course, they're your favorite."

Karah handed Shadir's crutch to him, and they shuffled to the busy markets. The chaotic noises of bartering merchants, creaky horse-drawn wagons upon cobblestone, the rhythmic clang of metal being molded by heavy hammers, and shouts for people to make way for passing lords and ladies got louder as they neared the market street. She bought bread from a nearby baker and handed it to her son before they crossed the street to the fruit stalls. Karah purchased several apples with her last coins, and as she turned to give one to Shadir, two riders caught her eye as they approached. Her heart skipped a beat when she glimpsed the face of the young guard.

"Kaden?" Karah asked as she stepped into the crowd.

"Watch where you're going!" someone said after Karah bumped into them.

Karah was jolted back to her surroundings but couldn't stop the apples from escaping her arms and dropping to the ground. Her heart dropped as she watched each apple get trampled by the crowd, but then she spied an apple rolling down the street, bruised but whole. She chased after it, determined to let her son have the treat she promised. However, Karah watched in horror as the apple was crushed beneath a wagon wheel when she reached to pick it up. With the last of her few coins from the morning gone, she dreaded telling her son he wouldn't get an apple.

Karah cried in the middle of the street with people jostling her from all sides as the words *"Shadir is better without you...you're cursed"* came to mind.

The jostling stopped as a horse snorted in front of Karah, startling her. Wondering why the rider hadn't passed by like everyone else, she looked up and was met with the kind hazel eyes of the young guard from earlier. His wavy chocolate hair and stubbled beard were similar to her late husband's looks, but now she wasn't sure how she could've mistaken him for Kaden.

"Your son is lucky to have you," the guard said, handing Karah a small leather pouch. "Have a good day, madam."

The guard coaxed his horse forward before Karah came out of her stunned silence. The courier scowled at Karah as he passed, but Karah was distracted by the weight of the pouch. She opened it and was met with the glitter of gold instead of silver or copper coins when she looked inside; more money than she had ever possessed.

Karah took the encounter as a sign Kaden was looking out for them. She dried her eyes and clutched the coin pouch close to her chest as she returned to her son. After repurchasing apples from the fruit seller, Karah herded her son eastward to follow the guard's path out of the city.

"Why are we going this way?" Shadir asked as he hobbled on his crutch and was handed an apple.

"To have an adventure," Karah said.

"Will it be dangerous?" Shadir asked, taking a bite of the apple and savoring the juicy morsel as he chewed.

"I foresee monsters and dragons, brave knight, but I pray thee not to forsake this noble quest..."

Shadir listened to his mother's tale while they walked down the street to the Dawn gate, and let his imagination take him to the land of make-believe, far from the world he knew.

The sun's rays warmed the well-weathered tree near Sargon's window as its tender leaves unfurled from their buds, a breeze tickling them. Many spies had been caught and executed for attempting to intercept secure communications, but no one suspected the tree had listened to every nearby whisper for generations. The trees trembled as they discussed the letter's contents and passed it along to warn the Wispryn Weald before the courier could deliver the dispatch. All their hopes rested on what Relvin would choose to do because none of the kings or queens, princes or princesses, lords or ladies, couriers, or emissaries who had passed through the keep's courtyard had a task more vital than his.

Chapter 1
CHOICE

LORD DARRICK TERSAN WAS DRESSED in his riding clothes, enjoying a cup of wine as the morning rays shined into his bed chambers. He looked northward from the balcony of the Wardrich keep, built on the border of the Nemoyid province and the Wispryn Weald. The Vol'aerai were rumored to dwell in this ancient forest, but they had kept to themselves for hundreds of years. Few believed they existed outside of fantastic fables of witchcraft, blood sacrifices, moving trees, and men turning into beasts, often told to frighten children into behaving. Strange animal encounters and weird feelings prevented most from venturing far within the forest, and the few who did never returned. However, folklore about the Wispryn Weald had little effect on how Darrick conducted his life.

A knock sounded on the heavy oak door of the lord's bed chambers, and the voice of one of his guards came through from the other side.

"The women are here for your selection, my Lord."

"Send them in."

The hinges groaned as the door was opened, and six women walked through the open portal into the room. A middle-aged and pleasantly plump woman named Cecelia, who managed Lord Darrick's companions, entered first. She stepped aside as five young women shuffled in like cattle to the slaughter and lined up with bowed heads to be inspected. The women were silent and kept their gaze on the ground as the lord's stout figure approached, holding his cup of wine.

"Strip!" Darrick said, causing Cecelia to wince and the women to startle at the abruptness.

The young women disrobed, losing all dignity that the clothes provided; they shook as Lord Darrick paced in front and eyed them up and down like pieces of meat. He forced their heads up one by one to see their faces and prodded their bodies until he selected the oldest of the five, a petite twenty-one-year-old redhead.

"She is…" Darrick said to Cecelia, even though he was still eyeing the young woman's naked frame.

"Yes, my Lord. I can attest to her purity."

"Bring her to my chambers tonight," he said before finishing the wine in his cup.

"Yes, my Lord."

Lord Darrick dismissed them with a wave of his hand, and the women grabbed their clothes and clutched them to their bodies as they exited the room, lowering their eyes as they passed the guards' lustful gazes. Darrick smirked when he saw the tears flowing down the face of his chosen entertainment as she was led away with Cecelia's arm around her. She was his property, and he would do what he liked with her, no matter what anyone thought. With his first agenda item completed, Lord Darrick strolled off to join the hunting party with a smile; the day was starting well for him.

Relvin Moriss mulled over his choices as he approached a split in the road. Due north was a lengthy rocky upthrust cutting the earth known as "The Scar," running for many miles to the east and west. A forest of trees grew around it like a bandage protecting it from infection. He brought his horse to a stop as he arrived at the crossroads where he could choose to go east, west, or north via a narrow passage through the scar.

Relvin turned and asked his companion, "Which way should we take?"

"The eastern path. It leads through Harholl, where we can rest and get a decent meal," Morgon said.

"But that will take two more days."

"It wasn't expressed to me that delivery was urgent. Besides, the northern passage is prone to ambush."

"Where is your sense of adventure, Morgon?"

"I'm neither a young man nor a fool, Relvin."

"Though your years are many, you're a fool to think adventure cares about your age when it calls. I'll ask our other companions to decide our path," Relvin said before leaning over to whisper into his horse's ear.

The mare nickered and took a few paces to the north. Relvin gave his horse a pat on the neck as he sat up.

"The horse says to take the northern path."

"The reins are there for you to lead the dumb horse, not for you to be dragged by it," Morgon said, gesturing towards the horse with his hands.

The mare looked at Morgon and snorted before turning away again.

"I agree," Relvin said to his horse as he stroked its neck, "He's an insufferable man. If you wish, I'll duel him on your behalf. I wouldn't want you to get your hooves dirty."

The mare let out a neigh similar to a laugh.

"I'm old, not deaf," Morgon said.

"For insulting my horse, you can take the rest of the journey alone or follow where the horse leads. I have reached my limit in accommodating you." Relvin coaxed his horse to walk the northern path, to the courier's chagrin. "I guess you don't want that early delivery bonus."

Relvin heard the creak of leather as Morgon gripped the reins tighter and growled before spurring his horse to follow.

"If I die, it will be on your head."

"And if you get that bonus, it will be because of me. I'm content with either outcome," Relvin said without turning around.

Morgon muttered curses as the path led them into the forest around the Scar, but Relvin was too wrapped up in his surroundings to notice. Sunlight filtered through the canopy and cast a warm glow as the soft clip-clop of the horse's hooves sounded from the dirt. Oak, pine, cedar, mushroom, and wildflower scents hung in the air, stirred up by the previous night's rainstorm. Squirrels and chipmunks scampered up the trees, chattering after their friends as they played games and searched for food. Choirs of birds competed over who sang their favorite songs the best. Rabbits followed their noses to the tastiest roots and greens while watching for anything new and exciting. Unlike the cantankerous courier he escorted, Relvin relished his time on the open road away from the greed for wealth, power, pleasure, death, and time that consumed many citizens of the Islatrian kingdom.

Relvin slowed the horse's pace as they approached the natural hall leading between two large rock faces of the Scar, only wide enough for one rider at a time. Royal guards were standing on either side of the opening. Relvin knew of no official posting in this area, but he didn't raise any alarm. Relvin stopped his horse in front of the guards.

"Good day!" Relvin said. "Is there any danger ahead?"

"Good day, travelers!" The guards said. "We need to see your papers before you can pass."

"Certainly, anything for the king's guards," Relvin said and handed their papers over for inspection.

"Official courier of the palace, I see," the guard said, inspecting the papers. "Good thing you have an escort. We heard several reports of thieves in these woods, but fear not, we've been sent to ensure safe passage along this trail."

"Guards doing their jobs instead of pointless audacity," Morgon said in a stab at Relvin, who didn't take the bait.

The soldier returned their papers, wished them a safe journey, and let them continue into the narrow opening; Relvin took the lead. The horses' hoof sounds striking the ground were amplified as they echoed between the stony walls. A flock of birds made a ruckus above them as they took to the air, drawing Relvin's attention to a flash of movement.

"As I suspected, they have a runner up there to alert the team on the other side of incoming travelers," Relvin said.

"Are you happy now? I told you not to take this road," Morgon said. "Now we'll both die."

"Oh, quit your whining. Fall back and continue at a saunter. Let me spring the trap."

Morgon pulled back on the reins to slow his horse. Once sufficient distance had formed, Relvin dismounted at a point where the fissure widened and smacked the mare's hind quarters. He extracted two large daggers from their sheaths on his hips before running as fast as he could behind his horse. At the other end of the narrow canyon, Relvin's horse exited and veered off out of view. Two marauders emerged from either side of the opening as Relvin arrived.

Among several buildings east of Wardrich keep was a place known as the Flower Garden. Inside the two-story atrium of the building, several ladies reclined on lounge chairs while conversing. Others entertained men in private side alcoves. While still more rested in their bed chambers behind the colonnaded hall, which wrapped around the second floor.

Within the chamber at the top of the stairs opposite the entrance, Cecelia Hobber prepared the young red-headed woman for the evening. Her melodious voice filled the room with soothing songs to calm her down as she braided white flowers into the maiden's hair. Cecelia watched as tears gently rolled down the young lady's cheeks.

"I know your sadness, but it would not do to have you crying in front of the lord tonight, my dear. Tears will not persuade him to be gentle. It may not be possible to hide your distress, but don't give him the satisfaction; he takes pleasure in causing pain."

Cecelia remembered her times in Darrick's bed and shuddered at the memories. Her experience taught her to empathize with the women in her care; she was like a grandmother to them.

"Oh, what a joy it would be to see Lord Darrick get what he is due for being so cruel," Cecelia said.

Cecelia's face beamed at the thought, and a chuckle escaped her lips. She saw a light break through the darkness that clouded the maiden's face as she smiled slightly.

"There you are, my dear. Find the strength you have inside, and never let it go. It will get you through the hard times and prevent the darkness from taking over your soul. Much can be taken from you, but the most important things can only be taken if you let them."

Cecelia sang another song, which stirred up feelings of home for both women as she braided the silky smooth hair in her hands.

"You sang this song as you embraced me the day I was brought here as a child," the maiden said.

"Oh, did I?" Cecelia said with a smile and sighed. "It makes me feel like I'm back in my mother's arms before Lord Darrick bought my sister and I. I can still see my parents' faces as we were carted away."

"Which lady is your sister?"

"She is one of many who never lived past this night."

"Sorry."

Cecelia finished the braid she was working on and brought a stool to sit in front of the young woman.

"There is little chance that I can stop the events of this night, but as I've told countless women before you, if I see an opportunity to help you escape the life you would be subjected to in this castle, I would take it in a heartbeat, even if it brings harm to myself. I can endure anything he does to me if my actions bring about good."

"Thank you for being so kind to me all these years, Cecelia," the maiden said as she hugged her. "It has kept my hope alive when otherwise I would've had none."

"You're most welcome, my dear," Cecelia said. "It makes me so happy to hear you say that. I don't like my role here, nor what they put us through, but to let that define who I am would be worse than dying." Cecelia rested her hand upon the face of the young woman. "I will be awake all night waiting to embrace you when you return, and I will mourn the loudest if you don't."

"Rookie mistake," Relvin mumbled, slashing the two marauder's throats at either side of the opening before they could correct their error in judgment.

Relvin leaped at his next target without hesitation, giving the remaining marauders no time to process that their trap had failed. The thieves were spread out and easy to pick off as he dodged their amateur attacks. This was a deadly dance he knew all the steps to. The gang leaders put up a decent fight, which increased the morale of the remaining members as they shouted encouragement from the sidelines. However, the underlings' hopes were shattered as Relvin pulled from his years of military training to take advantage of their lack of team coordination. The last two marauders fled, but they didn't get far before collapsing to the ground, writhing in agony after Relvin threw a dagger into each of their backs.

Relvin extracted his daggers from the two runners and ended their lives mercifully. He heard the squeaking leather of the Morgon's saddle as he cleaned his blades and hands of blood. He stood and turned to greet the courier as he returned his daggers to their sheaths.

"Perfect timing!" Relvin said as the courier approached, seemingly impressed with Relvin's prowess. "Let me get my horse so we can continue our journey."

Relvin's mare raised her head when he called and trotted from the sweet grass she had found in a nearby field. Relvin stuffed as many apples as possible from a nearby crate into his saddlebag but offered the best one to his horse, stroking her neck while she chewed the sweet treat. After mounting, Relvin led the mare towards the other side of the clearing to continue their journey, where Morgon joined him. While riding through the narrow exit from the clearing, a few lookouts with drawn swords made a foolhardy attempt to stop them from leaving.

"Your companions we passed are lying in puddles of blood," Relvin said. "Are you sure you wish to join them?" The men looked at each other before lowering their weapons as they stepped aside. "I commend you for choosing to extend your life. Clear out. I won't be lenient if you're still here when I return."

"Thank you for your mercy," the men said before turning tail to run away.

After almost an hour of riding, they cleared the tree line on the other side of the scar.

"See, that wasn't so bad," Relvin said. "Now, we have a straight ride to our destination. If we pick up the pace, we should be there before evening."

The shadows were long on the ground as the night watchmen prepared Wardrich Castle for the evening. The gates had been shut and barred, and the torches were lit when the tower guards announced the approach of two riders. All the known guests coming to the Lord's banquet were already in the great hall, so the two approaching riders made them leery even while standing within the castle's walls.

"Halt! State your name and business, or be on your way," the guard captain called down to the horsemen as they stopped before the gate.

"I, Morgon, am here to see Lord Darrick and deliver official correspondence from the king. My guard is Relvin."

"Open the gates!" The captain ordered his men before addressing the horsemen, "I'm sure Lord Darrick would be pleased to receive you this evening."

The gates groaned as they opened, and the captain, flanked by a couple of guards with halberds, stepped out to inspect the riders' papers before admitting them. Satisfied with their documents, the captain returned them.

"I will have the stable boy take care of your horses as I bring you to Lord Darrick. Follow me."

The two guards stepped aside to let the riders follow after their captain before taking the rear and closing the gates. Morgon and Relvin rode into the courtyard, where the stable boy took hold of the horses' reins as the riders dismounted. Morgon removed a sealed parcel from his saddlebag before joining Relvin and leaving their horses to be led to the stable. The captain escorted them to the Lord's private meeting chambers, where he was finishing up a few matters before the evening meal.

"I present Morgon, a courier of the king, and his guard, Relvin, to you, my Lord," the guard said before standing aside to allow the two visitors to enter.

"You may go," Darrick said, and the captain left to return to his post.

"I extend the King's greetings, Lord Darrick, and relinquish this package to you," Morgon said as he stepped towards the desk, placing the letter and sealed parcel on it and returning to his previous place beside Relvin.

As the letter was opened and the contents of it examined, a smile spread across Lord Darrick's face.

"Well, this is a good day indeed!" Darrick rose to his feet and walked around his desk towards the door. "Come, my friends. I insist you join tonight's banquet. I shall reward you later with payment for bringing this to me so swiftly, but tonight, I reward you with food, wine, songs, and dancing."

Lord Darrick led Morgon and Relvin out of the room to the great hall.

Attendants dispersed generous cups of wine from barrels in the colonnaded side areas as light danced around the walls from the many torches and chandeliers of the great hall. Arrangements of fruits, cheeses, and bread were distributed to each row of long tables that spanned the length of the perimeter colonnades. Within one of the large fireplaces at the side of the hall, cooks were basting a large stag with a buttery herb mixture, and on the other side, a couple of boars were being basted with honey and mustard, a popular delicacy in affluent estates imported from a remote monastery. The smells from the roasting carcasses at each fireplace made Relvin's mouth water, and he satisfied his hunger with a few bits of bread and cheese and a sip of wine as he waited for the event to begin. Once everything seemed to be in place, Lord Darrick stood. The conversations ceased as everyone turned their attention to the table at the end of the hall, where the wealthiest and most influential guests were seated next to the castle Lord.

The Lord's voice echoed through the hall, "I am honored to be with you all tonight as we celebrate my sixty-third year. Let us toast the year we have had together and the many more I hope to celebrate."

Lord Darrick raised his cup in the air before taking a drink. Relvin joined Darrick's guests in the toast though he only took a moderate drink before putting his cup down. He was not one to drink much because he knew how it affected his judgment.

Lord Darrick put his cup on the table and clapped his hands twice to signal the musicians to start the music. "Let the feast begin!"

One of the side doors under the west colonnade opened, and a long line of servants came streaming into the hall from the kitchen carrying large platters of roast chicken, duck, and rabbit, along with bowls of potatoes, parsnips, squash, and carrots. Attendants busied themselves distributing servings to each of the guests as requested. There was more than enough for everyone, and as the meal progressed, most called for additional helpings of their favorites.

"Fetch me more boar," a portly lord bellowed from across the room. The attendant scurried to the opposite side of the hall and gathered several choice cuts before the same man yelled, "Hurry up, useless wretch."

"My grandmother is faster than these servants," a young lord chimed in.

"Can I buy her?" The portly lord asked, bursting into laughter.

"The young are useful in…other ways," a third man said; his wife blushed with embarrassment.

The attendant returned with the boar meat he had been sent for and was immediately sent away for more wine without any thanks from the lord. Relvin heard many more rude conversations throughout the night. He felt bad for the attendants.

Cecelia watched from the eastern colonnade shadows as the guests gorged themselves on the food. She recognized all of the guests in the hall from previous years except the two late arrivals. While the older man didn't stand out from the crowd in any particular way, his younger guard companion did. His conduct was more noble than any lords or ladies around him. Though he hid his distaste well, Cecelia could tell he wasn't fond of the people within the room. Her hopes were elevated, but she needed more information.

Her attention was brought back to her role that evening as Lord Darrick signaled towards her from his table as the food consumption of the guests slowed down. Cecelia opened a side door to let a group of women into the hall to dance with the guests, or at least, the ones who weren't too drunk and didn't have their wives to dance with. She pulled aside one of the women.

"Find out what you can about that young man," Cecelia said to Sarai, a beautiful woman with curly brown hair.

"Yes, Cecelia," Sarai said before continuing into the hall.

Cecelia scrutinized the actions of the young man as he interacted with Sarai. The music and loud conversations drowned out any hope of hearing what was said, but she was more interested in his behavior as the man rose from his seat and joined Sarai. Through her body language, Sarai made it clear that the young man could avail himself of her services if he wished, but he never strayed from treating her with respect as they enjoyed their time on the floor. After several dances together, Cecelia saw him step back and bow to kiss her hand as Sarai curtsied, and they parted ways before Relvin retook his place at the table.

Cecelia listened to everything Sarai reported and a plan began to form in her mind as she paused to survey the room. Cecelia had no control over most of the plan, but she trusted it would come together even if she were only the first domino to fall. With prompting, Sarai exited the side door with Cecelia close behind.

As the celebration dragged on into the night, Lord Darrick noticed the mood of the room change. He surveyed the hall and saw most guests were feeling the effects of the wine and food. Several were already in a drunken sleep on the floor or in their chairs, and few were dancing or talking.

"My dear guests!" Darrick said as he stood to get the attention of any still awake. When the music stopped, he continued, "Again, thank you all for attending my celebration tonight, but I can see that many require rest. Lodgings will be provided for anyone without a place to stay if the floor hasn't accommodated them yet."

A chorus of laughter filled the room. A few sleeping drunks were stirred awake by the noise but nodded off soon after.

"I bid you all a good night," Darrick said.

Darrick exited the great hall and headed toward his chambers as servants dispersed among the guests to tend to their needs. Several guests were helped back to their housing in the castle complex, while others who had traveled to the event were escorted to their awaiting carriages in the courtyard. Most of those remaining were already sleeping on the floor and were covered by blankets to keep them warm during the night.

Chapter 2
OPPORTUNITY

ONE OF THE SERVANTS APPROACHED Relvin and motioned for him to follow while the others attended to the needs of the rest of the guests. The servant led him out of the banquet room and down a passage leading to an open courtyard west of the keep. The refreshing evening air was filled with a delicate, sweet scent of lilacs lining the courtyard perimeter, which was a welcome change from the stuffy air of the great hall. He couldn't help but smile as he took a deep breath. The servant led him up a flight of stairs to the second floor of the guest suites and stopped at the first heavy oak door to the right. He opened the door and showed Relvin inside the guest room.

The fireplace to the left had a merrily dancing blaze within, which cast a cheery glow and radiated its heat throughout. Woolen rugs and animal skins surrounded a four-poster bed. A couple of carved wardrobes and a matching desk camouflaged into the darker recesses of the room. However, Relvin enjoyed the starry view from the colonnaded balcony at the opposite side of the room, overlooking an orchard more than anything within the chambers. Beyond the orchard stood the north wall, and beyond that lay the Wispryn Weald split by the Snake River winding its way from the snowy northern mountains beyond.

"Your saddlebag and other belongings are in the trunk at the foot of the bed, and a bath has been prepared for you," the servant said. "Is there anything more you require?"

"No, thank you. You may leave," Relvin said.

"Rest well," the servant said while pulling the door shut on his way out.

Relvin walked onto the balcony and inhaled the cool evening air as he gazed towards the trees and mountains illuminated by bright moonlight. He felt peace and comfort, like a nostalgic longing for a home he always wanted. He contemplated exploring the Wispryn Weald, but he shook his head to clear his mind, thinking that the wine or exhaustion was playing tricks with him.

He could have spent hours on the balcony, but after the long journey, a bath to clean up was quite appealing. Relvin disrobed before entering a narrow archway to the right of the fireplace leading to a private washroom. He trimmed his beard before climbing a few steps into the generously sized bathtub. The tub was positioned behind the fireplace to keep the water comfortably warm by the heat radiating from the carved stone embracing the metal tub. Relvin relaxed in the warm water, which did wonders for his tired muscles, and he was almost asleep when a quiet creaking emanated from the direction of his room as if the door were opened and shut. He thought it too indistinct to be his door, and after no further sounds reached his ears, he thought nothing more of it. After a few more moments, he stood to get out of the tub to dry off and get to bed.

With the towel wrapped around his waist, Relvin exited the washroom and was startled by the presence of a petite woman, five years his junior, standing beside the bed. Her slight wavy red hair hung down to the small of her back with little white flowers woven into braids encircling the top of her head. The white silken nightdress she wore had loose-fitting shoulder coverings with flowery patterns along the dress hems with a laced center. She fidgeted with the sides of her dress as Relvin approached.

"Lord Darrick sends me with...to...uhh...to keep you warm tonight if I p-please you, my lord," she said.

When he was an arm's length away, Relvin reached out, and she recoiled at the movement. He paused before placing his curled right hand under her chin to lift her head until he looked upon her face. Her striking green eyes darted back and forth at first as he studied her and noticed a band of freckles from one cheek to the other across her nose that reminded him of the dense band of stars he often saw spanning the sky on moonless nights. A kind smile spread across Relvin's face, which seemed to help calm the woman enough to stop fidgeting with her dress. Relvin wondered if her nervousness was a product of her experiences within the castle. As a gift from the host, it would be an insult to refuse her company for the night, like he was inclined to do, and could subject her to unpleasant repercussions.

"I wasn't expecting any company tonight," Relvin said as he retracted his hand.

"It's customary for Lord Darrick to send a companion to fulfill his guests' desires... uh...so they know of his bountiful generosity, my lord, but if...if I don't please you, there—"

"I apologize if I seemed displeased," Relvin said, "I find you... alluring. I'm simply surprised because this wasn't mentioned beforehand."

She looked at the ground and fidgeted with her dress during the silence as Relvin turned and walked toward the fireplace, reveling in the warmth of the dying fire. He grasped the fireplace poker and stirred up the coals before putting it back on the stand to the left of the hearth. After crouching, Relvin removed several logs from the nearby wood rack and arranged them on the coals. He stared into the growing flames for a few minutes before standing.

"What is your name?" Relvin asked as he turned his attention to the woman again.

Relvin saw the maiden lift her head and look at him with surprise. He knew traditionally, the name of a woman in her position was requested only after performing sufficiently to be desired again, but to Relvin, the tradition seemed tantamount to telling her she was only an object, a tool to be thrown away if it didn't fit quite right. He had no desire to perpetuate the tradition after seeing what it could do to a person.

"My name is Tsorianya, my lord, but you may call me Tsoria if you wish."

"It is a pleasure to meet you, Tsoria. However, I request that you stop addressing me as 'my lord.' I'm only a soldier. Call me Relvin."

"As you wish, my...Relvin."

Relvin approached Tsoria, touched her cheek, and tasted the honeysuckle nectar on her lips as the hearth threw its heat into the room. After their lips parted, he drew back a little to gaze at her.

"Is anything wrong?" Tsoria asked as she looked up at him.

"No. I wanted to...long story, everything is fine," Relvin said with a smile, but the expression on Tsoria's face made him wonder if she knew he was lying.

"Perhaps I can make it better."

Tsoria loosened the lacing at the front of the dress and pulled the shoulder covers down, letting it fall to the floor. The firelight danced upon her body as Relvin watched her lay on the bed with her head on the pillows. Relvin removed the towel and lay beside her.

"How may I bring you pleasure tonight, Tsoria?" Relvin asked as he caressed her cheek.

Tsoria opened her mouth to speak but closed it and swallowed hard. Relvin felt her body tremble as he touched her.

"Are you—" Relvin said as he saw Tsoria's eyes get big.

Tsoria sat up abruptly and clutched her stomach as a loud gurgle emanated from her abdomen. Relvin fell to the floor when she pushed him away as she scrambled off the bed. Tsoria ran while she held a hand to her mouth, trying not to vomit before she got to the washroom.

Relvin looked up at the ceiling and chuckled at how he had ended up on the floor as he listened to Tsoria retching. The crackling fire was the only sound in the room for several minutes before he sat up and listened. The sound of sniffling and whimpering emanated from the washroom. Relvin collected the towel from the ground and wrapped it around his waist as he walked through the portal between the rooms.

Within the dimly lit washroom, Tsoria sat crying on the hardwood flooring beside the latrine with her back against the cold stone walls. She wondered how the other women made it look so easy, and if something was wrong with her. She feared Relvin would be angry for ruining the night, but tonight was her only chance, she had to talk with him.

The light from the opening to the room dimmed as Relvin stepped through and picked up the water basin, pitcher, cup, and cloth from the side counter. He knelt beside her and set them all on the floor. Tsoria pulled her knees closer to her chest for comfort as she prepared for the worst.

"Here, rinse with this," Relvin said as he poured water into a cup and handed it to her.

Tsoria took the cup, swished some water in her mouth, and spit the unpleasant taste into the basin as Relvin held it up. After she put down the cup, Relvin took the cloth, poured water on it, and wrung out any excess before brushing her hair back and gently wiping her mouth and chin of any residual spittle before setting the cloth on the edge of the basin.

"Are you feeling better?"

Tsoria didn't speak but had stopped crying enough to feel the cold stone walls extracting the heat from her naked frame sitting on the hardwood floor. Shivers rolled through her body, and her teeth chattered a little.

"I apologize," Relvin said as he withdrew the towel from his waist, wrapped it behind her back, and closed it around the front of her legs. "I should've known you would be cold. When you are ready, stand before the fire to warm up. We can talk if you are up to it, Tsoria, or you can sleep in the bed since you aren't feeling well tonight."

Relvin leaned over to kiss her forehead. Then he stood up and placed the basin and pitcher back on the counter. Tsoria watched as he exited the washroom, unmoving until he was out of sight. She laid her head on her knees and clutched the towel around her while rocking for comfort as she contemplated what had happened. The prospect of talking to him after that fiasco made her nervous. She feared that her deviation from Cecelia's plan had done irreparable harm, but the empathy she felt from Relvin made her want to salvage what she could. Tsoria stood and walked towards the archway to the bedroom while holding the towel wrapped tightly around her.

Relvin sat with his back resting against the headboard, waist under the covers, when Tsoria emerged from the washroom. The light dimmed as she stepped before the hearth and basked in its warmth for several minutes before turning and approaching the bed.

"Tsoria, you don't have to..." Relvin said, but she had already dropped the towel, slipped into the bed, and pulled the covers over her head. "Why are you hiding?"

"I want to climb into a deep dark hole and disappear," Tsoria's muffled voice came from beneath the covers.

Relvin chuckled as he slipped farther under the covers until he lay his head on the pillows facing Tsoria. He pulled the covers from her head and brushed the hair from her face until he could look into her eyes.

"You have nothing to be embarrassed about," Relvin said. "I'm glad that our night got interrupted like this."

Tsoria raised her head from the pillow and looked at him, "You wanted me to throw up?"

"No. I meant…" Relvin sighed. "While our dalliance might be pleasurable, the satisfaction would be fleeting since you are forced to be with me."

Tsoria rested her head on the pillow and said, "I feel mortified because it wasn't supposed to be this way. I never imagined I would be with a man like you for the first time, but—"

"Wait! You're chaste?"

"Yes."

"Now it makes sense. You were nervous. If I had known, I would have—"

"I…I was nervous because this would've been my first time, but there are things I was afraid to tell you about earlier." Tsoria pulled the covers closer to her face. "I still am."

Relvin reached out and caressed her cheek.

"Everything will stay private if that is your concern, I promise. I have no loyalty to Lord Darrick."

Tsoria opened her mouth to speak but then closed it again as she looked away. In the silence, she fidgeted with her hands under the covers and started without looking at Relvin.

"I wasn't supposed to be with you tonight." Tsoria turned her head and met his gaze and waited several moments before continuing, "Lord Darrick celebrates his birthday by bedding a chaste maiden, and he chose me for tonight. I have dreaded this day since I understood what I was bought for and how Darrick treats women. The more I relaxed, the less my built-up fear was suppressed until…it came out."

"I threw up the first time I killed someone…still not used to it. I know it's not the same as being forced to bed a loathsome man like Darrick…but I understand. How did you get away?"

"I was waiting in Lord Darrick's chambers when Cecelia came to see me. She had a lady dance with you to find out what kind of man—"

"Oh! That's why," Relvin said as he smiled. "Who's Cecelia?"

27

"She takes care of the castle companions. Cecelia told me about you and the risky plan she had put together. I was frightened because if the plan went badly..." Tsoria sighed and looked away. "But I agreed because I trust her. Cecelia drugged the wine cup in Lord Darrick's room and left before he arrived. When he had fallen asleep, I slipped from his chambers and crept to yours while other women distracted the guards along the way."

Tsoria paused and seemed afraid to say more. Relvin waited as she stumbled through whatever was stopping her from continuing.

"Relvin...I desire to return home to my family, my people. I have been a slave for longer than I have lived in the Wispryn Weald, but...I have no right to ask." Tsoria pulled his hand to her bare chest. "You can have my body in any fashion you wish in payment. Would you please help me escape? I fear this is my only chance."

Relvin felt her pounding heart and saw the tears well up in her eyes as she pled for his help.

"I would be happy to help you, Tsoria."

Her face lit up as she asked, "You will?"

"Yes."

Tsoria closed her eyes and Relvin watched as a few tears rolled down her nose. He pulled his hand from her chest to wipe her tears away.

"However, as lovely as you are, I won't disgrace you. The chance to thwart Lord Darrick's depravity is reward enough. Besides, I felt a strange sensation like the forest was calling me earlier tonight. I've never felt that before."

"I think you will like the Wispryn Weald. It is more than a forest."

"Then we should travel as far from Wardrich as possible before they realize we are gone. However, we need to avoid his men if we are to have any chance of success. Do you know a way to avoid the guards?"

"There is," Tsoria said after a moment of thought. "A stream runs through an opening under the north wall and flows out under the east."

"Won't there be a grate over each opening?"

"Men tend to get chatty in the Flower Garden, and one of the guards complained this afternoon that the north grate was loose. A vine has grown along the north wall for years, and an hour before sundown, the grate anchors dislodged from the wall. They weren't sure how long the vine had kept the grate in place, but it was too late in the day to do more than prop it up."

After some consideration, Relvin said, "Well then, we shall have to risk it, though they may have posted a guard. Do you have any clothes other than the evening dress?"

"Yes, in one of the wardrobes."

Tsoria peeled back the covers, got out of bed, and walked to a wardrobe to pull out a bundle of clothes stashed earlier. She proceeded to get dressed in sensible clothing for exploring the woods. Relvin donned a clean tunic from his saddlebag and the pants and leather armor he had arrived in, making sure to equip his daggers in case the plan went awry. Relvin converted one of his shirts into a sack to hold the remaining apples, gathered the waterskin and bedding, and left everything else behind as they left the room.

The moonlight was high overhead as they entered the orchard. A chorus of frog croaks from the pond near the livestock drowned out the sounds of their feet as they darted between the fruit trees' shadows. Once the pair managed to get to the wall, Relvin checked to see if any guards were paying attention to the water inlet before removing the grate. It was heavy, and he had to maneuver it to not bump into anything. They slipped into the cold, slow-moving stream up to their knees in depth. When they had ducked through the opening, Relvin turned back to reposition the grate so it wouldn't be apparent that it had been their exit point.

Relvin climbed out of the stream on the other side of the wall and lent Tsoria a hand while being careful not to splash water around or draw attention to themselves. The guards in the closest corner tower were distracted by wolves chasing a lone deer to the west, so they were unaware of the two figures trekking through the grass in the castle's shadow. The thick forest swallowed them, providing cover to wring their pants before continuing further.

It was a quiet night as they walked. They stopped to listen for signs of pursuit whenever they heard a twig snap, slowing their progress. The farther they got from Wardrich into the Wispryn Weald, the more relaxed they became. The occasional hoot of an owl or scurrying of some small animal in the underbrush drew their attention. Otherwise, it seemed that they had made a clean break and wouldn't have to worry about being pursued for the night, but they didn't speak above a whisper while they hiked through the woods.

Adrenaline kept them going throughout the night, but their exhaustion started overriding all efforts to stay awake. When the night was at its coldest, before the first rays of light pierced the darkness, they searched for a place to rest. After several minutes, they found a wide crevice in a boulder with a buildup of fallen forest foliage packed between, creating a decent springy place to bed down. Not far from the rocks, a soft wild plant added some fresh extra padding upon which Relvin unrolled the bedding he had brought. Almost as soon as they rested their heads and closed their eyes, they were fast asleep as they lay beside each other for warmth.

CHAPTER 3
JOURNEY

LORD DARRICK GROANED AS HE WOKE from his slumber with a throbbing headache. His eyes blinked at the bright mid-morning sun streaming into his room from the balcony, and he groaned again as his stiff back protested being subjected to a night of sleeping on the rug-covered floor. He felt pressure on his forehead, and pain shot from a swollen lump as his hand brushed against it. After rising from the floor with great effort, he shuffled to the washroom. Derrick was invigorated by the cold water he splashed upon his face, and the previous night's events started to come into focus.

He walked to his door and turned to face the bed as he retraced his steps of the previous evening to help him remember. He recalled that after he entered his room and bolted the door, he had drunk wine from his cup and ogled the beautiful red-haired woman in a lacy white night dress who would be his conquest for the night. After finishing his wine, he poured himself another cupful before walking closer. Before he reached her, he had felt more tired than usual, and his memory got fuzzy.

Slowly, he noted all that was wrong with the scene. His cup lay on the floor with a large spill next to it, as if it were almost filled when it had been dropped, which by itself was not particularly noteworthy because he had dropped his cup on several occasions. His bed was unkempt like he had slept in it, but there was no one else in his chamber and no staining upon the sheets, which struck him as odd as it had been his birthday the day before. He was also still clothed in the robes from the previous day. While he had woken on the floor in the past, most of those times were after vigorous activities, leaving him unclothed. The only conclusion he deduced from everything he could see and the painful lump he could feel soured his mood.

His nostrils flared, and his heart pounded with growing anger. If he was correct, the night didn't go as planned. He wanted answers, and the only person he knew who could give those answers wasn't in his chambers. He stormed to his door, which he noticed was not bolted, flung it open, and shouted for his guards.

"Find that red-haired woman who was in my chambers last night!" Darrick ordered before the guards could extend any morning pleasantries when he saw two guards approach.

"Right away, my Lord," the guards said as they turned and spread the word of the search to the rest of the guards.

Cecelia and many of the ladies under her care were sitting on lounge chairs having spirited discussions in the foyer of the Flower Garden when they were startled by the explosive intrusion of several guards. The men started searching every room and moving every piece of furniture large enough to hide behind, making a mess of the place. Undeterred by the vehement scolding they received, the guards shoved the women aside or dragged them out of their beds or baths as the search continued.

"What are you gentlemen looking for?" Cecelia asked with a forced pleasantness as she approached the guard in charge of the search. "Perhaps we can help you find what you are searching for without tearing this place apart."

Josier attempted to avoid Cecelia because he did not wish to be distracted from carrying out his orders. But Cecelia wouldn't let him dismiss her. Frustrated with her constant presence, the guard relented.

"Where is the woman?" Josier asked.

"Which particular maiden do you wish to please you?"

"Don't play with me! Where is the redhead sent to the Lord's chambers last night?"

"Oh, you have a good eye. If the lord is done with her, I am sure you can find her in his chambers, but you might want to—"

Josier slapped Cecelia across the face. "Do not lie to me, whore! The Lord has demanded that we find her for questioning! If you're concealing her, we'll find out, and your head will roll!"

The sting of the slap darkened Cecelia's already cloudy mood, and if looks could kill, Josier would have been dead at that moment. The revelation of Tsoria's missing status gave her a boldness she had never dared to unleash as she shoved the guard back without fear of reprisal.

"Get your hoard of jackals out of these chambers at once!" She continued to berate and push him back even when Josier reached for his sword. "You think your blade will keep me from beating you until even your mother doesn't recognize you? Who you seek is not here! Get out now! Go!"

The other guards thundered down the stairs to join Josier when they heard the heated exchange in the foyer.

"She is correct. We should go and leave them in peace," the guards said, attempting to deflate the situation.

Josier breathed heavily with fire in his eyes for several terrifying seconds before relenting when other ladies rallied behind Cecelia like a dam about to break and flood the room with their fury. The guards turned and exited the front door, leaving the mess they had made for the women to clean up, but Cecelia didn't care about the disorder.

The women extended their arms around Cecelia as she started crying. Cecelia smiled as she looked around at every lady encircling her when she was sure the guards were far enough from the door.

"I can die a happy woman. Tsoria is free," Cecelia said.

While Darrick's men searched the compound for signs of Tsoria, he paced in his room and drank wine, attempting to soothe his aching head. "They better find her. I paid good money for her," Darrick muttered.

"*She is yours...*" a voice inside said. "*Teach her a lesson...*"

"Ohhh, I will," Darrick said, pouring more wine into his cup. "No one will dare cross me once I'm done with her."

Darrick ruminated on the dark, uncontrollable thoughts in his mind and muttered for nearly an hour before two guards returned to report on their progress.

"We did not find her anywhere in the castle grounds, my Lord."

Darrick threw his wine cup, hitting the wall behind the guards, narrowly missing them, but they were not spared from the wine flung out as it flew by. "She has to be somewhere! Search outside the walls! Bring her to me so I can wring her neck myself!"

The guards exchanged glances with each other and continued, "Your guest, Relvin, is also missing, my Lord, and the courier doesn't know where he is. We found this dress on the floor of his chambers."

They presented the white evening dress they had found in Relvin's chamber for the lord to inspect. Lord Darrick shouted a lengthy string of curses as he recognized the dress, snatched it from their hands, and tore it to shreds.

"*Pursue her...*" the voice inside said. "*Don't be humiliated again...*"

"No one comes into my house and gets away with such disrespect! Form a hunting party, and drag them back alive! Or show me their heads if you can't!"

"Yes, my Lord," the guards said, exiting his chambers.

Commander Burmad joined his men at the forest edge where the hounds had picked up the trail.

"I estimate the trail is half a day old, Commander," his tracker said. "Two sets of prints, walking slow."

"Good," Burmad said turning to the rest of his small platoon. "Men, this is a hunt like any other. Our fugitives have never been in these woods before, but we all have. I expect to return by tomorrow." Burmad turned and gestured north. "Move out!"

The hounds led the men briskly into the woods. Two guards trailed behind with the two horses carrying their camp equipment.

Tsoria woke while the sun was still high in the sky after the most relaxing and comfortable sleep she had experienced in a long time. She found herself resting on her side with her head on Relvin's chest, listening to the steady rhythm of his beating heart with her arm draped over him. Being beside him reminded her of the several times she fell asleep with Cecelia's arms around her in the Flower Garden when she was younger. Tsoria basked in her feelings for a few more minutes before stretching her limbs and waking Relvin.

After greeting each other, their attention turned to the grumbling from their stomachs, which prompted Relvin to open his bundled shirt to produce the apples he had packed. While they ate, he told her how he had acquired the fruit the previous day. Though the meal satisfied their hunger, the water skin Relvin had brought was emptied during the night and would need to be refilled. Once Relvin had packed what little they had brought and donned the leather armor he had taken off to sleep more comfortably, they continued their journey, veering northwest to hasten crossing paths with the river.

The warm sunlight filtering through the leafy canopy above brightened their mood as they walked among the trees. Because of the distance they had gone the previous night, they openly conversed, which made the hours pass quicker and their journey more relaxing despite keeping a constant watch and ear for anyone who might be tracking them.

"I've heard many tales about this place, but I know no one wishing to live in the Wispryn Weald. What makes it so special that you would risk your life to get back?" Relvin said.

Tsoria thought a bit before she replied, "I may have only been a child at the time, but I remember my family lived simple lives in harmony with nature."

"Only your family? Must be isolating."

"No. My people have been living here for thousands of years. It provides everything we need as we take care of the forest and the creatures within. We are known as Vol'aerai."

"The Vol'aerai exist?" Relvin asked in astonishment. "I've been told stories about Vol'aerai, but I never thought they were real. You are nothing like the monstrous barbarians described in the tales. Are any of the stories about the Vol'aerai true?"

"You want to know if we worship the forest gods, perform ritualistic sacrifices in the woods, drink the blood of those we capture, and use magic to bend nature to our will?" Tsoria asked.

"Well, yes."

"That is what makes us Vol'aerai. Why do you think I lured you into the woods?" Tsoria said in a sinister voice with a straight face.

Tsoria walked several paces before stopping to look behind her and noticed Relvin tensed with large eyes as he looked around, hands gripping his dagger hilts. After a short pause, she couldn't stop herself from laughing.

"You should see your face!" Tsoria said as she pointed at Relvin.

Relvin narrowed his eyes and smiled like he was hiding something.

"You little vixen. I'm going to get you for that."

When Relvin started towards her, Tsoria ran off dancing between the trees, giggling, and said, "You'll have to catch me first!"

The hunters made good time as they followed their prey's trail. They regrouped when they found where the fugitives had slept, but they didn't pause long. The hounds were excited by the stronger scent of their prey and the trackers could tell they were catching up. An angry chorus of birds and squirrels accosted them from the trees as sunset neared but the men were so focussed on the hunt that they hardly noticed.

Half an hour later, they stopped when a large flock of crows cawed and dived at them for several minutes while the soldiers flailed their arms or swords to scare them away. The strange encounter delayed them but didn't persuade them to end their pursuit. At sunset, the hunters stopped again, bracing themselves for an encounter with something large crashing towards them through the forest under-brush.

Tsoria led Relvin on a merry chase before she was outmaneuvered and secured with her back to the trunk of an old oak, panting. She closed her eyes as Relvin put his hand on her cheek without warning and kissed her passionately. When their lips parted, he drew back with downcast eyes.

"I apologize. I shouldn't have done that," Relvin said, withdrawing his hand.

"Press me against the tree or kiss me?" Tsoria asked.

"Both."

"The bark is uncomfortable, but if you keep kissing me like that, I could be persuaded not to sacrifice you."

Tsoria giggled as she slipped from between Relvin and the tree.

"Trying to trick me again?" Relvin asked as he turned towards her.

"Enjoying the same joke."

"Still, I got carried away."

"Perhaps next time I will get carried away..." Tsoria said flashing a coy smile.

Relvin smiled as he turned to the weathered oak tree and touched the bark. "The stories this tree could tell if it could—"

"Oh, but they do talk," Tsoria said, stepping closer. "My people have talked with the trees for centuries. The ability to communicate with nature is what sets Vol'aerai apart."

Tsoria put her hand on the tree and rested her forehead on its bark as she closed her eyes. She felt a low vibration from the old oak.

"What is it saying?" Relvin asked.

"I don't know," she said after opening her eyes and stepping back. "I must have been away too long."

They reoriented themselves with their surroundings to be sure they were headed in the right direction before continuing their journey.

"What else can your people do?" Relvin asked.

"Most Vol'aerai can talk to animals. Some can see through the animal's eyes as if they were the creature. We have healers, crafters, cooks, and farmers like elsewhere. But the way we do it could be viewed as sorcery or magic, and perhaps this is where the rumors of us being witches and warlocks originated. However, since I was taken when I was young, I haven't heard all the stories or learned our entire history."

"Perhaps you will get your answers when you return."

Tsoria noticed Relvin run his hand along the fronds of a fern as they passed by. She had seen him feel the leaves of the bushes or stop to admire some delicate flower along the way several times before.

"For a soldier, you have an unusual fondness for nature."

Relvin looked down at his hand and smiled.

"They remind me of my mother. She cared for her plants like children. They always seemed...happier when she sang to them. I never understood her fascination until I left for military training. The plant my mother prized the most, Pyratsori Astranya, a wedding gift from my father, was in…" Relvin stopped and turned to Tsoria. "You were named after that plant, weren't you?"

Relvin waited for an answer, but Tsoria pushed him to continue his story, so he relented.

"It was blooming for the second time since I was born, and the intoxicating sweet fragrance from its flowers filled the house. I was fascinated by its crimson, orange, and yellow glass-like blooms. While in the army, touching and studying plants was my way of staying in touch with home. It might have been silly, but, I thought, if the plants knew I was well, they could tell my mother so she wouldn't worry."

"Awww…I like the reason behind it," Tsoria said, looking at Relvin admiringly. "My mother said I was a 'balm of grace' for her soul's longing and named me Tsorianya."

"Grace indeed. I seem to be snapping all the twigs while you hardly make a sound. Brothers or sisters?"

"No. I was their rare, fiery bloom. My parents were lucky enough to have me, or at least until they didn't."

Relvin looked around when the trees creaked and groaned as if they felt Tsoria's sadness. She rested a hand on the bark of a tall fir tree in passing and the forest quieted around them. Tsoria turned to find Relvin watching her as she caught up, but he didn't say what was on his mind.

"How would the enslavers know where to find Vol'aerai?" Relvin asked as they continued walking. "Hunters, perhaps?"

"I don't know," Tsoria said even though Relvin seemed to be talking to himself. "I was playing in the forest with eight friends when we were ambushed. Only three of us got away, and the slave market was the last place I saw those captured with me."

"I'm sorry you went through that," Relvin said as he held aside some branches for Tsoria.

"Where did you grow up, Relvin?"

"I was raised in the western province of Yashir in a city called Khuraja with two brothers and two sisters."

"Lucky you. I would've liked having a sister," Tsoria said. "Did you volunteer for the army?"

"I was sent as a tribute to King Dhar's army when I turned twelve. I spent the next decade training and learning all forms of combat."

"Were you ever in a war?"

"The only conflict of note was the Suraddin Uprising."

"I remember hearing about that. Duke Viktor Suraddin of the Ekbahn province defied the king and raised an army against him."

Relvin nodded.

"He didn't have as much backing as he thought. Many thousands died that day even though his army was subdued quickly. The Duke, Duchess, and their only male heir were publicly executed, while their four daughters were enslaved."

"That's horrible."

"I agree. The consequence of failed rebellions is meant to deter any more from occurring, but it can have the opposite effect. Sometimes it takes one person to inspire others to overthrow the monarchy, which the king fears."

Relvin stopped walking when a brightly colored fuzzy-backed caterpillar on an equally fuzzy-leafed plant caught his eye. They both crouched to watch for several moments while it crawled up the stem. Relvin reached out to touch it, but Tsoria yanked his hand back.

"Unless you want to scream in agony until nightfall, I suggest leaving it be," Tsoria said.

"I think I will. That doesn't sound pleasant," Relvin said as they stood and left the caterpillar alone. "After ten years, I collected the wages due for my service and returned to visit my family for a few weeks."

"You left the King's army?"

"Yes."

"Why?"

"The general who trained me recommended me for a position as a courier's guard while they transport valuables or sensitive messages."

Tsoria sighed and looked down as she walked for a few paces and startled when she nearly ran into Relvin. When she looked up his eyes seemed to probe the unspoken question from hers.

"You think there is more to it, don't you?" Relvin asked.

"Well, you gave an answer, but it doesn't explain why the general recommended you for that position."

"I was a good soldier," Relvin said as they resumed their journey. "The commanders were tough and unsympathetic to our pain. Many didn't get through the training, but I excelled in the challenges and duels. The platoon I was assigned to became my new family. I had found my purpose and was proud to be part of the army…"

"But?" Tsoria asked after Relvin stopped talking for some time.

"I was naive. Not every soldier was there for the goal of keeping the peace. Many got drunk on the power and thrill of pushing the boundaries of what they could get away with. They stole from the citizens, arrested or killed them under false accusations, or satisfied their lustful desires in shameful ways. I…" Relvin sighed as if a heavy weight rested on his shoulders. "I will never forget the terrified eyes of the woman in the mountain city of Drianfir. I wondered how many crimes I had been complicit in. How many innocent people could I have saved? Was I one of those once-decent men? I still second-guess everything I had been part of as a soldier. Escorting couriers lets me wander, think, and find a new path."

Tsoria caught Relvin's right hand in both of hers and paused in her tracks. She looked Relvin in the eyes when he turned back to look at her.

"What's wrong?" Relvin asked.

"No matter what happened in Drianfir, thank you for helping me escape. You gave my life back and made a dream come true for Cecelia. She had been looking for an opportunity like this for many years. I want to pass on her thanks in case she never gets to do so herself."

Relvin stepped towards Tsoria and pulled her into his arms. The leather armor wasn't comfortable garb to be drawn into, but his embrace was. Tsoria rested her head against him and closed her eyes.

"You are both welcome," Relvin said. "Perhaps one day I will have the pleasure of meeting Cecelia."

"I think she would enjoy meeting you as well."

Not long after they resumed their journey, they were greeted by the sounds of croaking frogs, dragonflies' humming wings, and humid air that they followed to the banks of Snake River. They took turns plunging cupped hands into the water until their thirst was satisfied. Relvin submerged the water skin to fill it before they left the river banks. A nearby search yielded several vines full of large, ripe berries to satisfy their hunger as they walked.

The hunters recoiled in fear as a monster of a bear burst into sight and sent the lead hound flying against a nearby tree with one swipe of its huge front paws, killing it on impact. The bear stood on its hind legs when it stopped, towering well above the tallest soldier. The men drew their swords as the bear slammed its front paws down, shaking the ground and roaring with a wide open mouth. The hounds barked wildly as they confronted the bear and the soldiers braced themselves for a fight, but after the bear finished its roar, it turned around, picked up the dog carcass in its mouth, and ran off. The remaining hounds pursued it a short distance before they were called back.

After the bear encounter, the men stopped to regroup, and lit torches before continuing their quest. The warm torchlight bolstered their rattled nerves, but the darker it got the stranger the forest became. They glimpsed eerie movements in the dark, but moving the torches to investigate changed the shadows and they couldn't uncover what was watching them.

Burmad ordered the men to set up camp once they reached the river late into the night. It was clear by the signs they followed the hunters were hours behind the fugitives, even though the tracks were fresher. A search of the area yielded nothing to hunt for the evening meal, and the berry vines they found seemed to have been picked clean by a group of animals no more than an hour before. The campfire was a welcome comfort and seemed to dispel the weird feelings they got from the forest, even though the rations they ate that night were far from enjoyable.

The men told stories around the fire to bolster their spirits, trying to outdo each other in "manliness" as they compared women, fights they won, and feats of strength. Everyone dismissed the tales of the Wispryn Weald as folklore and never admitted to being afraid of anything. Despite their bravado and words, they avoided eye contact that evening as much as possible because they feared their eyes would reveal their true feelings. Sentries were assigned around the camp while the rest of the men bedded down to get as much rest as they could before their round on watch.

CHAPTER 4
INSTINCT

COMMANDER BURMAD ROUSED HIS MEN early in the morning. Everyone seemed eager to be awake and ate their cold morning meal without complaint before dismantling their camp. The forest had been suspiciously quiet during the night: no owls hooted, no creatures scampered, no crickets chirped, no frogs croaked, and no leaves rustled. The men slept several hours, but despite this, no one felt well-rested because their dreams had been invaded by the trees' whispers, turning any dream into a nightmare. Once the horses were packed and the soldiers were fully assembled, the hounds were let loose, and the hunt resumed.

About a five-hour journey north of where the hunting party had camped, Relvin and Tsoria awoke when the warm morning sunlight peeked through the trees and shined upon their faces. They had slept well, and when they sat up, they were greeted by the most curious sight they had seen. On the ground in front of them was a female red squirrel waving its fluffy tail and staring at them with its beady eyes. Next to the squirrel on a flat rock lay a large pile of shelled mixed nuts and a couple of delicious-looking apples. When the squirrel saw they had awakened, it picked up a walnut in its front paws and presented the nut to Tsoria as it stood on its hind legs.

"For me?" Tsoria said with a smile as she reached out her hand to receive the nut from the squirrel. "Thank you!"

The squirrel squeaked a little and blinked as it dropped the nut in her hand, picked up a pecan, and offered it to Relvin, who graciously accepted. After they placed the nutty treats into their mouth, the squirrel pushed the pile of nuts towards them, ran up the nearest tree, and watched from a branch above as they enjoyed the meal they had been served.

"I have never met a friendlier squirrel in all my life," Relvin said.

"Nor a tinier chef," Tsoria said, and they both chuckled.

When they had finished the pile of nuts and apples, they got up and waved at the squirrel and thanked it again for the meal, to which it squeaked and ran off, jumping from tree to tree until it disappeared. Relvin rolled the bedding they had slept on before they continued north.

They hadn't gone many paces before a mother raccoon waddled in front of them with a litter of three. The day had barely started for the travelers but the sow looked overdue for a good sleep after a long night out. Curiosity got the better of the three kits, and they ambled over to examine Tsoria and Relvin. The mother scrambled to position herself between the wanderers and her babies. However, the kits were mischievous and less tired than their mother. The most determined troublemaker slipped past her to quench his curiosity while the other two distracted their mother. When the sow turned to search for her third kit after the first two were contained, she hissed a warning with arched back and bared teeth.

"You should listen to your mother, you rascal," Tsoria said as she scolded the baby raccoon, crouched down, and gently moved it within the mother's grasp.

The mother relaxed, sensing respect and no ill intent from either human. The sow allowed Tsoria and Relvin to pet her kits under close supervision, grateful for the assistance with her rebellious babies. After a few minutes, she herded her litter back to the den. When the kits were safely inside, she looked back at the travelers and chittered before disappearing down the hole, seemingly wishing them a good day.

Relvin and Tsoria had seen the occasional bird, watching them trek through the woods from a distance, or a flash of movement as something darted for cover when they passed. However, before the red squirrel and raccoons, they hadn't interacted with any woodland animals. But the deeper they went into the forest, the more frequently close encounters with the woodland dwellers happened. Each animal had a unique personality: the proud regality of the stag, the fierce loyalty of the wolf, the flighty playfulness of the chipmunks, and many others. Each encounter revealed different facets of Tsoria and Relvin's personalities and induced more than a few lively chases. However, the animal encounters occurred less often as evening approached until none appeared for over an hour. The quietness contrasted with the friendliness earlier in the day, making them uneasy.

They stopped more often to listen for danger. The first few times, nothing seemed concerning, but when Tsoria was about to write off her feelings as simple paranoia, she heard barking far too near for comfort. Based on the number of distinct barks, she estimated at least six hounds were closing in on their position. A loud whistle followed soon after, and Tsoria's heart fell because they were the prey; hunting parties never ventured this deep into the woods. Tsoria's heart pounded, and she ran north as fast as possible. Relvin followed after and dropped any nonessential items he had been carrying.

A woman stood on pine needle-covered ground in the mountains at the source of the Wyre River, northwest of the hunt. She seemed in perfect company with the short and hardy ancient pines surrounding the circle where she stood. Thick, multi-layered woven grass clothes protected her from the elements as she waited with her eyes closed and her arms outstretched to each side like she was feeling the surface of an invisible body of water. Her fingers twitched with slight, seemingly random movements as she listened to the forest's whispers and monitored the progress of the intruders within. Suddenly, her hands closed into fists by her side, and her eyes opened. Instead of seeing the trees that were in front of her, she was seeing the events unfolding in the south of the forest from the eyes of a creature on the prowl.

"Become prey," she muttered.

As evening fell, Commander Burmad was alerted to the proximity of their prey when the hounds started barking aggressively. He whistled a signal to the dogs, and they took off at full speed to corral and subdue their quarry. The hunting party picked up their pace so they wouldn't arrive too far behind the hounds. The soldiers were glad the hunt was nearing its end because the forest seemed less friendly the longer they remained in it. There was a palpable feeling of being watched and it hung in the trees around them.

When they started catching up to where the dogs had trapped their prey, the men heard fierce growls from the surrounding forest, and they stopped to peer into the growing darkness. Their minds played tricks on them as the shadows seemed to split and give birth to more shadows as gray ghostly blurs streaked toward them. Any confusion about what was stalking the hunters vanished from their mind as grey wolves leaped from the shadows around them. Panic set in as they realized the tables had turned, hunters were now the prey. They were no longer welcome in the Wispryn Weald.

Commander Burmad attempted to maintain control of his men, but he was defending himself from fierce wolf attacks like his men were and having a terrible time keeping his throat from being torn out. He cursed as he could do nothing but try to anticipate where to swing his sword next to ward off the attack. Eventually, he managed to edge his way south, and as soon as his path was clear, he ran like a madman. The wolves followed him briefly before abandoning pursuit, but Burmad ran until his legs could carry him no longer.

His men were not so lucky. Those on the group's outer edges had their throats torn out before they knew what had happened. Several men were in such a panic they could no longer distinguish between friends and foes, flailing their swords at anything that moved and killing several companions. The remaining few were the unluckiest of all, for their deaths were slow and painful as they were dragged away and torn apart piece by piece. The only calm party members were the two horses packed with equipment, watching the event unfold before their eyes while the wolves ignored them.

Relvin and Tsoria had been running as fast as possible but couldn't keep the pace for much longer. A small opening between two large boulders was spotted not far ahead, and Tsoria ran for it with what little energy remained. Relvin followed after, but instead of entering the crevice, he turned around outside the opening.

"What are you doing?" Tsoria asked when she noticed Relvin was staying outside.

Relvin turned towards her and felt transported back to that dark alley in Drianfir after seeing Tsoria's terrified expression.

"Stay there, Tsoria, no matter what happens!" Relvin said as he returned his attention to the incoming dogs.

Relvin reached for the daggers at his hips and drew them from their sheaths. He knew that being attacked by so many hunting dogs was a death sentence, but his mind was set. He would not allow another woman to be ravaged by animals while he still had breath in his body.

Relvin braced himself as the first dog neared. When it leaped, he slashed at the throat with the dagger in his right hand and pierced the brain with a backhand swing, killing it. He had enough time to reposition for the next dog, which stopped before reaching him, growling and barking while baring its teeth. Once the rest of the hounds took positions around him, they tested his defenses and feigned attacks before coordinating to subdue their prey.

Tsoria felt helpless as she watched Relvin fight the dogs. He was fast, but getting more injured as time passed because the hounds were well-trained, knowing every trick to expose their prey's weaknesses. Relvin might have been able to dodge more attacks if he moved away from the crevice opening, but he never let any dog past him. The hounds forced him to sacrifice himself to keep them from attacking her.

Tears streamed down Tsoria's face as she watched Relvin being punished for her actions, which had brought him into this situation. She shuddered with every scratch, bite, puncture, and rip of his flesh as if she were the one being attacked. Her desire to protect Relvin was strong, but she was unsure of how she could make any difference. Tsoria saw the worst possible scenario unfold before her eyes. Two dogs locked their jaws around his forearms, forcing him to let go of the daggers, while two more attacked his legs. He fell to his knees while another hound charged in for the kill. Tsoria felt her heart jump into her throat as time seemed to slow down, cruelly etching every detail of the moment into her memory. Then she felt a warm feeling embrace her from behind like the strong hug of a supportive father picking their child up from a great fall and giving them the strength to get back up. Her steely eyes reflected her determination to protect what she loved. An unexpected power swept through her, and an ancient instinct took over.

"Leave him alone!" Tsoria screamed at the top of her lungs as she slammed both hands, palms down, onto the dirt and dug in her fingers.

The ground shook as numerous roots burst from the ground in front of Relvin, blocking the dog from killing. The hounds that gripped his extremities let go and yelped as they writhed from being pierced by roots. The roots curled outward away from the rocks and slammed down, crushing the rest of the dogs and dragging the dead dogs' remains with them as they disappeared into the earth. It was silent.

Relvin turned to Tsoria mouth agape as he gestured while short of breath, trying to vocalize the questions in his head, but he failed to get any complete thought out of his mouth in shock from what had happened before his eyes.

Tsoria lifted her hands from the ground, staring at them before looking up at Relvin. "Did I do that?" Tsoria asked before fainting.

After seeing Tsoria collapse, Relvin rushed in and dragged her from between the rocks and tried to wake her but was unable to get a response. Tsoria was breathing, but Relvin noticed she had a high temperature when he touched her forehead. Relvin knew he was in no shape to carry her far and was at a loss for options.

He heard approaching horse hooves on the ground behind him. Relvin turned around and braced for a fight despite having little energy left. He saw a mare packed with camping gear standing there and recognized a distinct mark on its leg. It was the same horse he had ridden from Islatria. The horse pawed the ground and let out a whinny as it tossed its head, encouraging him to hurry up. Relvin's mind flooded with questions, but the mare was right, none of that mattered. He removed the camping gear from the horse, lifted Tsoria over its back, and mounted wrapping both arms around her and clutching the saddle horn.

Relvin wasn't sure which direction he should go to reach help in time, but without prompting, the horse started walking northeast. Something inside told him not to worry; he entrusted his path to the horse. He tried to stay conscious to ensure Tsoria did not fall, but he was still bleeding from his wounds, and it was not long before he passed out.

Relvin awoke in a dwelling the following day, the sun shining through the doorway. The bedding he lay on was soft but felt different than anything he knew. His wounds were wrapped with healing poultices. His leather armor had been removed, leaving his looser-fitting, blood-stained clothes. A villager entered through the doorway with a water bowl and placed it on a small table beside the bed.

"Where am I? Who are you?" Relvin asked, attempting to sit, but his wounds hurt when he moved, causing him to cry out from the pain.

"Careful…" The villager rushed to sit beside Relvin before he hurt himself; he eased Relvin into a sitting position. "You're safe now. I'm a healer, and my name is Macias. What should I call you?"

"Relvin."

"Many of your wounds are deep, Relvin, and they will heal faster if you rest, but first, you need water."

Relvin didn't remember Macias bringing a cup with the bowl, but as he drank from the cup, he realized how thirsty he was. Macias refilled the cup many times until Relvin was satisfied, and the previous night's events flooded back to him. He looked around for Tsoria.

"Tsoria! Where is she? Is she well?" Relvin asked.

"She is experiencing what is known to us as aliuscerai within our sacred clearing," Macias said.

"Can I see her?"

"You should rest, but I will find the elder and ask her."

Macias lowered Relvin until he lay upon the bed, rose to his feet, and stepped through the doorway. After several minutes, a woman who looked spry for her age entered.

"My name is Lellia," the elder said in a strong, wisened voice, "I was told that you have asked to see Tsoria. I will lead you to her."

Macias reentered, helped Relvin to stand, and supported him as they walked through the doorway. During the slow and painful walk east to where Tsoria lay, Lellia continued the conversation. "As Macias has told you, Tsoria is going through a process most Vol'aerai experience."

"He said it was… alluseri?" Relvin said, attempting to remember what Macias had said.

"Aliuscerai," Lellia said, correcting Relvin's mispronunciation.

"I don't know the word. What does it mean?"

"I wouldn't expect you to," Lellia said, with a gentle smile, "it comes from the old tongue rarely spoken today. The full meaning is complex, but in the simplest terms, it means to call forth and imbue. Aliuscerai is experienced by those who use the abilities entrusted to them by the forest for the first time. It's a rite of passage when they dedicate themselves to the forest."

"Has anyone failed to complete aliuscerai?"

"Everyone has a choice and isn't forced to commit, but they won't be able to do more than talk with the animals or each other through the forest network."

"Last night Tsoria brought roots from the ground to attack the dogs," Relvin said motioning with his hands to reenact what happened. "Can all of you do that?"

Lellia looked at Relvin with a hint of surprise at his description of events before answering, "Not everyone is the same. Most only get common gifts from the forest, while others get rare abilities."

They arrived and entered a circle of trees surrounding an intricate bed that seemed to have grown out of the ground. Tsoria lay shaking and unconscious on the bed, which concerned Relvin, but he held back from acting until he knew more to avoid doing something offensive.

"How long does aliuscerai take?" Relvin asked.

"No more than it takes to prepare a meal for most. The longest I've known it to take was half a day, until now. Tsoria has been there since you arrived last night." Lellia turned away from Tsoria to face Relvin. "I'm also worried."

"Are there any rules forbidding me from holding her so she isn't alone?" Relvin asked, meeting Lellia's gaze.

"I hoped you would ask such a question when you saw her. Aliuscerai has historically been a solitary process, but no law says it must be. I brought you here because there is a chance your presence will help her move beyond her fears. I feel she is about to give up."

"Then let me try."

Lellia's shoulders relaxed and her mouth showed a hint of a smile at Relvin's response. She nodded to Macias before exiting the clearing. Relvin climbed onto the bed beside Tsoria with Macias's help, and despite the painful wounds, he snuggled close and embraced her. In less than a minute, her body stopped shaking, and even though her fever had not broken, she rested peacefully. With his worries eased, Relvin sighed and rested his head. He didn't feel tired after sleeping since the previous night, but he drifted off as doves sang a lullaby and the wind whispered through the trees.

CHAPTER 5
COALESCE

BEFORE MIDNIGHT, AS THE MOON shined a silvery light into the clearing the ancient trees surrounded, Tsoria opened her eyes. She felt Relvin's warmth encircling her and his slow, quiet breathing. She turned around in his arms to face him, put a hand on his chest, and felt his heart beating strong and steady. She smiled as she remembered waking with her head on his chest days earlier. Tsoria moved her hand from his chest to caress the side of his face.

"I'm glad you are alive," Tsoria whispered. "Time to wake up."

At first, nothing happened as she studied the details of his face. She played with his beard and ran her fingers through his hair until Relvin's eyes fluttered open.

"Tsoria, you're awake. Are you well?"

"I am," Tsoria said as she nodded. "Your wounds should be healed as well."

Relvin sat up, peeled back the poultices wrapped around him, and inspected his wounds in the moonlight. They were healed; the only indications of injury were slight scars.

"Incredible…" Relvin said as he continued inspecting his body.

"I had the forest accelerate your healing while you slept," Tsoria said.

"Thank you," Relvin said, turning his attention to Tsoria.

"It was the least I could do for protecting me," Tsoria said as she sat up to face him.

"What was aliuscerai like?"

"I want to tell you everything," Tsoria said, "but there is something else I wish to discuss."

"Sounds serious," Relvin said.

"You have done what I asked and more," Tsoria said." You are free to return to the Islatrian Kingdom."

"What if I don't want to leave?" Relvin asked.

Tsoria smiled, fiddling with her blouse laces. "You may stay in the Wispryn Weald. The Vol'aerai have welcomed many who sought to live here in peace."

"I don't know much about the Vol'aerai, but I want to know more." Relvin surveyed the trees surrounding them before returning his attention to Tsoria. "I feel at peace here. Even when the dogs were about to kill me, I felt an inexplicable calm inside. I want to stay."

"I'm glad, but is that the only reason you wish to stay?" Tsoria asked. Relvin looked confused by the question. "After our first chase in the forest, you kissed me. I know it was in the heat of the moment, but it felt real. Despite the many opportunities I gave you after, you didn't kiss me again—making me think our connection was imagined."

"I didn't want to assume…When we talked in Wardrich you were desperate."

"I wanted out—"

Relvin and Tsoria looked up when something came between them and the moon, casting a shadow as it passed. They watched an owl fly to one of the trees and alight on one of the lower branches. It swiveled its head to look at Relvin and Tsoria before flying off toward the distant call of its mate.

Tsoria took Relvin's hand in hers. "This isn't desperation…or payment. Do you desire all of me?"

Relvin put his hand on Tsoria's cheek and pulled her in for a deep kiss. Tsoria lost herself in the warmth of his passion and touch until their lips parted.

"More than ever," Relvin said.

"I need you to know, Relvin," Tsoria said, "for Vol'aerai, sex isn't only a physical act. It is a promise to grow together and support each other as long as we breathe."

"It sounds like you are saying we would be married."

"That is what I'm saying, which is why being forced to bed a man like Darrick and then be used as a commodity for any man after would have been…debasing." Cricket chirps, frog croaks, owl hoots, and the rustling and squeaking of scampering creatures filled the silence as Tsoria paused. "If you don't wish to—"

"It is a lot to ask from someone you have not known long," Relvin said.

"I know…" Tsoria said, hanging her head.

Relvin breathed deeply. "I suppose it's not much different than marrying someone you hardly know based on an arrangement by your parents long before coming of age."

"Have your parents arranged a marriage for you?" Tsoria asked.

"No. My parents arranged their marriage after a chance encounter, perhaps it affected their views on life."

Tsoria pulled Relvin's left hand close to her heart as she interlocked her fingers with his. "Do you want to be married to me?" Tsoria asked, looking into Relvin's eyes.

"Yes. I wouldn't want anything less with you," Relvin said reaching out to caress Tsoria's cheek before pulling her in for a kiss.

Tsoria smiled when she saw a twinkle in Relvin's eyes when he pulled back, and giggled as he stared at her with a mischievous smile. "What?"

"Do you have any of that honeysuckle nectar for your lips?" Relvin asked.

"I know you love how my lips taste," Tsoria said with a giggle before letting him taste them again.

Relvin chuckled. "Indeed I do."

"I will get you back for that comment, though," Tsoria said as she loosened the lacing of her blouse.

"I await your punishment, my lady," Relvin said.

Tsoria was nervous, but none of the curious forest creatures passing by would have known. Relvin and Tsoria had fun together like their journey into the forest. They giggled, nipping and rolling with each other like playful pups, dancing together in the moonlight until they could take no more.

After a short rest apart to catch their breath, Relvin pulled Tsoria into his arms. His hands and lips caressed her body as she purred with delight, moving in response to the pleasure he had introduced her to. Before the high wore off, she took ahold of his left hand and stretched it over the side of the bed.

"What are you—" Relvin asked.

Tsoria shushed him and said, "Wait for it."

As they watched, a single root grew from the ground and split into two strands not much thicker than coarse hair. One strand wove around Relvin's ring finger and the other around Tsoria's. Numerous gems were pulled from the earth and set within each ring. Once completed, the roots detached and retreated.

They both rolled over to lay on their backs and held up their hands in the moonlight, marveling at the intricacy of each ring. At the center of Tsoria's ring was a tree with leaves made from tiny diamond, emerald, and peridot gems. The tree trunk was a mixture of woven roots and deep brown tourmaline, and the tree's roots curled around and merged into the band. The top side of the band, near the leaves, was embedded with sapphires, topaz, and moonstones, like the sky with clouds. The lower portion of the ring contained tiny flowers of amethyst, morganite, and rubies, and if they looked close, they could see deer, wolves, hawks, and other forest creatures formed along the band as it wrapped around her finger. Relvin's ring was intricately woven like a Celtic knot and embedded with diamonds, rubies, sapphires, emeralds, and amethyst. Both rings sparkled from gold fused within the root fibers, and though the gems were uncut, they were well polished from their journey through the ground and reflected the moonlight.

"What kind of root is this?" Relvin asked.

"It comes from the crystal tree," Tsoria said.

"I've never heard of it."

"The only crystal tree is here in the Wispryn Weald. I've never seen anything scratch or burn crystal root."

"Fascinating."

Tsoria rolled over, draped her arm around Relvin, and lay her head on his chest. She closed her eyes and relished his warmth.

"The bond is complete," Tsoria said. "With the forest as our witness, we are now joined together as husband and wife."

"Do Vol'aerai have wedding ceremonies?" Relvin asked.

"After a couple has learned how to live as one we have a celebration called fírha'achíd. They happen weeks, sometimes months after the first physical bond."

"Wedding or not, tonight was far better than the night we met."

Tsoria lifted her head to look at him and said, "Did you have to bring up that embarrassing moment?"

Tsoria punched Relvin in the chest and he pretended to be hurt but couldn't hide his smile before she lay her head back down.

"Truthfully, Cecelia told me asking you for help would be enough, but I was afraid you would say no if you weren't given something in return. I had nothing but my body to give, so I changed the plan. Perhaps if…" Tsoria trailed off as she sighed and clung to Relvin. "No, I wouldn't change a thing. Tonight was better than I imagined, and I like our story. Even though I was mortified then, now I'm grateful."

"I like our story, too," Relvin said. 'Dashing hero saves the princess from certain death' has a nice ring to it, don't you think?"

Tsoria laughed. "Sure, if it were true. The story is closer to, 'Gorgeous princess saves the reckless hero from a painful death.'

"Reckless? You wound me," Relvin said as he chuckled. "Let's call it even and say, 'Hero and princess work together to save each other from the jaws of certain death."

"Yeah, that is more like it." Tsoria kissed Relvin before they held each other and listened to the sounds of the forest nightlife. "I wish we could be like this forever, but our marriage wasn't all that changed tonight."

"What else happened?"

"You asked earlier about what aliuscerai was like, and the closest I could say is that it was like millions of voices…no…feelings is a better term. I could feel everything in the forest at once, what each creature or plant wanted, the joy, sorrow, and desires each felt, and I finally understood what happened when the dogs attacked you last night."

"I'm glad you figured it out because I still can't wrap my head around it," Relvin said as he adjusted to lay on his side to look at Tsoria.

Tsoria reached to touch Relvin's face as she studied him.

"I felt helpless as you fought the dogs, but when I saw you fall to your knees, I became aware of a presence around me, like an army with more soldiers than I could count, waiting for my command. As I dug my fingers into the ground, they took my feelings as an order to protect you."

"An army…"

Tsoria nodded. "It scared me to have that much power in my hands, to be appointed as Queen of the Vol'aerai."

Relvin's eyes got big, and his jaw dropped. "Queen? That is quite the honor."

"It is, but it was overwhelming. I'm a young woman, a little girl at heart, and I haven't been in the forest for as long as most other Vol'aerai. I didn't understand why I would be chosen for that position, and I wanted to refuse their offer," Tsoria snuggled close to her husband with her head tucked under his chin, "but then you lay beside me and held me close. I felt your pain, concern, desire, and joy. I felt you…That's when I knew everything would be alright with you by my side. I made a covenant with the forest that if you agreed to be my husband, I would accept the honor of becoming the Vol'aerai queen."

"If I had refused, you wouldn't be queen, and you would have lost the power entrusted to you?" Relvin asked.

Tsoria retreated from Relvin's embrace to look at him and rested her hand on his cheek.

"I wanted to tell you earlier but didn't want to burden you with that choice. I wanted you to choose because you desired me, not because I would become queen. I hope you understand."

"I do. Tsoria, you are fierce, caring, wise, and beautiful beyond comparison. You will be a great queen."

Tsoria smiled as she pulled Relvin's face closer before kissing his lips.

"Thank you, my husband. I will need your support so much."

"You're welcome, Tsoria, my wife, my queen."

The early morning light roused the newlyweds within the ancient circle. Tsoria yawned and stretched her limbs. She greeted and kissed Relvin before tearing herself from his warm embrace. Instead of donning her previous clothes, Tsoria stood next to the bed and held her arms to either side as the forest clothed her in the most splendid garb Relvin had ever seen any royal wearing.

Soft grasses grew and wove themselves together into a living dress that embraced her body, covered her arms, and flowed elegantly almost to the forest floor. Thousands of tiny royal blue and violet-purple flowers bloomed from and layered on top of the woven grasses, while white and gold flowers bloomed to trim and accent the dress. The flowers gave off the most delicious, sweet fragrance that hung in the air. Hundreds of roots combed through and styled her hair with braids to control how her hair flowed down the back and sides of her face. Around her feet grew a pair of intricate crystal root shoes with gold accents, lined with soft grasses and flowers to match the dress.

Once fully dressed, Tsoria turned to her husband with a huge smile.

"Look at this dress! This is the most beautiful thing I have ever seen or worn!"

Relvin could not help but stare at how elegant his wife looked standing before him.

"Wow! I have known good seamstresses, but this makes them all look like amateurs."

Tsoria danced, twirled, and giggled as she marveled at how light, airy, and comfortable the dress felt. After a few minutes, she motioned to Relvin and smiled.

"Now it's your turn."

"The forest is going to dress me, too?" Relvin asked, a little surprised.

"Yes! You may not be king of the forest, but you are the queen's husband. Therefore, you have its respect."

Tsoria excitedly reached for his hand and pulled at him until he got off the bed and stood up. Relvin embraced and kissed Tsoria as he told her how beautiful she was before she stepped back to watch, clapping her hands in delight.

The clothes created for Relvin were sturdier by design but no less intricate or spectacular next to the queen's dress. The tunic was primarily royal blue with trim like Tsoria's dress, but the pants were more earthy with root fibers running through them, as were the bracers on his arms, the shoulder pads, and the boots that grew around his feet. The last thing to be created was a narrow cape matching the tunic, which hung from the shoulders and was trimmed in white and gold flowers.

"Clothes fit for a king," Tsoria said when Relvin was dressed.

"Since I'm not a king, doesn't that make me overdressed for my role?"

"A dashing hero needs to look the part, as long as they don't out-shine the queen, of course."

"I don't think that's possible."

Tsoria giggled and kissed Relvin as the village elder walked into the clearing.

"I figured there was something special about you for the aliuscerai to take so long," Lellia said, "but I never expected to witness a new queen's appointment. It's been hundreds of years since our last queen. This is cause for celebration, but it means the forest is unsettled, which troubles me." Lellia closed her eyes and was silent for a moment before opening them. "Come, we need to get you to the crowning ceremony. I have let the other village elders know we have a new queen."

Relvin hadn't noticed anything about the village the previous evening since he was preoccupied with getting to Tsoria, but as they followed Lellia, he was amazed by what he saw. He expected to see rough-hewn structures arranged with minimal sophistication, but instead, he witnessed a careful arrangement of charming buildings. A natural spring brought water to the village from the west, opposite the ancient circle where they had spent the night. Delicious smells drifted from a large gazebo-like central structure that was abuzz with multiple villagers as they baked bread, cooked porridge in several stone caul-drons, and prepared other menu items for the morning meal. Support structures for crafting, storage, and baths were in the south, and the dwellings were in the north.

Each structure was functional and a beautiful work of organic frac-tal artistry. Most buildings were grown from the ground, though some dwellings were in the trees. Every one of the structures seemed to morph or move based on need: doors and windows grew or dissolved instead of opening or closing; chairs conformed to their occupants, and the heavy stone cauldrons were carried by roots or vines instead of needing to be picked up for serving or cleanup. Everyone wore woven grass and root clothes, each with their unique style which matched their personalities, though none sported the royal purple and blue colors afforded to Tsoria and Relvin. Forest animals roamed the village and helped bring rare ingredients for the meals.

When the adults saw the newlyweds walking hand in hand into the village wearing such splendid garb, they knew a queen had been chosen and respectfully greeted them. When the young girls saw the dress, they thought it the prettiest thing in the world and gaily danced around Tsoria, telling her how pretty she looked and asking how they could get one like it. The young boys admired the clothes, but most were shy about saying it out loud. All the attention set Tsoria off in giggles of delight as she enjoyed interacting with the kids.

Relvin smiled as he watched Tsoria be so girlish and happy compared to when they first met. Now that she could relax, her personality bloomed like snowdrops, bringing life and beauty into a frozen world despite her soon-to-be queen status. He was sure she would be one of the best Vol'aerai queens, even though he didn't have any information about the past queens to make a rational comparison.

Relvin was happy to stay in the background and didn't mind that Tsoria was the center of attention. When questions arose about how they got to the village, Tsoria told stories to the kids about their journey. When she got to the night they arrived, she told the kids that Relvin single-handedly fought off a whole pack of ferocious dogs to protect her, and she left out her part in the ordeal. This brought a chorus of gasps and exclamations from the kids, and though Relvin attempted to correct the story, they crowded around him, asking questions all at once not allowing him to finish the story.

After shooting a playfully annoyed look at Tsoria, Relvin gave in and played along with the story. He answered their many questions, making it as fun as possible for the kids and overhyping his feats in many places. It was Tsoria's turn to stand on the sidelines and watch with a smile as he told his tales.

The kids groaned as their parents called them away for the morning meal before their lessons. When the last child walked away, Tsoria threw her arms around Relvin's neck and stood on her toes to kiss his cheek. With a satisfied smile, she rested her head on his chest and stared after the kids as he put his arms around her.

"Thank you for indulging me," she said, "I had a lot of fun with the children."

"You're welcome," Relvin said and continued after a short pause, "You know, one day, they are going to find out the truth about that night."

Tsoria smiled and said, "Yeah, but they should stay kids as long as possible before learning the realities of this world."

"I suppose you are going to want children so you can all gang up on me."

Tsoria giggled at the thought. "Yeah, one day we will have children."

"With my luck, they will all be girls, and I will be powerless against you all."

"Think of all the fun you will have frightening all their potential suitors."

"Or perhaps you can use the forest powers to keep them as children forever, so I don't have to worry about that."

"The forest powers don't work that way, my dear, and even if I could keep them as children, there is no guarantee they would never be hurt. Besides, if we kept them young, they would miss out on all the good that life offers."

"Very true. Shall we get some food in us before we leave?"

The couple joined the rest of the village at the tables for a morning meal of porridge, tree nuts, fruit, bread, and soft herb-flavored cheese. Relvin enjoyed the experience of everyone together at the same table during meal time. In the cities he was familiar with, the class divisions were most evident at meal times. Those who dared to eat with anyone above their status without an invitation were quickly put in their place. Relvin had grown to detest how most Islatrians treated each other. He thought that what someone does for society doesn't make them any more or less important. Seeing everyone sitting together, talking, and eating the same food was a refreshing change.

When they were ready to travel, a few horses trotted into the camp to take Lellia, Relvin, and Tsoria to the ceremonial clearing used for crowning. Saddles grew upon the horses' backs like the forest plants had dressed the newlyweds. Relvin helped Tsoria mount her horse sidesaddle before he turned to help Lellia, but the elder had already mounted her horse without assistance. Since both ladies were ready, Relvin mounted his horse, and they began their journey west.

CHAPTER 6
ASCENSION

ELVIN WAS USED TO LEADING as a courier guard but followed behind Tsoria and Lellia because navigating the thick woods seemed difficult, and he couldn't see the trail. However, when Tsoria came within twenty feet of the trees, an opening appeared in the forest, providing an unobstructed passage. Relvin thought this was some illusion he had somehow missed, but as he took a closer look, he realized that the trees were moving aside through the earth, as if a person was wading through shallow water to clear a path for the Queen. The leafy giants bowed their arms above them to create a canopy over the passage toward their destination. The tunnel remained open after they passed through. Relvin would have thought he was hallucinating or dreaming days before, but today, he was eager to learn about his new home.

"How are the trees moving? I've only known trees to be entrenched and unmovable," Relvin said.

"The trees only move when there is a Queen," Lellia said. "They will not move for anyone else anymore."

"So the legends from thousands of years ago are true? Wispryn Weald trees can move?"

"Yes, they are true, or at least what the legends are based on," Lellia said. "People have forgotten because it has been so long since there was a Queen to wake the patient giants."

"Why such a large gap between queens?"

"The forest's experience with time is different than ours. We tend to be impatient and fleeting in our planning because our lives are short and fragile, but the trees see hundreds or thousands of years at a time. Their memories and history are written within them as they grow. When they feel the time is right to step in to change the direction of the world, they appoint a queen."

"Why doesn't the forest act on its own and bring the change it feels is best instead of appointing a queen?" Tsoria asked. "Why does it need our help when it has the power?"

"The world was influenced by the forest when it came to be," Lellia said, "though there is much I don't know about the early years."

Relvin and Tsoria listened to Lellia tell the forest's history: how the trees tilled the soil and enriched it for other plants to grow, making the lands livable for animals and people alike. The tale was occasionally interrupted by a neigh or whinny from the horses, and Lellia would thank them before voicing their input.

"Those beginning years seem peaceful. I wish it were like that now," Relvin said.

"As do I," Lellia said. "We have enjoyed a peaceful life within the Wispryn Weald, but as Tsoria knows all too well, there are times when that peace is disrupted."

"What happened?" Tsoria asked.

"Many questions remain about the early years when the first queen, Voletia, was appointed, but what is known is that she was needed to solve some crisis, like all other queens. Voletia was the first to talk with the trees and animals. She taught many to do the same, and—"

"They became the Vol'aerai..." Relvin said.

"Yes. I imagine, what they learned was supposed to bring peace and quell the unrest in the world, but it seemed to have the opposite effect," Lellia said.

Lellia explained how many never opened themselves to the voice and instruction of the forest and were not entrusted with gifts. They thought the Vol'aerai were discriminating against them and hoarding the power for themselves. Their envy turned into distrust, which became fear and hate. They fabricated stories to discredit Voletia and instill distrust in her motivations. The people stopped listening to reason and turned against us.

"They built walled cities to protect themselves from the Vol'aerai, but that didn't protect them from their internal divisions," Lellia said.

"The fires of hatred never unite people for long and don't discriminate against any fuel source," Relvin said.

"Yes," Lellia said. "Instead of using their differences to strengthen them, they became the new fuel for their hatred. Many factions split off to find a home of their own."

Relvin and Tsoria listened as the Elder told of the many past wars. Each conflict had a heavy toll on both sides and pushed the trees and Vol'aerai farther north. She listed the successes and failures of the past queens in their attempts to negotiate peace with the people south of the Wispryn Weald and how none was successful for long.

"The forest can't force people to change their hearts if they've closed their minds to its voice. That's why you're needed, Tsoria. You're the voice of the forest to the people who won't listen," Lellia said.

"But what can I do if there have been so many failures?" Tsoria asked.

"My dear child," Lellia said as a grandmother might soothe their grandchild. "Even if you didn't possess the gifts of the forest, you aren't as powerless as you may feel, so don't count your influence on the world as meaningless. You were picked for a reason, and in time, you will discover what makes you uniquely qualified to bring about the change needed in the world."

There were many light-hearted conversations about the forest, animals, and villages sprinkled among the more serious questions as they continued through the woods. There were also plenty of silent pauses, allowing Tsoria to contemplate the enormous weight of responsibility upon her shoulders.

It was a humbling experience for Tsoria to see the wise giants creating a path and bowing in respect to her; she was a mere sprout compared to them. The steady rhythm of the horse hooves and various animal chatter around them lulled her into a peaceful calm as she closed her eyes and connected to nature. The way the trees conversed with her felt like they were all her grandparents, doting on a visiting grandchild and assuring her along the way. The more time she spent communicating with nature around her, the easier it was for her to differentiate between each voice within the forest. Each tree and animal she connected to had a new lesson to teach her or words of advice so she could become acquainted with her kingdom, its laws, and how to manage it. However, the amount of information she was taught overwhelmed her, and after a polite exit, she opened her eyes as the sky began to change colors.

When evening fell, they dismounted in a small clearing off the path. Lellia connected to Tsoria through the forest network to teach her how to grow dwellings.

"As Queen, you are entrusted with all of the gifts of the forest. There are many you can't learn from me or any other elder, but I can teach you the basics. In time, you will learn the rest as you need them," Lellia said.

"It is strange not only hearing you in my head but also feeling your emotions," Tsoria said.

"Talking through the forest network is one of the basic gifts that most inherit if they open themselves to the voice of the forest, even before going through aliuscerai. Talking to animals works similarly, but getting used *to how they speak might take practice. You connected to the trees on your way here, which makes what you are about to do easier."*

While Tsoria learned from the experience of the elder, Relvin wandered into the woods to gather dry branches and grass to start a fire. Two small dwellings had been grown for them when Relvin returned to camp, and they were ready to prepare the evening meal.

The night watch at the northern gate of Wardrich Castle was prepared to have an uneventful evening, which was almost always the case, and why guards were attracted to being posted there. Only hunting parties used the northern gate facing the forest, and although Commander Burmad had led a party through the gate in search of two fugitives four days prior, the guards had forgotten already. The torches on the walls emitted a warm yellow glow, which kept their spirits up as they milled about conversing and joking to keep themselves awake through the long night ahead.

About an hour after evening turned into the dark of night with the stars shining overhead, a rustling sound came from the forest. Since it was home to many animals, the soldiers upon the wall took no notice until it was clear that something potentially dangerous was approaching their position. The tower crossbowmen readied their weapons and waited for orders as two men came out above the gate and prepared an arrow on the string to be loosed at the first sign of danger. They warily scanned the tree line for whatever was causing the commotion. A figure resembling a man stumbled from the trees after a few minutes.

"Halt!" The captain called out. "Identify yourself and your business here."

No intelligible response was received from the figure as he spouted gibberish while approaching the gate. At the officer's signal, the archers drew back their strings and aimed at the unfortunate soul nearing the castle.

"This is your final warning! Identify yourself at once!" The officer waited with his hand, ready to give the order, but this time, they got something like words from the figure.

"Com-m-mand...B-Bur-Burmad...f-forest...attack...w-water..." the figure stammered out as the rest of what he said became unintelligible.

The officer turned to shout to his men near the gate to open it and ordered the archers to stand down but stay alert. After descending the stairs, he grabbed a torch from the wall before joining four guards with swords drawn as they walked through the gate. Within the torchlight, the man appeared crazed and wild. His hair was disheveled and matted with leaves, large sections of his leather armor and trousers were shredded, dried blood and dirty wounds were all over his body, and somewhere in the forest, he had lost his sword. There was no mistaking that this man was indeed Burmad.

The two closest guards sheathed their swords as they rushed in to wrap their arms around the commander before he collapsed. The officer led the way back to the gate as the other two guards walked backward with their eyes to the forest and swords in hand for anything that might have been chasing Burmad. After the last of them had returned through the gate, it was barred shut.

"Bring water for the commander! Rouse the surgeon! Bring that cart over here!" The officer ordered as he gestured to different men under his command; the men rushed to carry out the orders.

Lord Darrick was in bed with a companion when there was a loud knock on his door.

"What now?" Darrick asked.

"I apologize for the disturbance at this late hour, my Lord, but Commander Burmad has returned—"

"Send him in," Darrick said with a cheerier tone as he sat up and reached for his robe.

"He is being treated by the surgeon, my Lord."

"What happened?"

Darrick's mood soured as he listened to the guard explain the situation. He got out of bed, threw on his robe, and ordered the woman to stay in the room before exiting his chambers and following the guard to the surgeon.

When he got to where Burmad's wounds were being cleaned and treated, Lord Darrick could hardly believe the state of his commander. By this time, it had been a couple of hours since they had brought Burmad in for treatment, and he was more alert. Once he relayed his account of what had happened, Lord Darrick cursed, stormed back to his quarters, and ordered the guards at his door not to disturb him again until morning. He shut and bolted the door before filling his cup with wine and gulping it down.

"The bed is still warm, my Lord," Raven said, laying seductively across the bed. "I'll help you forget your troubles."

Darrick wasn't in the mood anymore and it showed in his eyes as he turned to glare at Raven. He wanted blood after his men failed to retrieve the fugitives. He approached his bed like a predator stalking its prey.

"My Lord..." Raven said, gripping the bedpost between them after sitting up.

Raven's eyes widened in fear causing a twisted smile to grow on Darrick's lips as he got closer.

"Please...I can..." Raven pleaded weakly, attempting to placate him but causing him to turn more beastly as he pounced.

The echoes of her screams haunted the halls even after she was silenced that night.

A little after noon on the second day of their journey, Tsoria, Relvin, and Lellia exited the passage into a large clearing. At the center grew the tallest and oldest tree Tsoria or Relvin had ever seen. The deep brown smooth trunk was a massive forty feet in diameter at the base and over two hundred feet tall, with twelve large roots cutting into the ground around the circumference. The lowest branches jutted from the trunk thirty feet up and spread sixty feet in all directions. The oblong evergreen leaves were smooth and densely spaced, containing large crystal clear veins that sparkled in the sun, which was how the tree became known as a crystal tree. Nestled between two roots on the south side sat an intricate and slender throne made from crystal tree roots. Like the rings on the couple's fingers, this throne sparkled with precious metals and was adorned with large, flawless gemstones.

Once the trio had dismounted and their horses trotted away, Lellia joined Tsoria in the forest network to prepare the grounds for the ceremony.

"Connecting through the network seems easier for you today," Lellia said.

"It is," Tsoria said.

"Good. In time, it will become second nature, like moving your arms and legs, negating the need to close your eyes. Even if you can visualize what you want in your head, it can be helpful to pair physical actions with your thoughts for better communication with the forest. Practice this when you call forth chairs for the ceremony."

Tsoria drew a semicircle with her hands while she concentrated, and chairs grew from the ground facing the throne arranged in the shape she had gestured. She then used her hands to locate and grow tables for the food around the perimeter of the chairs. When everything was set up for the ceremony, Tsoria opened her eyes and saw the results.

"You will need to create tables after the ceremony for people to eat at, Tsoria, but as you are done for now, perhaps use the area at the opposite side of the crystal tree to practice or whatever you wish while we wait for everyone to arrive."

"Thank you for the instruction, Lellia."

"You're welcome. I am available for help any time, but I now need to talk to your husband about the small part he will play during the ceremony."

After Lellia left to meet with Relvin, Tsoria walked to the north side of the crystal tree and sat in solitude. The crystal tree's trunk hummed and felt warm against her back despite it being in the shade. Tsoria continued to learn from the wisdom of the forest and prepared for her new role.

A large crowd of Vol'aerai representatives from the villages were gathered by late afternoon for the crowning. The tables around the edges had been covered with various foods for the evening meal, and the air was filled with the most delicious smells. Parents attempted to contain their children as the excitement of seeing a queen's crowning was too much for the young ones to bottle up inside. At least two of every kind of creature that dwelt within emerged from the forest, from meek mouse to burly bear to majestic eagle. Each animal was treated with respect and welcomed by the Vol'aerai like family and without fear.

When late afternoon turned into evening, the elders called for everyone to take their places. A hush fell over the crowd as they turned and watched Tsoria walk down the center aisle toward the crystal tree with her hand in the crook of Relvin's arm. Before reaching the throne, the couple turned to face the crowd. Relvin felt Tsoria's hand quiver, but he squeezed her hand in assurance before she let go and stepped toward her people.

"I come before the Vol'aerai today at this sacred forest clearing, pledging myself to you and the forest we dwell within. With the council of the elders and the wisdom of the forest to guide me, I vow to protect and serve to the best of my abilities. I, Tsorianya, solemnly promise, in front of all the witnesses here, to be your queen until I can no longer serve."

After the last words were spoken, Tsoria knelt, and the audience watched crystal tree roots grow from the ground and weave a delicate crown onto her head adorned with precious jewels. The crystal roots receded when the crown was completed. Relvin reached down to take her hand, and Tsoria stood, turned, and approached the throne.

When she was seated, Relvin announced, "I introduce to you all my wife, Tsorianya, Queen of the Vol'aerai!"

The crowd stood as they cheered and clapped, and the animals joined in to celebrate and support their newly crowned queen. Tsoria's eyes sparkled while smiling as the Vol'aerai welcomed her ascension. After a minute, she stood, walked to the front of the crowd, and motioned for silence.

"I know most of you haven't spent any time with me or my husband Relvin, but I am happy that despite this fact, you are here representing your villages this evening and have shown such strong support. We look forward to meeting you all and hope we will become great friends and prove that your trust is well placed. Until then, let us join together to feast on the food you have brought tonight because if you are like me, the smells have been making your mouth water for quite some time."

Tsoria motioned for everyone to clear the chairs and move to the sides near the food tables, and while Tsoria and Relvin walked down the center aisle, the semicircle of chairs retreated into the ground. Round tables grew around the perimeter of the crystal tree, resembling lacy fractal-mesh flat-top mushrooms with chairs around them. Intricate centerpieces with diverse flowers emanating sweet scents adorned each table. Pitcher plants grew around the base of each centerpiece and produced mildly sweet and fruity nectar to drink. Glassy, light yellow mushrooms sprouted from the top of each centerpiece with stems gracefully curving downward before ending in large upturned caps, which started glowing a warm light that was more noticeable the darker it became.

When Tsoria and Relvin reached the first table of food at the back, they began filling bread bowls with a thick savory stew from large stone cauldrons and passing them to the attendees. Once everyone had been served and found seats, they served each other and found a place to sit, eat, and converse. Berries, fruits, nuts, and cheeses were acquired from other food tables when opportunities arose between conversations. The meal ended with delicately sweet and spongy hazelnut honey cakes.

Throughout the evening, Tsoria and Relvin mingled and spent hours talking to as many attendees as possible. Tsoria was delighted to catch up with several from the village where she was raised but disappointed her parents hadn't attended. Before Tsoria left the table to socialize with others, her friends promised to keep her return secret until she could personally break the news to her parents.

The animals present also greeted and conversed with them, though Tsoria had to relay to Relvin what they were saying so that he could also participate. The same red squirrel that had fed them nuts on their journey greeted them from the table of nuts and fruits, along with her mate. They were the most chatty of the animal families they talked with, though Tsoria did almost all of the conversing since there weren't many breaks long enough to convey what was said.

There was one notable animal conversation that was directed to Relvin that evening. The alpha male and female gray wolves approached the couple and greeted the Queen first.

"Alpha Tsorianya. I'm Grryffan, alpha of the prime pack. My mate Frrynner and I welcome you as leader of the forest."

The wolves bowed their heads.

"Thank you! I am pleased to meet you," Tsoria said.

"We wish to speak with your mate Relvin, but since he's not attuned to the forest, we humbly ask that you speak for us," Frrynner said.

"I will relay anything you say to my husband." Tsoria turned to Relvin and started with the introductions. "Relvin, the alphas of the prime pack Grryffan and Frrynner, are here to speak with you."

"Alphas Grryffan and Frrynner, it is a pleasure to make your acquaintance," Relvin said.

Tsoria began relaying their words, "They watched from the shadows as you fought the pack of hounds and would like to express their admiration for how you stood your ground against overwhelming odds. A true alpha."

"Thank you. I'm honored to be considered an alpha by you," Relvin said with a slight head bow.

"They would also like to express their apologies for not stepping in to help, but it was decided by the one watching through their eyes, the forest, and the wolf pack that it was necessary to test you. It was important to know how far you, an outsider, would go to protect those you had no obligation to protect. They could tell by your eyes that you knew your life would be forfeit if you fought, but you didn't hesitate to put your life on the line, unlike the 'alpha' hunting you." Grryffan let out a low, growling gag. "He ran like a coward instead of standing with his pack. He wasn't worth killing."

"I wondered what had happened to the men hunting us," Relvin said.

"They became food for several wolf packs," Tsoria said, shuddering at the thought.

"*Apologies, alpha Tsorianya, that is what happened,*" Frrynner said.

"*I know. I wish they didn't have to die,*" Tsoria said.

"*They didn't,*" Grryffan said. "*Several attempts to scare them off were made, but they sealed their fate when they pressed on anyway.*"

Tsoria continued relaying what the wolves said after the small private side note.

"The wolves say that I was tested as well because I was not initially on the list of candidates to be queen, but during our escape, I was viewed as the best choice. The wolves will proudly fight by our side if they are summoned."

"We would do the same for you," Relvin said.

The alphas bowed their heads as Relvin and Tsoria did the same in response before the wolves turned to leave.

"*Why me?*" Tsoria asked.

Grryffan turned back to look at Tsoria.

"*Despite the painful and dire circumstances you both experienced, your motivation for attacking and killing the hounds was never hatred, anger, or revenge. You and Relvin protected each other out of love.*"

Grryffan turned and trotted off to catch up to his mate before they disappeared into the woods.

The conversations and revelry continued late into the night, but when the celebrations waned, dwellings were grown to accommodate each family's needs.

CHAPTER 7

REUNION

A FEW WEEKS AFTER TSORIANYA'S ASCENSION, she and Relvin had settled into a routine while they visited each village for three to four days. A meeting was the first agenda item at each location and was an opportunity for those who hadn't attended the ascension to get to know their new queen. Tsoria and Relvin then toured with the village elder to discuss issues or things that needed to be addressed by the queen while she was there. Tsoria and Relvin spent the remainder of the days working on separate activities and rejoined in their dwelling at night to discuss the day's events before falling asleep.

Tsoria acclimated to her duties and the Vol'aerai way of life quickly since she had grown up in the Wispryn Weald. Expanding the farming fields was one of the chief concerns—the population had grown considerably since the last queen—and Tsoria asked the trees surrounding the fields to spread out to give the people more arable land. Of the many tasks requested of the Queen, none could compare with giving the parents a much-needed break and spending a day with the children. She often took them on hikes through the woods, told them stories, played games with them, and listened to each of their tales. The kids were always eager to learn anything new, and their wonderment was contagious and made Tsoria feel like a kid again.

At first, Relvin felt out of place due to his inexperience with the Vol'aerai way of life, but with each passing day, he felt more at ease after experiencing their culture. He joined groups for simple tasks like gathering dead branches shed from the trees for firewood, gathering food, or hauling water for the cooks. He watched in fascination as roots from the trees surrounding the fields enriched them with mulch and tilled the soil before he joined the Vol'aerai in sowing seeds. He learned to appreciate how much work it takes to make a meal from scratch and accompanied the cooks as they milled grain into flour, baked bread, made soup, and grilled vegetables. Every tool used was grown from crystal roots and was reclaimed by the forest when unneeded.

Education was as integral to the children's lives as playtime, and almost every moment became an opportunity for elders, parents, or animals to impart wisdom. The children learned practical topics for their life in the Wispryn Weald about plants, animals, insects, cooking, and farming. Advanced subjects like history, philosophy, anatomy, poetry, astronomy, and many others were taught as they advanced in their studies. Everyone seemed to have incredible memories because most knowledge was passed down orally or through hands-on experience. Everyone learned to read and write, but instead of keeping books or scrolls, the forest historians—some of the oldest trees in the forest—recorded everything within them as they grew.

Conflicts among the Vol'aerai were uncommon but did occur, usually among children, and they often worked themselves out. If necessary, a parent or the elder guided them toward an amicable solution. Relvin was glad to be part of such a harmonious community and hoped the conflicts of the Islatrian kingdom would not seek him out.

A large group of hunters entered the Wispryn Weald before dawn between the Foracian River and the Scar. Their horses were left behind outside the forest in the care of a few who would help load their catch into their wagon upon their return. They split into several smaller groups as they went deeper and watched for tracks that might lead them to the best hunting grounds. Eventually, each small group found places to hide and wait.

When the sun peaked through the trees and warmed the ground below, forest creatures came out of their burrows or thickets to forage for food, and still, the hunters waited. A family of wild pigs wandered close to a group and a herd of deer near another, but the hunters stayed hidden. After several hours, a unique bird call rang through the misty forest air, piquing the interest of each group of hunters, who signaled back with similar calls in confirmation. Their prey had been spotted, and every group was ready.

A merry group of children wandered through the forest noisily chattering about different topics, randomly stopping to examine a funny-looking bug, pluck juicy berries off a vine to eat, or watch whatever animal crossed their path. The teenager, Brune, who accompanied them, was kept busy trying to herd them along and prevent them from straying far away.

"Over here," one of the boys said.

The children all rushed over to look at the discovery, eager to get a first look at what they had been sent to find by their teacher. Brune examined the plant as the rest of the kids huddled around.

"Did I find it?" Thad asked.

"Yes, Thad, good job!" Brune said.

The boy beamed with pride, having been the one to find the plant before anyone else. Brune picked a few leaves and passed them to the kids to examine.

"Notice the yellow around the outside edge of the leaf, the dark green center, and the hairy purple stem and veins. Remember how this plant looks. If you ever get a wound, this plant will help stop the bleeding and protect the wound."

"My mother makes tea from the flowers to make my tummy better when I don't feel good," a little girl said.

"Excellent, Artie! You have been paying attention. Now, each of you gather several leaves, and once we get back, the elder will show us how to prepare them."

Brune led the group back toward the village when each child had a handful of the leaves. After several paces, a thrashing sound accompanied by a muffled scream came from behind the group. Brune whirled around and saw a wide-eyed Artie squirming with a hand over her mouth as she was held fast by what appeared to be a hunter.

"Let her go!" Brune said as he lunged to save her.

Two more men leaped from their hiding place and roughly secured the teen. With the strongest in the group subdued, the other children screamed and attempted to run back to the village, but by then, the rest of the enslavers had emerged from hiding and moved to cut off their escape. One by one, the frightened children were rounded up and secured. The enslavers holding the children hurried out of the forest with the remaining enslavers close behind, guarding their retreat.

Tsoria was teaching a group of kids when she stopped mid-sentence and looked south with a faraway look. This had happened many times before, usually at night, when the forest would show her a concerning event occurring within the Wispryn Weald that needed to be addressed. Most of the time, these sudden interruptions ended in no need for action, but sometimes, she would get wolves, skunks, porcupines, bears, or hawks to scare off those with ill intent. This time, however, the color drained from her face, and she broke out in a cold sweat as she muttered "no" repeatedly.

The sudden change in the Queen's demeanor frightened the younger kids, and they tugged at Tsoria's dress, asking what was wrong out of concern. One of the teens ran off to find Relvin, while others pulled the young children away from Tsoria and assured them everything would be fine.

The scene unfolding before Tsoria's eyes brought back long-suppressed feelings from when she had been taken as a child years before, and as eager as she was to save the children from having the same fate as her, all it took was a glimpse of one of the enslavers' faces to freeze her with fear before she could act. She had recognized Teivel as the one who hauled her off, and despite being free and not thinking of him in years, the face that taught her to fear had come back to haunt her again. By the time Tsoria had gotten past the fear, it was too late to send in animals to prevent the capture, but she did send a pack of wolves to pick off several of the enslavers that protected the retreat of those hauling off the children. Tsoria decided to personally ensure the kids made it home safely instead of having the wolves pursue the enslavers.

Relvin arrived as two horses trotted into the camp, and Tsoria snapped out of the forest connection. Her dress reconfigured itself into something better suited for riding as saddles grew on the horses, and she mounted the nearest mare.

"Tsoria, are you—" Relvin asked.

"Get on the horse, Relvin, we are leaving!" Tsoria said as she urged her horse in a southern direction without waiting for her husband.

Relvin mounted his horse and followed after without question. Trees moved out of the way in front of them and returned to normal behind as the horses cantered down the path being made for them. Tears flowed down Tsoria's face, but she knew that being sad at this point would not help her act when she needed to, so instead, she screamed until all she felt was determination.

After several hours and a few horse changes, they broke through the tree line, where they switched to the final set of horses called to wait for them. The journey seemed like an eternity to Tsoria as they followed the cart's tracks, and as time wore on, she closed her eyes and talked to the mare to pass the time.

"I have only been queen for a few weeks, and enslavers come to steal our children," Tsoria said.

"Enslavers? They are a scourge upon the earth. I hope you teach them a lesson," the mare said.

"I thought I had gotten past the fear of my captors from long ago when I was taken. Maybe I buried it."

"Fear is an insatiable leach. It is slippery and painful to face, but the longer it stays attached, the deeper it buries its fangs until it controls you with the pain it inflicts."

"Today is the day I face my fear no matter what it takes," Tsoria said.

"Good. I can hear the squeaky wheels of their cart in the distance, Queen Tsorianya. Get ready for a hard gallop once we get closer."

When the enslavers were spotted ahead, the horses squealed and dug deep into their energy reserves, straining every muscle until they were at full gallop. The enslavers on horseback turned their horses around to confront their pursuers while the cart continued. Tsoria reached out with her hands, and before the two sides met, she raised them and closed her fists. Roots burst from the ground to snatch the enslavers from their saddles. The queen left them dangling midair as she passed them and connected to the horses harnessed to the cart, ordering them to slow to a stop. The bewildered drivers picked up a whip to force the horses forward, but before they could use it, Tsoria used roots to pluck them from the front seat and left them midair like the other enslavers. Tsoria and Relvin's horses slowed until they were next to the cart, and then she and Relvin dismounted.

"Thank you for helping us get here so quickly," Tsoria said to both horses as she hugged them.

"Happy to be of service, Queen Tsorianya. Is there anything else you require of us?" The horses asked.

"No, you may return home and rest with your families. We will use the other horses to pull the cart back home."

"Very well, safe journeys to you."

"And to you as well."

As the horses turned and walked back to the forest, Tsoria stretched her arms towards the cart and articulated fine movements with her hands, directing roots to curl around the cage in the back and tear it open. Once she confirmed the children were unharmed, she spent a few minutes calming them down and had Relvin stand guard. She turned around and took several deep breaths with her eyes closed to calm herself before motioning for the roots to bring all the enslavers close together in front of her to address them.

"I am Tsorianya, Queen of the Vol'aerai, and you have attacked my people and stolen children from their families. If you had caused harm to any one of them, nothing would have stopped me from ripping you open and letting the buzzards pick you apart while your heart still beat in your chest. Since they are all unharmed, I will be merciful and leave you with a parting gift to remind you never to return to the Wispryn Weald."

Tsoria faced her open hands to the ground and slowly lifted them as she turned them palm up. Multiple strands of crystal root grew from the ground until they reached each slaver's forearms and burrowed into and under their skin, creating a raised tattoo of a chain circling their arm. The process was painful, and several of them begged for her to stop, to no avail. When the marks were complete, she addressed them once more.

"I think the mark is fitting for how you chain your victims into a life of slavery. However, this isn't only a symbol. It is a promise from the Vol'aerai that if you ever place even one toe into our territory again, you will be bound in servitude to the earth until it has reclaimed everything it has given to you. When the water is extracted from your body, each bone is shattered into tiny fragments, and every organ is invaded by roots for the nutrients within while you are still alive, you will know what true pain is."

Tsoria turned toward the man who had snatched her from the forest and motioned for the roots to bring him face-to-face with her.

"You may not remember me from twelve years ago, Teivel, but I remember you. You were the man of my nightmares for years, but you will be no longer. Get a good look at my face. From now on, I will be the woman of your nightmares." Tsoria stepped back and addressed the group, "Tell King Dhar I wish to speak to him. Now, get out of sight before I withdraw my grace."

The queen motioned for the roots holding the enslavers to throw them to the ground in a southern direction before retreating. The men ran off as quickly as they could while she watched. Tsoria's attention returned to the cart once the men had reached a comfortable distance away. As she got close, a girl about ten years old stepped forward to where the cage door had been. She was staring at Tsoria with her head cocked to the side.

"Are you my big sister?" The girl asked.

Taken aback at the question and the fact that this girl's red hair and green eyes hadn't popped out at her earlier, Tsoria replied, "I don't know, but perhaps when we get you back home, we will find out. Does that sound good to you?"

The little girl beamed and nodded her head, "I've always wanted to meet my big sister, but I don't even know her name. My father always looks sad and says she is traveling, and my mother starts crying if I ask..." she paused and looked at the ground before speaking with sadness in her voice, "I don't ask anymore. I don't like it when Mother cries."

"Would you like to ride with us in the front seat on the way home as if I were your big sister?"

"Oh, may I?" The girl asked.

"Of course. Would you tell me your name?"

"My name is Eviara, and I am ten and one half."

"What a wonderful name," Tsoria said as she helped the girl down from the back of the cart. "You may call me Tsoria. I wanted a sister to talk to when I was younger, but enslavers took me. I don't know if my parents had any children after me."

"Like me?" Eviara asked as she followed Tsoria to the front of the cart.

"Yes, by the very same men who took you."

"Will they come back?"

"No, they will not bother you ever again. I told the trees to stop them if they ever try to step into the forest again," Tsoria said as she helped Eviara onto the front seat of the cart.

"I wish I could talk to the trees and animals."

"Maybe I can teach you," Tsoria said as she and Relvin climbed up to the seat on each side of Eviara. "The important thing is to listen for the forest and feel its voice inside you."

"I would like to learn from you. I like having a big sister," Eviara said as she hugged Tsoria.

The queen put her arm around Eviara's shoulders and squeezed as she said, "And I think I will enjoy being a big sister to you."

Relvin grabbed the reins and prompted the horses to pull the cart around. The trip was much longer at a walking pace on the way back to the forest than it was in pursuit of the enslavers. However, the journey felt much shorter than it was as they spent the time laughing and storytelling and getting to know the children.

The southern village had been filled with the sounds of grief felt by everyone within that morning. Although only some of the families were directly affected, the pain of loss was felt by everyone, for they had all spent time raising each other's children. Tasks went undone, and food had lost its taste because everything reminded them of their children, but before evening, they watched the forest part to allow a cart into the village center. When the children leaped from the back and ran into their parents' awaiting arms, happy exclamations filled the village as their sadness turned into joy.

Tsoria got down from the cart and helped Eviara to the ground, and as the girl ran off to her parents, Relvin and Tsoria unhitched the horses and let them run off in freedom. With the children returned to their parents, Tsoria ran into Relvin's arms with tears streaming down her face as she let herself feel all the emotions she had suppressed during the ordeal.

"I'm supposed to be strong…protect my people…fear prevented me from acting…What kind of Queen allows…? I feel…failed…by letting these…" Tsoria blubbered between sobs.

Upon hearing that, Relvin reached out for her head with both hands and turned it up until he looked directly into her teary eyes.

"My love, you haven't failed. Letting those enslavers get away and not fighting to recover the children would have been a failure. You fought for the children as only you could. A queen can't always prevent bad from befalling their kingdom, but they can help their people recover. Tsoria, you have succeeded already."

Relvin kissed her on the forehead and tightly wrapped her in his arms as she digested what he had told her. Even though her tears did not immediately stop, his warm and caring embrace gave her a safe spot to let herself feel her emotions and calm down.

After several minutes, Eviara came up behind Relvin with her mother and father in tow and excitedly said, "Come on, Mother, Father! I want you to meet my big sister, who saved us all this morning."

Tsoria pulled away from Relvin and wiped away her tears before stepping around her husband to meet Eviara's parents, but as she looked, she recognized the faces that greeted her as those of her parents.

"Tsorianya? Is that you?" Her mother asked.

"Yes, Mother, I'm finally home," Tsoria said as she started crying for a new reason when she ran into her parents' embrace.

"You *are* my older sister?" Eviara's eyes got big, and her face lit up. "Hooray! I have a sister!" Eviara said as she joined the group hug, and the family was whole again.

Tsoria and Relvin spent the rest of the day with her family, reciting stories of the events they had missed during her absence, what happened while she was growing up in captivity, Lord Darrick, and all the ladies who raised her. Her family was enthralled by the stories of her escape from Wardrich Castle and how Relvin aided her flight from there. When her parents heard the tales of her aliuscerai, marriage, and ascension, they couldn't help but express their pride in who she had grown to become, though they were saddened they hadn't traveled to see her crowning. Tsoria's parents welcomed Relvin into the family with open arms and thanked him for helping to make their family whole again.

Tsoria's return from captivity gave renewed hope that the missing children from years past were alive and waiting for their chance to return. The whole village put on a feast that night to celebrate the presence of Queen Tsorianya, the return of their children, and honor the memory of those who had not yet returned. Everyone danced, laughed, sang, and enjoyed the merriment late into the night.

Relvin sat on the bed as he watched Tsoria pacing back and forth in front of him within the glow of the mushrooms illuminating their dwelling interior.

"What is on your mind, my love?" Relvin asked.

Tsoria paused her pacing and turned to Relvin. "I can't let this attack on my people go. We may have recovered the children, but what is to prevent future attacks? I feel a clear message is needed to deter further aggressions."

"What response are you contemplating?"

"I want to close our borders to all outsiders, no matter their intent."

Relvin played with his beard. "For how long?"

"As long as it takes to attract King Dhar's attention."

"It is possible you already have his attention if Darrick reported the loss of his guards and hounds. But if that isn't enough, attacking the enslavers on his sovereign soil should get his attention."

"Is closing our border too much?"

Relvin put his hand down and looked up to his wife. "No...it is a logical fortification of Vol'aerai territory. No matter what you do, the accumulation of actions against his kingdom will force King Dhar to see it as aggression."

Tsoria began pacing again. "I feel the pain endured by the forest over thousands of years more than most." Tsoria paused to look at Relvin and gesture to the north. "The forest can't take this much longer. I need to do something before the pain becomes unbearable and the forest unleashes its fury." Tsoria resumed pacing with animated arm gestures. "If it means we must go to war, then we go to war. I can't sit by as queen and let my people be slandered, bullied, kidnapped, or attacked for being who they are without doing something." Tsoria pointed to the ground and drew a line in the air. "The line has been drawn, and I won't suffer their aggression any longer."

"Then it is decided, and I will be on the battlefield alongside you," Relvin said. "I can't wait to see King Dhar's face when he underestimates you, my queen."

Tsoria closed her eyes and reached out to the entirety of the forest as she told every tree and creature within to shut and protect all borders. When Relvin saw Tsoria open her eyes, he reached out and pulled her onto his lap on the bed.

"I admire you more every day, Queen Tsorianya. May I be of any further assistance to you tonight?" Relvin asked, smiling.

Tsoria giggled as she draped her arms around Relvin's neck and kissed him. "I think you know exactly how you can serve me, but as my servant, I expect you to be thorough."

"I'm always thorough, my queen, but there might not be an opening in your schedule. It's been quite hectic."

"My schedule is always open for admiration."

"As you wish, my queen."

The day's tension seemed to melt away as their clothes dissolved. The glow of the mushrooms faded, and Relvin took his wife to be her servant for the night.

CHAPTER 8
PREPARATION

IN A CIRCULAR ARRANGEMENT OF CHAIRS grown beneath the shade of the crystal tree, Queen Tsorianya stood as she told the village elders about the kidnapping, which had occurred two days prior. They were appalled by the latest brazen attack on the children.

"I have closed our borders to outsiders to prevent further attacks on our people until a permanent arrangement is made with the Islatrian Kingdom," Tsoria said. "However, Relvin is most familiar with the king's behavior and has informed me we can expect retaliation from King Dhar."

Tsoria turned and gestured to her husband to take over as she walked to her chair and sat. Relvin stood, stepped toward the center, and addressed the elders.

"I've never met King Dhar, but from what I have been told and observed while in his army, I can say that he is a proud man who has outlasted several rebellions and coup attempts because he deals with them swiftly and harshly." Relvin emphasized his point with a chopping motion of his hands. "With the attack on Darrick's men, the attack on the enslavers on his sovereign land, and the closing of the forest borders to hunters and gatherers, Dhar will be obligated to respond," Relvin said.

Elder Oren stood to be acknowledged, and Relvin gestured for him to speak.

"I'm sure you're aware, but I would like to point out that we are neither trained nor equipped for war. We don't have soldiers, weaponry, armor, siege engines, or fortifications. We have built our lives around peace and the balance of life," Oren said and sat when finished.

"Thank you for that reminder, Elder Oren. We can hope that King Dhar will send a delegation to negotiate with us first, but I would expect him to send a large army in an appearance of strength," Relvin said.

Elder Nemica stood, and Relvin acknowledged her.

"Could you train us to fight?" Nemica asked before returning to her seat.

"Yes, but as Elder Oren pointed out," Relvin gestured to Oren, "there isn't a standing Vol'aerai army, and we won't have time to train one from scratch."

Tsoria stood, and Relvin turned to face her.

"We have no allies to call on. How do we get an army?" Tsoria asked and sat.

"I never said we needed an army to beat him," Relvin said and saw a perplexed look on Tsoria's face. "I know that seems like an odd thing to say. Let me explain." Relvin paused to survey the elders around him. "My mentor told me: 'Battles are won or lost in the hearts and minds of men, not with the number of soldiers on the field.'" Relvin paused to let the words sink in. "I see two possible paths to victory. The enslavers were told to let King Dhar know we are open to negotiating before bloodshed is necessary. However, the enslavers look out for their interests; I wouldn't rely on them to deliver the message."

Tsoria stood again and said, "Do you think he would be willing to talk if we sent emissaries directly to him?"

"Even if we sent a delegation to Islatria, what can we trade him for peace? He could see it as a sign of weakness and not submit to our demands." Tsoria looked defeated when she sat. "The Vol'aerai are relegated to fairy tales. Will he believe they are Vol'aerai or part of a rebel group taking advantage of the tales to get something out of him? The most likely option is to defeat Dhar in battle and force him to negotiate a favorable treaty."

Elder Yarah stood, and Relvin turned around to hear her question.

"This brings us back to what Oren said. How do we fight without becoming as savage as them? And how do we do it with no army?" Yarah said before returning to her seat.

Relvin sighed.

"I don't have an answer to that problem yet. I was trained to tackle problems with brute force in King Dhar's army. Since we don't have that luxury, we will need to use what we have." Relvin grasped his chin and paced as he thought for a time before looking up. "I have an idea, but I need a better understanding of the abilities granted by the forest. Based on the time it takes to send messages and form an army from all provinces, we will have at least one month to devise a strategy."

Elder Lellia stood and was acknowledged.

"Assuming we get him to the negotiating table. Who will do the negotiations?" Lellia said before sitting.

"Queen Tsorianya. If we send anyone else, it will look like we aren't serious, and that she is afraid to face him," Relvin said.

Elder Torin stood, and Relvin turned towards him.

"How do we get him to agree to our terms, whatever they may be? Can we trust Dhar to honor a treaty?" Torin said before sitting.

"The specifics of the negotiations will depend on the information gleaned with the help of the forest historians and your advice as elders. I believe Dhar will honor his end of whatever deal is struck. He may be proud and not wish to look weak, but to my knowledge, he has never reneged on his word without a good reason."

Elder Vellios stood next.

"What if negotiations don't convince him to leave in peace?" Vellios asked before retaking his place.

"Good question, Elder Vellios, we need to be prepared for every outcome. War is ugly and I don't wish any to be exposed to it if they don't have to be, which leaves me, the trees, and the predators of the forest as soldiers. Like you, I would prefer it doesn't come down to killing. I know many of the soldiers of Dhar's army and their families. I don't wish to make widows or orphans of anyone unnecessarily. However, I will unleash the full fury of the forest upon them if it comes to it..." Relvin sighed and briefly looked at the ground before raising his head to look at the elders. "At least that is how I would do it. However, I'm an outsider and the forest isn't mine to command. I want to learn to communicate with the forest to discuss this matter and develop a bloodless plan while you search for the best way to negotiate with the king," Relvin said.

Pearla stood to ask a question.

"Since we haven't yet seen an army amassing at our threshold, I suggest we not alarm anyone in the villages until we know what will happen. We should go about our normal activities as if nothing is of concern," Pearla said before sitting.

"I agree," Tsoria said as she stood from her chair and took the floor as Relvin retreated to his seat. "After another few days with my parents' village, Relvin and I will continue making our rounds and taking care of issues we have not addressed." Tsoria paused and looked around to see if anyone else had any comments or questions. "Well, that is all I wanted to discuss today. If no one else has anything to address, I will let you get back to your villages."

It had been several days since the meeting, and Relvin and Tsoria had moved to the next village to help where they were needed. Relvin spent more time each day in class with the children as they learned to be with nature. Although he had joined under the pretense of helping the teachers handle the children, which he was good at, he listened to every lesson as if he were also a student. In the evening, he also spent time with the village elder for private lessons to accelerate his training.

Early one morning, before the sun was visible above the horizon, Relvin slipped out of bed so he would not wake Tsoria and got dressed before walking east to the ancient circle of trees. When he reached the center, he got down on one knee, pressed his fingers into the ground, and listened to the forest sounds around him with his eyes closed. He had made Tsoria his world by marrying her, but now was the time to open up to her home that he was now within. The sun ascended, and its warm light filtered into the circle through the leaves of the surrounding trees, and still, Relvin waited.

"Welcome to the forest, Relvin. We are pleased you have joined us," the Elder trees around him said in unison with deep, woody voices as a warm feeling embraced him.

"I hear you," Relvin said. *"This is incredible."*

"We know why you have come, but the time is not yet upon us to speak on such matters."

"I understand." Relvin said. *"This is only a first step to trust. I have more to learn."*

"Queen Tsorianya also," the elder trees said. *"Your bond will be tested. You will need each other for the coming conflicts."*

"Thank you for your wisdom, elder trees. I hope to learn more in the coming days."

"We look forward to the next time we speak. Your wife will wake soon. Go to her."

Before getting up, Relvin reached out to the one person with whom he had the closest connection. It didn't take long to connect with Tsoria, who was still asleep.

Tsoria was awakened by the warm feeling of Relvin close by and the sound of his voice bidding her a good morning. She enjoyed waking up with Relvin beside her and smiled in satisfaction from the restful night she had received. She let out a moan as she stretched her limbs before rolling over to kiss her husband, but her arm only touched the bedspread, and when she opened her eyes, he was not in bed with her. She sat up, confused and panicked, but Tsoria still felt his warmth embrace her. She closed her eyes again and followed the feeling.

"*Surprise,*" Relvin said.

"*You scared me a little by not being here this morning,*" Tsoria said.

"*Yeah…I felt your panic. I'm sorry. I wanted to try something out before rejoining you this morning now that I have connected with the forest.*"

"*Well, now that you had fun, Relvin, I expect a proper greeting before we join everyone for the morning meal.*"

"*Yes, my gorgeous flower. I would not want you to start your day without one. See you soon.*"

Tsoria lay on the bed as she awaited her husband with a smile, happy that Relvin had become part of the Vol'aerai.

The main hall of Islatria's keep was an impressive sight for anyone summoned before the king. The massive carved oak inner doors trimmed in gold between larger-than-life statues depicting knight heroes of the kingdom would be enough to intimidate anyone from going further. However, today, the doors were open, and a crowd was waiting inside to have the king hear their grievances. At the other end, past the large overbuilt columns and the many immaculate gold candelabras hanging from the tall vaulted ceiling above, was the platform where grandiose statues depicting the first king and queen of the kingdom stood. King Dhar sat between the statues upon one of two carved white marble gilded thrones with royal blue pillows on the seats.

The king was anxious for the afternoon court session to end. It was one of his least favorite royal duties, but every once in a while, there was some bit of information that piqued his interest. More than a few times, he learned of unrest within the kingdom that would have led to a coup or rebellion had he not been alerted early and able to squelch the threat before it got out of hand.

Dhar ruled on the matter brought before him and the citizens turned to exit the hall as he gestured for the next group to come forward. The councilor attending to the line of waiting subjects stepped aside to allow several lesser lords to approach the king. They bowed their heads before the steps leading up to the platform upon which the throne stood.

"Speak your complaint," King Dhar said.

"Thank you for seeing us, Your Majesty. We represent the northern towns and cities close to the Wispryn Weald, where hunters and gatherers have returned with wild game and produce to sell for many years. Many rely on what is found within to feed their families or to sell at market, but in recent weeks, they have been denied access to these rich lands."

"Denied? By whom?"

"We aren't sure, Sire. It's like the forest has come alive. There are reports of trees and vines moving to block the way inside no matter where people try to enter, wolves growl from the shadows and chase anyone out if they manage to step inside, hawks dive and claw at your citizens, or skunks spray them. Everything within has lost all fear and is hostile towards those who dare to enter."

"Are they drunk or hallucinating? The Wispryn Weald has been silent for—"

"Begging your pardon, Sire," interrupted the lords, "but we assure you we would not waste your time with such trivial things as hallucinations. Each of us witnessed the hostile nature of the Wispryn Weald when we accompanied your subjects to the forest. It does not matter which day we go or how carefully sobriety is ensured. We are always met with a hostile denial of entry."

"What could have triggered this?" Dhar wondered out loud.

"Apologies, Your Majesty, for speaking out of turn. If you permit us an audience—" said one of the subjects in line.

The councilor chastised those breaking court decorum. The king signaled to the councilor to cease berating his subject, then turned to one of his nearby attendants.

"Find out who else has a complaint about the Wispryn Weald and permit them all to approach."

The attendant nodded in acknowledgment and hurried to carry out the command. A small crowd of about thirty came forward and took a position behind the lords already there. The king was now fully attentive since this was bigger than he had believed.

The king addressed those who had spoken from the line, "Please, tell me what you know of this situation."

"Your Majesty, like the lords before us, my men and I hunted in the Wispryn Weald two weeks ago," Fasik said. "A pack of wolves chased us out and killed a third of us as we ran for our lives. While journeying to the market with our wares, we were torn from our saddles in a manner that can only be described as witchcraft and assaulted by a redhead woman and her guard.

"Did they say who they were and what they wanted?"

"The woman identified herself as Tsorianya, Queen of the Vol'aerai, Sire. They chased off our horses, stole our cart, and marked us for death should we ever attempt to re-enter the forest."

At this last comment, a group of seventeen held up their arms to show the chain grown into their forearms.

"They did all this because you hunted in the woods?"

"Yes, Sire. They gave no reason or warning before they attacked. The Queen had a blood lust in her eyes and no regard for your laws nor desire to negotiate peace."

King Dhar fell silent as he contemplated the reports brought before him. The king recalled the letter from Lord Darrick delivered to him several weeks prior about an incident in the Wispryn Weald. Since Darrick had described the red-headed woman as a witch offering blood sacrifices to appease the forest gods, the king had dismissed the letter as the drunken ramblings of an old friend partying a little too hard on his birthday. However, he was starting to think he might have been wrong to dismiss the letter since Lord Darrick was not known to believe in fairytales. The king snapped back to his surroundings when someone in the crowd sneezed and apologized for the interruption.

"Thank you all for bringing this matter to my attention. I assure you that I will look further into this issue and do something about it."

"Thank you, Your Majesty," the crowd replied as they bowed.

The king turned to his attendant.

"Take these citizens to the treasury so that they and their subjects may be fairly compensated for their troubles."

"It shall be done, Sire," the attendant said as he bowed his head, then told the small crowd to follow him out of the great hall.

The king addressed his nearby councilor, "Cancel the rest of my schedule and summon my generals, advisor, and head treasurer to my council chambers immediately. Tell my historian to bring every book and scroll about the Wispryn Weald and Vol'aerai."

"Yes, Sire," the councilor said before shooing everyone not yet seen away.

Dhar remained seated as the last of his subjects exited the hall and the doors closed, leaving him to contemplate his options. Since the Vol'aerai had not been a threat for hundreds of years, he had doubted their existence as a prince and failed to see the need to study them in his history lessons. He had always assumed that the stories of the Vol'aerai were nonsense because he knew of no one who had personally witnessed evidence supporting the fantastic tales everyone readily told. However, after the northern attacks and access to the forest cut off, he began to think he had made a mistake not learning more about them.

Dhar rose from his throne and motioned for his guards to accompany him to his council room, where he would meet his advisors and generals.

When King Dhar entered the room, almost everyone he had summoned was waiting within. His four highest-ranking generals, Torridol, Rashe, Fasid, and Norrik, stood near the table, speculating that a war or new campaign was the reason for their presence. His head treasurer and advisor, Mordrid and Gouste, kept to themselves at the side of the room. Petre, the royal historian, was the only absentee.

"Advisors, generals," King Dhar said, "you have been summoned because of a matter brought to my attention. Since Petre has not arrived, Torridol, what is happening on our western border?"

"Your Majesty, the Kalumat border raids continue to test our armies. We have increased our patrols and recruited more soldiers for our border towns," Torridol said before reaching for several flag markers and placing them on the painted table map of the kingdom. "These recent raids show they are pushing the skirmishes further north each year, but our armies continue to repel them with few losses."

"How many do they send?" Dhar asked.

"Small parties of twenty to thirty men, Sire. They seem to be testing our weaknesses and responses. They could be readying for a larger attack soon," Torridol said.

"A troubling development." Dhar motioned to General Fasid. "You studied the Tashtari capabilities during our negotiations. Enlighten us with a review."

"Sire, the Tashtari Islands are a small but formidable kingdom. I'm glad we signed a treaty with them."

"And if the treaty were dissolved?" Dhar asked.

"Their naval vessels are aging, but they outnumber ours two to one. I would advise against challenging them at sea, Sire," Fasid said. "Even under the best circumstances in a war on land, we would sustain heavy losses, and there is no guarantee of repelling them. Tashtari citizens are trained for combat from childhood. Even if we took the fight to them, every citizen would be a threat."

The door to the room opened, and Petre entered with his arms full of old scrolls and books. He placed them at the far end of the table and then turned to King Dhar.

"My apologies for my late arrival, Your Majesty. There was much to review," Petre said.

"To the contrary, Petre, you arrived as I was getting to the heart of the matter."

King Dhar picked up a flag marker from the table's edge and walked around to place it at the border of the Wispryn Weald. He looked up at the generals opposite his position.

"The Vol'aerai have appointed a new queen, and she is already making moves. She has awakened the trees of the Wispryn Weald, attacked citizens both inside and outside the forest, and is denying our citizens access to the hunting and foraging grounds of the forest. If this continues, our treaty with the Tashtari will be in jeopardy, and we could have a three-front war on our hands, a war that will spread our forces thin and be difficult to win."

The generals digested the news as they studied the map.

"Any demands or reason given for the attacks?" Rashe asked.

"None that have been reported," Dhar said.

"Can the source of the reports be trusted, Sire?" Rashe asked. "Someone could be—"

"I doubt the accuracy of the enslavers' report," Dhar said, "but the report from Lord Darrick and other northern lords are trustworthy."

"Regardless of the accuracy, Sire, attacks on your citizens must be dealt with," Torridol said. "We can't afford another uprising like in Ekbahn."

"I agree," Norrik said. "The Tashtari and Kalumat are not a problem now, but if we don't respond to these Vol'aerai attacks, they might exploit your apparent weakness, Sire."

"A war to pacify the Vol'aerai to prevent a larger war is a shrewd move," Fasid said to Norrik before turning to the king. "However, I'm concerned about how little we know about their capabilities outside children's tales. How can we prepare?"

"Petre?" King Dhar said as he turned to the historian.

"Sire, generals, many records about the Vol'aerai have been lost to the elements or worms over the years before they could be duplicated," Petre said, "but I have searched the available records, and nothing concerning stood out. While there have been many conflicts with the Vol'aerai, most of the time, they retreat instead of fighting back."

"Don't they possess mystical abilities?" Torridol asked.

"There was one ancient reference in a damaged scroll to walking trees and sinking armies, but there wasn't sufficient context. Likely, it was about traps instead of any mystical powers because no other records mention anything to suggest the Vol'aerai are magicians or sorcerers," Peter said. "My conclusion is that they are as human and vulnerable as us."

"Any suggestions on how we beat them?" Dhar asked.

"There are three ways the past kings have dealt with the Vol'aerai. We could choose to leave them alone, and they will keep to themselves, but since the Tashtari treaty is at stake, I wouldn't suggest that. This leaves only two possibilities: meet them on the battlefield and force them into a treaty that favors our side, or if you get close enough, you could kill their queen. There are verified accounts where the Vol'aerai queen was killed, and without their queen, they retreat."

"Is there any opposition to fighting the Vol'aerai?" Dhar asked after giving time for the information to settle in each mind. No one spoke up. "Mordrid, how is the treasury?"

"We can fund a short campaign without issue, Your Majesty, but I will have a financial plan for every eventuality by the end of the day," Mordrid said.

"I suggest creating provision waypoints to speed your armies along the route," Rashe said.

"Good, I want this campaign to be as quick as possible," Dhar said. "Gouste, send word for each province to mobilize my armies in the north."

"Yes, Sire," Gouste said.

"I will arrange for our best spies to scout the border. If the Vol'aerai have a weakness, they will find it," Torridol said.

"Have them begin where the enslavers encountered the Vol'aerai Queen," Norrik said.

"Since this is not our usual campaign, I want to hear some plans by the time I arrive," Dhar said.

The room emptied as everyone dispersed to start on the tasks each had been given.

In an isolated stretch of the coast in the far eastern reaches of the Wispryn Weald, Gafre worked in the nursery he had established a few weeks prior. The seclusion helped him attune to the delicate work he was tasked with. As a plant specialist, he knew that creating a whole new type of tree was usually a long process that required years of hard work and many failures to get the desired result, but from what Queen Tsorianya said when she contacted him, he didn't have that kind of time. If he were to succeed in his mission, he would have to put every ability granted to him by the forest on the table for this project.

"Terril, come here a minute," Gafre said to his assistant.

His fifteen-year-old apprentice, who had been at a desk extracting new seeds, put down the seedpod he was working on and came to see what Gafre wanted.

"Why aren't you watering these seedlings?" Gaffe said as he pointed to a few containers that felt dry.

"I water them daily, but they are a fickle variety," Terril said. "At first, they thrived with abundant water, but more recently, they seem to do better with less."

"Their growth has slowed considerably compared with the other varieties."

"I noticed that, too. I found a mushroom growing near the base of one of them, removed it, and reduced the amount of water I used, thinking that perhaps the soil was too moist and a fungus was attacking the tree."

"What kind of mushroom was it?" Gafre asked.

"An edible salt-dependent mushroom variety," Terril said.

"Salt-dependent? Interesting…"

Gafre picked up one of the containers for a closer inspection. The seedling was at least a foot shorter than the other varieties they had been working with and seemed like it was struggling to get enough nutrients. They were his most ambitious variety, and Gafre knew they would likely fail, but he was not yet at the point of giving up.

"Too young for a voice…what can we do?" Gafre said as he vocalized his thought process, an oddity that Terril was used to though sometimes it was difficult to distinguish when Gafre was talking to himself. "Forced to test before I was prepared to…have no choice now." Gafre shrugged and turned to his apprentice. "Bring a bucket of seawater."

"Are you sure, Gafre?" Terril asked. "You taught me that salt—"

"I know what I taught you, and I stand by it, but in this case, we need it to be salt tolerant and have to take risks."

Terril picked up a bucket, headed for the beach, and returned with sea water soon after. Gafre took a cupful of the brine and watered the container in his hand. When they checked the seedling later in the afternoon, it seemed healthier than the two seedlings of the same variety they had not yet watered with seawater.

"I rarely see seedlings tolerate salt this well, let alone thrive best in its presence. There is still hope for this variety, but this is only the beginning, Terril. There is still much work to be done. Set aside these three trees and water them exclusively with seawater."

"Yes, Gafre."

Terril watered the remaining two seedlings with salt water as Gafre had done before returning to harvesting seeds.

CHAPTER 9
CONFLICT

QUEEN ISIDA WAS ENJOYING A QUIET morning in the royal garden, reading a book of poetry under the gazebo shade as she waited for Dhar to approach and announce his departure for the battlefield as per tradition. Her lady-in-waiting embroidered a pillowcase while sitting across from Isida along with one of her handmaidens. The weeks since Dhar had formally begun war preparations were filled with restless nights for the Queen, leaving her with puffy eyes and a terrible foreboding. She was glad for the sweet smell of flowers in full bloom filling the air and the melodious songs of the birds that calmed her down as she rested her head against the nearby post.

When Isida opened her eyes, the book of poetry had fallen to her feet, and the pleasant morning had turned eerie. The sky was an ominous red-orange color, and the breeze brought a putrid smell to her nose instead of the sweet flowers she had been enjoying seemingly moments ago. She stood and looked around as she called out for her lady-in-waiting, but there was no answer.

She turned back to where she had sat, intending to pick up her book before returning to her chambers in the castle, but suddenly found herself next to the keep. Thousands of roots emerged from the ground as she watched. They tore apart the walls, and the keep started to collapse. Isida's heart raced in her chest as an avalanche of stones and timber tumbled toward her, and she brought her hands up in front of her face to protect herself. However, the queen found herself near the top of the rubble pile instead of being crushed by the stones. The war-torn Islatrian flag—three white rectangles separated by vertical and horizontal blue stripes meeting at a center golden sun—hung from its mangled pole. A plant emerged from the rubble below and produced a beautiful, sweet-smelling red flower. The plant grew taller until the flower touched the flag, causing it to burst into flames that consumed everything as it spread in an ever-widening circle.

Isida turned to run from the fire but tripped and fell as she lost her footing when something crunched and gave way under her foot. She reached down and grabbed the first thing her hand touched in the ash-covered ground, bringing it up until she was face-to-face with a skull that King Dhar's mangled crown hung cockeyed upon. As she looked into the gaping eye sockets, it spoke:

> Life or death the flower brings,
> Heed her words as the bell rings.
> One last chance, Islatria's fate,
> Warn King Dhar before, too late.

The sea of skulls she stood within repeated the poem. The Queen tried to scream, but the only sound that came out of her mouth were the words of the ominous poem as she felt herself disintegrate into a pile of bones.

Isida's eyes flew open as she awoke within the gazebo screaming. Her lady-in-waiting and handmaiden flew to her side and grasped her hands, trying to calm her down.

"Your Majesty! It was only a dream! You are safe, you are safe," the lady-in-waiting said.

"I saw..." the Queen paused to breathe.

"That's it, breathe…breathe…" the lady-in-waiting said as she breathed with her.

"…the end."

"You are safe, nothing to worry—"

"No! I must speak with Dhar now!"

"I will send for His Majesty at once," the handmaiden said as she stood and held her dress up a little to make running easier, leaving the queen to catch her breath and calm down with her lady-in-waiting.

Dhar slowed as he approached the clearing where Isida waited in the gazebo. Isida's lady-in-waiting left the queen's presence and curtsied as Dhar passed before walking a short distance away to join the handmaiden to give the monarchs privacy. Isida paced in the shade, wringing her hands, and reminding herself to breathe as Dhar climbed the steps to join his wife. Upon seeing her husband, the queen forsook typical royal protocol and embraced Dhar. The closeness surprised him. Their wedding may have been a political affair, as most royal weddings were, but they had grown to love each other despite their many disagreements. However, there seemed to be more fights than pleasant interactions in recent years. It became easier to avoid each other on most days unless their interaction was necessary for royal functions.

After several moments, King Dhar spoke, "Isida, my queen, what has gotten you so agitated this morning that you sent your handmaiden to summon me with such haste?"

Isida withdrew from his embrace and wiped her tears before looking at him.

"Dreams have been disturbing my rest for some time, but this morning, as I was reading, I had a most vivid and terrible vision I must tell you about before you leave."

Isida described every scene she had experienced within the dream as she paced and motioned with her hands to express the horror to her husband.

"That was the poetic warning from the dream. The only conclusion is you will face a choice that will decide the fate of this kingdom."

"Isida, my queen, do not trouble yourself further." Dhar reached and placed a hand on Isida's arm. "It was but a dream. You are tired, and your fears are manifest—"

Isida stepped back and pointed a finger at Dhar. "I wouldn't disturb you with this unless I felt it was important, Dhar, and you know it."

"But—"

"How many times did I wake screaming from dreams before your other fights?"

"None, that I am aware."

"How many battles did I ask you not to wage?"

"Two before this, but—"

"I was right about both of those wasn't I?" Isida asked. Isida's eyes seemed to bore holes through Dhar as she waited for the answer he was reluctant to give.

"Yes..."

"Something about this battle is different. There is still time to stop this before it happens," Isida said as she grasped his hand, pleading with her eyes for him to listen to her.

"Isida, I can't let this go without action. This isn't only about the Vol'aerai." Isida pulled away and threw a hand in the air as she paced again. "I can't fulfill my agreement with the Tashtari without the lumber of the Wisp—"

"There are other woods—"

"None are as vast and strong. You know I don't relish war, but my hand is forced," Dhar said. "There's no other way."

Isida spun around to face Dhar.

"No one is forcing you into battle except your ego, Dhar," Isida said. "Obsession with strength and bravado is why you can't think of an alternative. Aren't you tired of the constant fighting and tit-for-tat exchanges that never end?"

"The Vol'aerai could have sent someone to negotiate if they wanted to avoid war, why didn't they?"

"Because they know you won't listen! Like you aren't listening to me now...and I'm your queen! They have even less chance you will listen as an adversary...or mythical people." Dhar tried to think of something to say but before he could Isida continued. "If they wanted war, why would they wait centuries to start it? They are defending themselves. Have you considered that?"

King Dhar stepped towards Isida to reason with her further.

"Isida—"

"I have said all I have to say, Your Majesty," Isida said as she turned away and threw her hands in the air, letting out a growl before grasping the gazebo railing to look out at the garden to calm herself. "Whether this kingdom lives or dies will depend on your choice. Go! Have your war; if death comes for us, it's all on you."

King Dhar knew there was no point in talking further unless he was willing to apologize and admit she was right. In private conversations, Isida only addressed him as "Your Majesty" when she was angry with him and wouldn't budge. He didn't want to admit it, but the dream was difficult to dismiss from his mind. With a heavy sigh, Dhar turned and exited to rejoin his procession of soldiers waiting for him in the courtyard.

The weeks flew by for Tsoria and Relvin. Meal times were the closest thing to leisure breaks, and even then, they seemed rushed. In each village they visited, needs were prioritized and finished as soon as possible, leaving time for Tsoria and Relvin to prepare for the upcoming war they were sure was coming.

After the daily tasks and people's concerns were addressed, Tsoria spent her time communicating with trees of the forest, poring over every detail of their records in search of anything that would help prepare her for the confrontation with King Dhar. Relvin spent his time in the woods at secluded training grounds to practice his skills by training with the forest. They were often so wrapped up in their tasks that they would lose track of time well into the night and would go to bed exhausted with little time together other than sleeping in the same bed, and it took its toll on them.

On the day the spies in Islatria sent word that King Dhar had begun his journey to join the army, Tsoria called for a meeting of the elders in the afternoon so that everyone was clear on their roles and duties as they defended their home. Relvin was also summoned to join them in the forest network, but he never joined even though Tsoria delayed the meeting to wait. She held the meeting without him, which seemed less productive without his military knowledge.

After disconnecting from the elders Tsoria sat in their dwelling alone with her thoughts. The disconnect over the weeks left her feeling alone and angry at his apparent abandonment of his vow to be on this journey with her. She needed his support more than ever at this pivotal juncture before the clash with King Dhar and he was nowhere to be found.

"Why didn't you show? You knew how important this meeting was, Relvin," Tsoria said, *"and you abandoned me."* Tsoria wiped away a few tears from her eyes as she sat waiting for any sign Relvin heard her or was coming home. *"I don't want to do this without you, please return to me."*

Tsoria pondered the weeks of waking up to an empty place beside her and coming home to Relvin already asleep before they could discuss their day. He seemed to be pulling away from her and she couldn't figure out what she had done to deserve this treatment.

"Is your training more important to you than me?" Tsoria stood and paced, angry and jealous at the time he spent with the forest instead of her. *"Answer me, Relvin! I'm your wife, your Queen, I deserve an explanation!"*

Tsoria exited their dwelling and walked around the village to clear her head since there was continued silence from Relvin. The smiling faces of the villagers and pleasant conversations distracted her for a few hours, but when the daylight faded, she returned to her dwelling. The thoughts she pushed to the recesses of her mind had festered and one phrase crept to the forefront: *he's a spy.* She tried to ignore the thought but it kept returning and the more time she dwelt on it, the more sense it made.

"You planned this, didn't you? I was your way into the Wispryn Weald. You've been spying the whole time, finding our weaknesses, plotting against us, and using my body as you pleased. I've been so naive. I'll bet you are on your way to Islatria to report what you know, but I won't let you get far. You'll regret crossing paths with me!"

Tsoria reached out her hands in the light of the glowing mushrooms of the dwelling. The forest network had become so tangible to her in the weeks of studying that she felt like it was an extension of her body as she sent signals through it, probing for any sign of Relvin within the forest.

"Found you, traitor," Tsoria said as roots enveloped her in a protective pod and pulled her into the ground.

The pod burst from the forest floor and unraveled, leaving Tsoria beside her husband, who lay unmoving on the ground. She fell to her knees beside Relvin checking for vitals as she hovered over him detecting the signs of aliuscerai. Tsoria lay a hand on the side of his face and looked upon it as she realized how far her mind had wandered in her anger.

"How could I think such terrible things about you? You have never shown any sign of betrayal," Tsoria said as tears fell from her eyes and splashed onto his face. "I'm sorry...I'm so sorry..."

Tsoria stepped back and grew a bed under Relvin, raising him from the forest floor, and a dwelling with no entrance to isolate them. Since she had him to herself now, she was determined to protect this time with him from any more interruptions. Tsoria wrapped her arms around Relvin as she lay beside him; she poured her heart out as she cried herself to sleep.

In the morning, Tsoria stirred as Relvin caressed her face. She nuzzled against his hand without opening her eyes as she relished the touch she had been denied access to for so long; she was afraid that if she opened her eyes it would be a dream. Tsoria reached up and confirmed that his hand was on her cheek before she opened her eyes, feeling immense relief. For many silent moments, she lay staring into his eyes, trying to decide what she should say until she caught a glint of light shining off something on his nose, and as she moved her hand to touch his face, she felt the warm wet tears on his nose and cheek.

Before Tsoria could say anything, Relvin began, "I'm sorry for everything I put you through in the last weeks, for the loneliness, the pain, and the heartache. I should have prepared you for how my training could affect you." Relvin blinked squeezing more tears from his eyes which dripped from the end of his nose. "I was concentrating on my training, not trying to shut you out. I still want to do this together with you. I heard everything you yelled at me yesterday, and I deserved—"

Tsoria pulled Relvin close and kissed him before he could finish his apology. Relvin opened his mouth to continue when she pulled back to look at him, but Tsoria put a finger to his lips.

"No...you didn't deserve to be falsely accused of things you would never do," Tsoria said as she withdrew her finger from his mouth.

"It wouldn't be the first time, but you are right about me being a traitor. Though to King Dhar, not to you."

"Even so, it was wrong of me, and I'm sorry I doubted you. I know this distance between us wasn't all your fault. Our devotion to duty drove a wedge between us. We're both to blame."

"We've been working too hard. I forgive you and I'm sorry for my part."

"I forgive you too," Tsoria said as she ran her fingers through his hair and closed the gap between them until their noses touched. "I want to take advantage of this time without responsibilities, training, meetings, or anything interfering."

"Me too," Relvin said.

The forest's mood brightened with the growing light as the birds trilled sweet melodies and the flowers invited the bees to drink their nectar.

Relvin and Tsoria talked and laughed for hours after the tension between them was released as they made up for lost time. Tsoria stared at the sunlight filtering between the fibers that formed the dwelling during a lull in their conversation.

"I wasn't prepared for how intense it would be with you," Tsoria said.

"How so?" Relvin asked.

Tsoria rolled over to look at her husband.

"Jealousy. I've felt it before but I was jealous of what others had or could do—"

"Perhaps you are thinking of envy?" Relvin asked.

"Hmm…I suppose that is a better word." Tsoria said. "This time it felt like you were being pulled from my arms and I wanted you back."

"There will be times that we are apart—"

"I know but—"

"This was different." Relvin pulled Tsoria into his arms and kissed her forehead. "I know. We hadn't spent quality time together for weeks."

With an ear to Relvin's chest, Tsoria heard the familiar and reassuring sound of his heartbeat. Tsoria closed her eyes and lost herself in the rhythm for several moments before pulling back.

"We won't be much help to our people if we're fighting each other when they need us the most," Tsoria said.

"What if we retreated from our duties and spent some time alone for a few days?" Relvin asked.

Tsoria propped herself up and looked at her husband.

"I like that idea, but won't we fight Dhar any day now?"

"It should be another week more before his armies are assembled. The elders can handle anything else while we are gone."

"There is a waterfall with a clear pool at the base for swimming up the Trifalls River. It should be teaming with birds, butterflies, flowers, and other wildlife about this time." Tsoria's hand moved in the light as if dancing with a butterfly as they watched before she turned her eyes to Relvin. "It's a half-day ride by horse if we hurry, more if we take our time to enjoy the journey," Tsoria said.

"Which gives us time to catch the midday meal in the village and we can still catch the sunset by the pool."

"It feels like it will be a warm day. Maybe we cool down in the water after the long ride as the sun sets," Tsoria said.

"Are you sure? The water will be quite cold from the melting snow."

"That's why I have you to keep me warm," Tsoria said with a smile.

Relvin kissed Tsoria in response but was interrupted by a loud growl from each of their stomachs, and they laughed.

"Perhaps we should start with the midday meal," Relvin said.

Tsoria motioned for the hut to dissolve back into the ground, and they blinked as their eyes adjusted to the late morning light shining around them. Tsoria summoned a couple of horses, and they got off the bed to dress. When the horses arrived, the forest reclaimed the bed, and they mounted and rode the horses back to the village before continuing upriver to their retreat.

Almost a week later, Eviara was helping to prepare the evening meal with her mother and other villagers in the afternoon. She watched the faces of the adults and could see the worry etched upon them while they all chatted with each other. Since the adults never spoke openly about what worried them, Eviara listened to the whispers and the quiet conversations to find out what was happening, even though she pretended not to pay attention.

Once King Dhar's army started assembling to the south, the village atmosphere changed overnight. Adults seemed on edge even though they pretended nothing worried them. Children were no longer allowed outside of the village perimeter without an adult. Even inside the village, parents kept close tabs on their children, and several families took this time to visit relatives that lived deeper within the forest. The children didn't like seeing their parents worry so much and took it upon themselves to be on their best behavior while attempting to cheer up their parents. Their efforts seemed to work for a while, but there was no lasting relief from the cloud hanging over each adult's head.

When the meal was ready and the villagers started gathering at the tables, the forest trees to the north parted to give way for Queen Tsoria and Relvin as they arrived on horseback from their private retreat. Eviara's face lit up with an enormous smile as she leaped from her seat.

"Welcome back, Tsoria!" Eviara said while running to her sister as she dismounted her horse.

Tsoria embraced her younger sister as Eviara leaped up and wrapped her arms around her.

"Eviara, I'm so glad to see you as well. It seems so long ago that we were here," Tsoria said as she put her sister back down on the ground.

"How long are you going to stay?" Eviara said as they walked together to the center of the village.

"I will be here as long as it takes to deal with the king and his army. So it might be a while."

"Good, everyone seems so unhappy. I hope you cheer them up."

Tsoria chuckled. "I will certainly try."

Eviara sat beside her parents as Tsoria and Relvin joined them to partake in the evening meal. The cloud of impending doom seemed to lift from the villagers with the queen's arrival. The conversations seemed livelier and focused on the fun events that happened since the queen's last visit: birthdays, marriages, pregnancies, births, and funny stories. That evening it was like old times again; Eviara listened to the laughter and looked around at the smiling faces that were now free from the worry that had been there for so long.

After the conversations died down and the villagers retired to their beds for the night, Eviara stayed up talking with her sister next to the fire. Before Relvin bid them a good night, Eviara hugged him, and Tsoria kissed Relvin before the sisters resumed their conversation.

"I wish we had grown up together," Eviara said, looking at Tsoria as she watched Relvin walk away, "but your eyes sparkle whenever you look at Relvin and I know it was for the best."

"I would have found someone—" Tsoria said as she turned to her sister.

"Maybe, but not like him. Relvin makes you happy, far more than I have felt from the villagers here lately."

"Is it that obvious?"

"All over your face…" Eviara said, moving her hand in a circle as she gestured at her sister.

Tsoria looked into the warm glow of the fire. Her smile faded several moments before speaking, "When the battle starts, most adults will be away from the village, Eviara," Tsoria said, turning towards her sister, "I need you and the older children to stay and keep the younger kids calm. They don't yet understand what is happening and will be scared."

"What if the village gets attacked?" Eviara asked.

"I won't let them get that close," Tsoria smiled reassuringly at her sister, "but I will grow a shield around the village to stop any stray projectiles—even though Relvin assures me they can't reach here from the catapult positions."

"A shield is a good idea. It will ease the adults' fears."

Tsoria chuckled. "I think you're right. It is more for their benefit."

Tsoria and Relvin spent the subsequent days letting the villagers know how they fit into the battle plan, telling them they wouldn't have to fight and assuring them that, one way or another, everything would be over soon. Tsoria kept an eye on the enemy camp and the roads leading to it through the eyes of hawks to stay up to date on troop movements. During one of these surveillance sessions, two days after King Dhar arrived with his guards, Tsoria noticed an emissary of the king riding a horse on the field and stopping at the midway point between the two sides. Tsoria spoke to Relvin without disconnecting from the hawk.

"Relvin, there is a representative from the king on the field. Could you go see what they want?" Tsoria said.

"Yes, my queen."

Relvin mounted a horse and rode through the forest to the battlefield. When he emerged from the tree line, the hawk that Tsoria was connected to circled down and alighted upon Relvin's right shoulder pad. When the two sides met, the king's emissary spoke first.

"For attacking His Majesty's citizens without provocation, Queen Tsorianya and her guard are summoned to submit to King Dhar for justice. If they fail to surrender themselves to pay for their crimes, the king will be forced to make the Vol'aerai pay for their treachery. This is your one chance to surrender and live," the emissary said.

The hawk screeched at the emissary before Relvin replied. "Without provocation? Is King Dhar ignorant, or is he stupid?"

The expression on the emissary's face darkened. "Be careful what you say—"

"The question still stands," Relvin said. "The king's citizens attacked the Vol'aerai first, and we had every right to defend ourselves. Neither Queen Tsorianya nor any other Vol'aerai will submit to the 'justice' of your king. Dhar has until his army is fully assembled to withdraw his claims and be shown mercy. If he does not, the blood that flows will be on his head."

Relvin abruptly returned to the forest before the emissary could respond. The hawk spread its wings and launched from his shoulder into the sky.

"Any chance Dhar will back down from his claims and leave in peace?" Tsoria said.

"I highly doubt it, especially after I insulted him with that exchange," Relvin said.

"Then war is inevitable."

"Yes, we'll be forced to show him our resolve soon."

Chapter 10
Skirmish

Before the first morning rays shone over King Dhar's army, the sound of a horn rang out from the center of the camp. The horn blast was followed by several more throughout the camp until every tent occupant was roused and preparing for battle. The cooks, who had awakened before the signal, distributed rations from caldrons and bread rolls baked the previous day.

The soldiers gathered their equipment and assembled in formation for inspection by their captain after their meal. Each company that passed scrutiny was then marched to its designated area on the battle-field. Support personnel distributed supplies along the battlegrounds with haste, and oil-filled jars bound in hay and pitch were carted to each of the catapults, along with torches to light them.

When the sun had been up for about an hour, King Dhar sat on a horse with his four generals and his guards overlooking his army from a hill towards the rear as messengers reported to them when each army legion was ready.

"So, are any barbarians going to show up today?" King Dhar asked with a chuckle.

"They probably ran as fast as they could when they saw the might of your army, Sire," Norrik said.

"You might want to look again," Torridol said as he nodded toward the forest.

A soldier and a red-headed woman in a dress emerged from the forest. The two figures stopped about a hundred feet from the trees, and the whole tree line came alive as hundreds of figures stepped out from the trees' shadows.

"I guess we will fight after all," Norrik said, "but it doesn't seem like they have a large army."

"Things aren't always as they seem," Rashe said. "I don't think we should underestimate them."

"I know, it is probably part of their strategy since we couldn't assess their capabilities," Norrik said.

"Perhaps we should tease out the answer with fire?" Fasid said.

"I don't like the thought of fighting them on their terms. I agree with General Fasid. Launch the fire jars and see if we can burn them out to the open field," King Dhar said.

Relvin stood guard as Tsoria surveyed the field of battle from the eyes of the hawks above to see what King Dhar would order first. A great deal of activity by each of the catapults suggested an answer. Tsoria disconnected from the birds and turned to the villagers standing at the ready, waiting for any signal from their queen.

"Get ready, everyone. Think of your families, for we do this for them, but do not linger on fear or worry, for you also have tasks you have been given to accomplish. I give you my word, no harm will befall your children," Tsoria said.

The Vol'aerai shouted in confirmation and support of their queen. Tsoria looked toward the forest and gestured with her hands. The trees inched forward, making it seem like the Vol'aerai floated backward without moving until they disappeared among the trees. Once the villagers were out of sight, Tsoria extended her arms and brought them around, as if she was hugging something in front of her, before clasping her hands together and pulling them towards her heart.

Eviara and the other older children were playing with the youngest children when the earth started trembling, and large crystal roots burst from the ground encircling the village. The roots formed a protective dome above, while smaller roots wove together and formed an impenetrable barrier above and to the south. The young kids started to whimper as they didn't understand what was happening. Eviara gathered the youngest kids and smiled as she crouched down to look them in the eyes.

"Don't worry, this is my big sister protecting us. We will be safe inside the village," Eviara said.

"Are you sure?" A little girl asked.

"Queen Tsorianya is my sister, and with the forest, she is powerful. Look at me. Do I look frightened?"

The kids shook their heads.

"I trust my sister and she said that we will be safe here." Eviara reached out, took the hands of the two nearest children, and smiled. "Who wants to hear a story?"

The faces of the kids lit up as they replied "me" or "I do" and jumped up and down in excitement.

"Come, let's gather around the fire, and we can tell stories and sing together while the queen sorts this out."

Eviara led the way to the fire, and after the older kids sat down, the little ones climbed onto their laps and snuggled in their arms. One at a time, they told stories or sang songs. The nursing mothers within the village joined in while they rocked and nursed their babies and let their minds be distracted from the dangers of the battle to the south.

The creaking and groaning of wood under great strain, followed by a solid thud, fell upon every ear as the catapults sprang to life one by one and launched their destructive payloads toward the forest. The pitch and hay-bound jars bathed in fire flew through the air as black smoke trailed behind. The siege crews worked to reset the catapults for the next round. Cheers rang through the ranks as each fireball disappeared within the forest and released its liquid fire upon impact.

Volley after volley was thrown toward the forest, and black smoke billowed from the fires they started. The king and three of his generals joined in the chorus of cheers, but General Rashe's attention was fixed upon the two figures standing outside the forest, his only window into their opponent's mind. He had witnessed many reactions over the years to attacks, but none as unconcerned as he saw from these two, leading him to think he was missing some vital information.

Tsoria soared above the battlefield through the eyes of a hawk as she watched the attack unfold. The extra dense formation of trees at the border successfully blocked the opposition from seeing what was occurring in the forest behind. The jars launched into the trees were harmlessly splashing their fiery contents onto large swaths of earthen clearings abandoned by the trees in the dead of night. Since the range and trajectory of each projectile could not be predicted ahead of time, Tsoria called out corrections to the trees as needed to prevent any needless damage. Between volleys, some of the villagers were tasked with stoking the fires with branches left by the trees, causing large clouds of smoke to billow high into the sky.

"*Queen Tsorianya, the bombs are ready,*" one of the villagers said.

"*Good. Proceed as planned after launch,*" Tsoria said.

"*Understood.*"

"After the next volley, Relvin," Tsoria said.

"Yes, my queen," Relvin said.

"Sire, we have launched five rounds, and the fires we have started behind their lines are not flushing them out as we had hoped," Torridol said.

"I don't wish to be drawn into their territory yet," King Dhar said. "Before we are forced into a ground assault, are there any suggestions?"

"We should target those two near the forest," Rashe said. "We have been targeting the forest while they stand there. Perhaps we need to go after the leaders."

"Yes. Perhaps turning up the heat on them will make things interesting," Norrik said.

Horse messengers were dispatched, and the catapults were rotated and adjusted to follow the new orders. When ready, the levers were released, and their fire jars sailed through the air toward the Vol'aerai leaders. Most projectiles were off target by a significant distance, but one jar sailed true and impacted where the Queen and her guard stood. Shouts rang through the ranks as they celebrated the good fortune of getting a direct hit on the opponent's leadership.

"Rashe, you've won the war for us," King Dhar said as he clasped the general on the shoulder. "We will feast tonight and break out the good wine to toast our fortune!"

"Thank you, Sire, but I didn't think that would work. I was—"

"Well, it did," Torridol said. "Celebrate, you earned it! You will be back with your family before you know it."

As the fire consumed the oil and pitch that had splashed around where Tsoria and Relvin had stood, the earth in the center of the fires was agitated from below. The dirt churned and seemed to consume the fire, starting from the center and rippling outward. Two root pods slowly emerged from the ground where the fire had been put out as the earth continued to extinguish the flames around them. Grasses quickly grew to replace what had been scorched earth moments before as the root pods unraveled and retreated into the ground, leaving their occupants standing in a lush green field indistinguishable from what had been there before the fire.

Large crystal root daggers grew within each of Relvin's fists before he fell to one knee and stabbed the ground with them.

The king swore as he watched their assured victory be extinguished along with the flames.

"I knew it was too easy," Rashe said.

"We all saw them take a direct hit. What kind of sorcery is this?" Norrik said.

"Sorcery or not, I have a feeling we are about to find that we poked the bear in the wrong spot," Rashe said.

A slight breeze had been blowing the smoke from the oil fires in a southwestern direction, which concealed numerous incoming projectiles from view until they were well on their way. The commanders scrambled to send a warning as hundreds of melon-sized balls pierced the smoke screen and pelted the ground surrounding each catapult. The projectiles burst open upon impact, and a powdery yellow cloud billowed forth from each, spreading and engulfing everything within thirty paces of the catapults.

At first, everyone outside the yellow clouds could see no reason to fear since those who managed to find their way out experienced nothing more than sneezing fits from exposure. However, not long after the clouds were at their thickest, vibrations in the ground could be felt from all around, loud sounds like the breaking and splintering of great beams of wood came from within, and numerous screams rang out from each of the clouds for a couple of minutes before silence fell on everyone's ears.

No one could believe the sight before their eyes after the clouds had settled. Nothing but a few splinters remained of the catapults, and every soldier within the densest parts of the clouds had vanished almost without a trace. The only sign that people used to be there was the random dropped sword or shield lying on the ground.

Messengers flooded the king's mound with reports of the losses sustained by the Vol'aerai attack. Preliminary numbers indicated over four thousand troops, including more than a hundred officers, had been consumed by the clouds in addition to the loss of every catapult. Seasoned officers stepped in to reorganize the lines and control the level of panic among the soldiers, but the belief that this would be an easy win was shattered by one attack.

Relvin pulled the crystal root daggers from the ground and stood. The attack was unconventional and effective at destroying their opponent's long-range weapons and hiding the true nature of their capabilities for at least a little longer. With the catapults out of commission, the villagers could manage their remaining tasks without the threat of death.

Relvin turned to Tsoria. "Next phase?"

"Yes," the Queen said with a smile.

"Time to corral a king."

Relvin turned and walked towards the front lines with daggers in hand as a helmet grew around his head from the crystal leaf mail and root armor he wore.

Relvin turned and walked towards the front lines with daggers in hand as a helmet grew around his head from the crystal leaf mail and root armor he wore.

"What did they throw at us, and how?" Dhar asked, turning to his generals.

"We don't know, Sire," Torridol said. "As you know, our spies couldn't pierce their borders, so we had to speculate about their capabilities. Besides, I've never seen any projectile that spews forth clouds like that and then dissolves everything within."

"It couldn't have dissolved them," Norrik said, "many escaped without being affected. They were covered by a—"

"Perhaps it is witchcraft after all," Fasid said. "You know the stories—"

"It's not witchcraft," Rashe said. "It's tactics. They used the smoke from the fires we started to their advantage, and knowing what happened within the yellow dust will not help us right now. Perhaps we will know later, but it looks like they are initiating the ground attack," Rashe said and nodded toward the forest.

"One soldier? What kind of madness is this?" Torridol asked.

As Relvin approached the opposite side, he could see the lines rearranging to bring the archers to the front. When he reached their bow range, a cloud of arrows was loosed in his direction. Relvin tapped his daggers' pummels together, causing the blades to grow into a shield he held in front and continued to advance as the arrows rained down upon his position. The ground around him looked like a pin cushion as each volley of arrows pierced the ground.

When he continued advancing despite multiple waves of arrows, the commanders reordered the front lineup to bring the infantry forward. With the shield no longer needed, Relvin pulled the handles apart, and they returned to their original dagger form. When he was within a hundred feet of the front, he beat his chest and motioned for the soldiers to attack him.

While the front line advanced, many soldiers turned to each other and expressed confusion before the sides clashed. They weren't sure if this was a joke, a trap, or if this champion was so good he could defeat them all alone. His boldness made the soldiers hesitant to cross blades with him, but when he started taunting them, the strongest among them couldn't help but wish to prove themselves to their commanders.

One zealous soldier broke ranks and rushed at the warrior with his sword at the ready. The soldier swung his sword, but when Relvin blocked the blade with one of his daggers, it shattered as if made of glass. The soldier had little time to process what had happened because Relvin punched him with his other fist. Roots encased the soldier, pulling him into the earth.

The rest of the soldiers hesitated, unsure of how to process what had happened, but the commanders ordered them to rush this warrior and would not stand for deserting their duty. The next couple of soldiers wishing to prove themselves advanced from opposite sides, but with dodging and well-placed punches from Relvin, they were also pulled into the ground. Subsequent waves brought more soldiers until the circle of soldiers rushed at Relvin from every angle to overwhelm him.

The circle was drawn tighter and tighter despite the losses incurred, but when the soldiers were about to pounce, the champion fell to one knee and punched the ground with both fists. Roots came up from the earth, forming a protective pod around Relvin, and pulled him into the ground before the soldiers could lay a hand upon him.

A root pod emerged from the ground silently between the rear guard and the army camp while the commanders debated what to do next. After unraveling and retreating into the dirt, Relvin advanced with soft footfalls until he stood behind them.

"See any action yet?" Relvin said between a couple of the soldiers.

Without turning, one of the soldiers replied, "Ha, there is no way we'll see any action back here."

"Yeah, the battle will be over long before we are called to fight," the other soldier said.

"Fifty gold says you will experience combat before you can count to ten," Relvin said.

With their interest piqued by the absurd bet and timeframe, several rear guards turned to look at who could afford stakes that high.

"Wait, who are you?" The soldiers said when they saw that Relvin wasn't one of theirs.

"I'm the action. You owe me fifty gold," Relvin said as he punched the closest soldiers, and they were pulled down.

The commotion and soldiers' shouts drew attention to the rear as Relvin's daggers grew into swords and he attacked without missing a beat. The rear guard scrambled into action as a horn was blown to alert everyone to the enemy attacking behind the lines. Relvin braced himself for the onslaught after he was surrounded. Each soldier that he landed a blow upon was wrapped in roots and pulled into the ground. Since these were seasoned soldiers, it didn't take long for them to change tactics once they witnessed the ineffectiveness of their weapons against Relvin's armor. They tightened their perimeter around Relvin with shields in front, and although they didn't hold up to Relvin's crystal weapons any more than their swords did, they provided a degree of protection and a way to box Relvin in.

Relvin adjusted to the change in tactics and attacked what their shields did not protect or broke their barrier with one blow followed by a second, marking them to be claimed by roots. The ring of soldiers constricted after each man was removed from the circle, either by being pulled into the ground or retreating after their shield was broken.

Tsoria watched the confusion and chaos Relvin sowed on the battlefield from the eyes of a hawk. She had witnessed Relvin's skills during the fight with the hounds, but that night, he had been hampered by the desire to protect her. Today, he was fearless, free to fight without holding back at each random location where he appeared. He was chipping away at the army's morale, and from the tone of Dhar's voice as he talked with his generals, they were almost at a breaking point.

"…but you aren't ready to give up," Tsoria said as the hawk's gaze shifted.

Tsoria disconnected from the hawk and looked toward the front lines. Cavalry thundered toward her from each side, taking advantage of her assumed vulnerability.

"While my guard is away, Dhar comes to play. I guess I can't expect my husband to do everything."

Tsoria thrust her open hands out towards the cavalry as if she were pushing on invisible walls and connected with every charging war horse.

"I am Tsorianya, Queen of the forest and all creatures within. I command you to return to camp. Comply and be spared. Refuse and forfeit your life." The horses continued to charge. "You have been taught to fear the whip and spur in captivity." Tsoria relaxed her arms to her sides but made a fist in each hand. "Last chance…"

Tsoria thrust her hands out to each side and opened them as if she were throwing invisible darts at the lead horses. Spiked roots burst from the ground and impaled the lead horses at each flank, stopping them instantly and causing their riders to be thrown from their backs. Roots caught the cavalrymen in midair and pulled them under. The remaining horses needed no further persuasion and changed course toward the camp. The angry and bewildered soldiers upon their backs whipped, spurred, or pulled their reins in an attempt to redirect them, but nothing convinced the horses to go against the queen. The cavalry cut through the ranks as ground troops jumped aside and didn't stop until they reached the corrals within the camp, never to return to the front lines.

Relvin timed his final retreat to take advantage of the chaos of the cavalry cutting through Dhar's army. During the subsequent lull, commanders assessed losses, regrouped, and watched for any sign of where the fight would commence next.

The guards surrounding King Dhar and the generals felt vibrations beneath their feet before a root pod erupted from the earth like a small volcano. Relvin was launched into the air and came down swinging as the unraveled roots pulled those thrown aside into the ground. Although Relvin was exhausted from all of the energy spent at the previous locations, he gave everything that he had left into this round as he unleashed a whirlwind of attacks without weapons, using punches and kicks to mark each guard for the roots to pull into the ground in his progression towards Dhar's position.

It didn't take long for the guards to abandon their weapons in favor of containment as they threw themselves at his extremities to protect their king at all costs. Even with depleted energy, it took the strength of several men to hold onto Relvin's arms and legs to stop his forward momentum. Once Relvin was contained, the soldiers bound him to a post with arms behind his back.

Before the soldiers left, Relvin spoke, "Tell King Dhar that I come with a message for him should he wish to leave this battlefield alive."

Relvin had several minutes to catch his breath before he saw King Dhar approach, flanked by his generals.

"Queen Tsorianya sends her greetings, Your Majesty," Relvin said as soon as the king stood before him. "She will be on her way soon to negotiate a treaty."

"Why should I negotiate anything with the likes of her? I have overpowered you, her champion, and I still have most of my army left."

"True, but do you have a large enough army to stop all her champions after seeing what one can do?" Relvin asked as he locked eyes with the king.

Even though King Dhar tried hard to prevent his fear from showing, Relvin noticed a slight twitch in reaction to what he had said and could tell his comment had the desired effect.

"Set up a tent for the negotiations anywhere you wish, then blow a horn three times. She will give you until noon before she unleashes the one hundred champions that have emerged from the forest during our conversation. If you subdue them, the next wave will be a thousand. I suggest you heed her words," Relvin said.

The king stared at Relvin for several moments, studying what little he could see of the mysterious warrior protected by the natural armor he wore before retreating to his private tent with his four generals to discuss the situation.

"They have to be bluffing, Sire," Fasid said in the king's private tent along with Torridol, Norrik, and Rashe. "There is no way they have that many champi—"

"Did you see what happened on the field today?" Dhar explosively interrupted the general and pointed towards the battlefield. "They killed over four thousand men when they destroyed our catapults! Then, one soldier kills two hundred more before we can contain him! Not to mention, whatever happened to my cavalry!" Dhar pointed at Fasid. "Do you know how many Vol'aerai we have killed?"

Fasid looked at the king and shook his head. Dhar looked around and gestured to the other generals.

"Does anyone want to guess?" Dhar asked, waiting for an answer. When no one spoke Dhar continued, "Based on what has happened so far, I will wager that we haven't touched a single hair on their heads! Even if this next wave of champions is only half as good as the first, they will decimate the already shaky morale of the army, and that alone would win the war for them!"

There was silence in the tent as the king ended his rant.

"An enemy that can jump from the front lines to right next to the king at will…" Torridol said. "I don't know how they can do—"

"Don't forget the armor he wore. All our best blades couldn't pierce it," Norrik said.

"Right," Torridol said, pointing at Norrik. "We aren't prepared to defend against that. We were lucky the soldier—"

"Lucky...ha!" Rashe said, pacing while grasping his chin.

"General Rashe, care to elaborate on your thoughts?" Torridol asked.

"Oh...sorry," Rashe said as he stopped pacing and looked up. "This morning has perplexed me." He looked and gestured to Torridol. "You mention luck...as if everything they have done was random. The more time goes on, the less I think that is true. While they might be bluffing, this champion is too relaxed for luck to have played a part. I believe we've been playing their game from the beginning."

"Please go on," Torridol said.

"With his ability to disappear and reappear anywhere on the field at will, why was he captured?" Rashe asked as he looked at each of the other generals. "He could've started by assassinating the king and retreating without us touching him. If they have the number of champions he mentioned, why didn't they release them all and decimate our army? I am not a betting man, but if I were, I would wager that their goal today isn't to defeat you, King Dhar."

"What would you say it is?" Dhar asked.

"To send you a strong message," Rashe said.

"Which is?" Dhar asked.

"Negotiate..." Rashe said as he looked the king in the eyes, "...or die."

King Dhar shifted uneasily as a shiver ran down his spine.

"The champion reminds me of a young soldier I trained several years back," Rashe said, "a fighter you wouldn't want to meet on the field. He gets more dangerous the closer you are, and he doesn't fear death." Rashe paused. "Sire, I recommend we hear Queen Tsorianya out. It might be the puzzle piece that lets us see the whole picture."

"Rashe, I appreciate your counsel," Dhar said. "I also fear that we have been playing their game, but we can still come out on top in negotiations. I will meet Queen Tsorianya. Rashe, you will be my guard. Perhaps you will see what I don't."

Chapter 11
Face-off

TSORIA WAITED AT THE FOREST EDGE for the signal to be sent from King Dhar's camp. The battle had gone according to plan with some adjustments to counter what they couldn't have predicted, but if the negotiations didn't go well…She shook her head. She didn't want to think of their backup plan. Tsoria paced as she knew the success depended on her preparation, but doubts lingered in her head. She took long, slow breaths and tried to calm herself as she reached out to Relvin.

"*Relvin, I'm nervous. After coming this far, what if I—*"

"*Don't finish that thought, Tsoria,*" Relvin said. "*'What if' should only be used to prepare, not to doubt. 'What if' doubts paralyze your mind and prevent you from doing what is necessary. The better question to ask is this: 'What is?' That prepares you for the present.*"

"*I wish this was all behind us,*" Tsoria said.

"*As do I, but here we are. You are prepared. You can do this.*"

"*I'll do my best.*"

"*With the children, the dogs, and on the night we met, you moved beyond your fears and took action. You'll do it again—*"

Tsoria stopped pacing and turned her attention to King Dhar's camp when three short horn blasts rang out.

"Good. He's chosen the bloodless path," Tsoria said, feeling a burden lift from her shoulders. *"Time to keep him on it."*

"No matter what happens in that tent, Tsoria, you aren't alone," Relvin said. *"Trust yourself, my queen, and if you can't do that, trust the forest. See you soon."*

Two white doves alighted on Tsoria's shoulders as she began to cross the open divide between the two sides. The soft cooing of the birds kept her thoughts from wandering from the task ahead and calmed her nerves. Four soldiers met Tsoria at the mouth of a flagged path leading to the negotiating tent.

"Queen Tsorianya, we'll escort you to King Dhar," one of the guards said.

"Lead the way," Tsoria said.

The soldiers formed a square around the queen and escorted her down the path. Tsoria could see the soldiers murmuring as they watched the procession from the edges, but the doves' cooing kept her from hearing what was said. The envoy escorting Tsoria stopped at the end of the path and stepped aside to let her proceed alone. Ahead was a square royal blue tent with its side flaps tied to the corner poles with small gold ropes that matched the trim. Before the queen entered, both doves flew up from her shoulders and perched at the tent peak.

General Rashe stood in the corner of the sparsely furnished tent to the right of King Dhar as they faced the north entrance, watching Queen Tsorianya approach. Rashe and Dhar wore mail armor, and a sword hung at Rashe's side. A small table occupied the center with high-backed chairs on the north and south sides. A scribe occupied a small desk with ink and parchment on the western side, with a councilor mirroring Rashe's corner position. All eyes were on the young queen as she entered the tent's shade.

"Your Highness, Queen Tsorianya, I presume," Dhar said as he extended his hand to her.

"You presume correctly, Your Majesty, King Dhar," Tsoria said as they shook hands.

The monarchs parted and sat in the chairs.

Rashe warily scrutinized Tsoria's actions. Her choice to appear without a guard or visible armor was surprising. The lack of reaction to Dhar's subtle disrespect by greeting her with the lesser royal title puzzled him. She was either naive or hiding her cards well.

"I requested this meeting to negotiate peace between our people and end our conflict," Tsoria said.

"You ask for a peace treaty after I have defeated your champion. From my perspective, it seems you realize that you cannot win," Dhar said. "Perhaps you are confusing a treaty with surrender."

"I see why you think that, but I am neither surrendering nor defeated. I do not wish to shed any more blood."

Dhar postured strength as he sparred words with Tsoria, but he was getting nowhere with this young queen. Rashe heard the subtle changes to the king's tone as he became more flustered the longer they talked.

"What terms are you proposing?" Dhar asked.

"My simple terms are that the land and forest in the north, from the current tree line to beyond the mountains, be recorded as Vol'aerai territory. No one will be allowed to cross the border from either side without permission. If any were to transgress this boundary, their lives would be forfeit. You and your remaining army get to walk away with your lives intact."

"You are in no position to demand such terms. Most of my army still stands, and I don't concede defeat. Therefore, you will lay down arms and surrender if there is to be any peace between our people."

"The number of soldiers you have now or in the future makes no difference. You will not win this war."

"You think I will lose?" King Dhar asked, scoffing at her confidence. "Your army is incapable of matching my strength of numbers."

"I see where your confusion lies. Regarding human troops, you are correct. However, the entirety of the forest is at my command, and it would be a grave mistake on your part to force me to mobilize it."

Tsoria maintained her composure, seemingly unaffected by the barbs of their exchange. Still, Rashe noticed subtle changes to the scent emanating from her dress, giving him clues to her mood as she talked.

"You have provoked this war between us by attacking my citizens, breaking the peace that we had."

"I suppose you expect me and my guard to surrender to your court for 'justice' so we can be flogged or executed for our 'crimes?'" Tsoria asked and paused while she watched Dhar's reaction. "Tell me, King Dhar, is it against your laws for a monarch to defend themself or their citizens? Because if it is, you have broken the same law. Will you submit to my court for justice?"

Dhar shifted in his chair. Rashe had never seen him so uncomfortable during negotiations before.

"Give me a reason I should relinquish the timberland you demand for nothing in return?"

"The land and trees in the north were never yours to give away. Your previous monarchs drew it as part of the Islatrian Kingdom without consulting the Vol'aerai, and we have been more than accommodating to your people despite this. Besides, you have plenty of trees in your kingdom to fulfill any *obligation*." The way she worded her response made Rashe think Tsoria was referring to the Tashtari trade agreement. "You are leaving here with peace and your life, King Dhar, but if you think your life has no value—as you stated—I can take it from you."

Dhar stood in a huff. "Witch, I tire of this charade you are playing. If this is what you call negotiation, these talks are over."

"Witch? That is what you think I am?" Tsoria asked and chuckled. "No, dear king, I am human like any other in this tent. If I am thrown into a fire, held underwater, or *stabbed* in the heart, I will die like everyone else. *Please* sit so we can continue these talks *civilly.*"

Rashe didn't like where the talks were heading. Dhar was angry, and it seemed like she had him exactly where she wanted him. How she emphasized certain words and the changes to the scent in the air, made him nervous. He could feel his body tensing for action as Tsoria stood after Dhar refused to rejoin her at the table.

"I would prefer not to prolong this war any further, King Dhar, but I fully expected this conclusion. Before we part today, you should know that if I leave and return to the forest alive before a treaty is agreed upon, you will not live to see tomorrow. Without me, the forest is only trees with an unarmed population, and you will not get another chance to kill me. It should not be hard for you to accomplish that feat. Thank you for your time, King Dhar," Tsoria said and turned to exit the negotiating tent.

"*She's taunting you. She thinks you're weak, pathetic, tiny...*" a voice said to Dhar, feeding his anger.

Dhar reached towards his waist.

"*Yes...show her power...show her strength...show her who is king...*" the voice said.

Rashe's focus on Tsoria as she turned to leave distracted him from noticing Dhar had drawn his poniard. A glint of light from the dagger as the king darted around the table and lunged for Tsoria made Rashe realize his mistake.

"It's a trap, Sire!" Rashe said, but it was already too late.

The King's aim was perfect, and the dagger struck its intended target, but any hope of ending the war with the attack shattered at the moment the dagger did when it impacted the queen's floral dress.

Tsoria whipped around with her jaw set and eyes that bored into Dhar like a miner digging for precious metals. The queen's dress dissolved to reveal her battle armor, and the flowery smell dissipated in the breeze. Crystal roots grew around her right arm as quick as it took for her to shoot out her hand and lift the King off the ground by his neck. Dhar grabbed her forearm to prevent his weight from hanging on his neck, though he could have strangled Tsoria with his superior reach.

General Rashe stepped forward to protect his king, but as he did, he saw Queen Tsorianya make a quick motion with her left hand. Rashe felt the ground beneath him grumble before a root pod burst from below and forced him back. When the roots retreated, the Queen's champion they had fought so hard to capture stood unbound and ready for action. Rashe's hand was already grasping his sword's hilt, but before he could draw it, the champion had stepped forward, and Rashe felt a dagger pressing against his throat and groin.

Rashe glimpsed hazel eyes through the slit in the helmet as the champion shook his head without speaking. He was sure he recognized those eyes. Rashe had seen that look before on a young man who wouldn't let failure be an option even if it cost him his life. The general decided not to test the soldier's resolve, released the hilt, and let the sword slide back into its sheath. The champion nodded as Rashe raised his hands to the panicked army, signaling them not to interfere.

The king felt small for the first time as Tsoria held him in the air. She stared him down for what seemed like forever as Dhar wondered how this petite woman could lift his entire six-foot armored frame off the ground as if he were a bunny. His mind raced to figure out how he could turn the situation around.

"I have abided by all your kingdom's laws," Tsoria said with a commanding voice, "and you dare to break them by attacking me, the legal representative of the Vol'aerai. Did you think I wouldn't learn from the past and allow you to harm me in your house?"

"What harm in the past did we do to you?" Dhar asked with difficulty since his neck was constricted by Tsoria's hand.

"Have you not learned your history? Or have you conveniently forgotten?" Tsoria asked.

The king couldn't think of anything to say due to his lack of knowledge about the Vol'aerai.

"My historians could list numerous wrongs your people have done to mine, but I will settle on one relevant example. After centuries of conflicts between our people, the fifth Vol'aerai queen, Cassie, attempted to negotiate. Peace was almost assured after the talks, but an ambitious prince decided to get something from the deal for himself. Prince Agera lusted after Cassie. The queen refused his advances because her hand was already promised to another. Agera was enraged at her rejection and stabbed Cassie in the back, killing her as you intended for me. Jeran Taurille, Agera's younger brother, inherited the throne. I wonder why?"

Dhar knew Tsoria's question was rhetorical. His family's genealogy recorded Agera's death, but he was always curious why the cause was omitted. Now that he knew, Dhar began to sweat.

"However, these talks are not about the past, nor were previous negotiations. This is about now and the future," Tsoria said. "What is the penalty for attacking or killing a delegate protected under a diplomatic flag, King Dhar?"

The King stayed silent because he knew the law and the consequences. He hoped Tsoria didn't and that his councilor would keep his tongue.

"Have you forgotten your laws as well? Then I will have to educate you again. Your law states: 'Attacks on delegates under a diplomatic flag are prohibited until all negotiations have ceased and they have returned to their side. Anyone who violates this diplomatic treaty and attacks a delegate of either side without first being attacked will be surrendered to the aggrieved party for any punishment deemed fair by that party unless an alternative agreement is negotiated.'" The queen then addressed the king's councilor while staring at the king, "Isn't that correct, council?"

"I'm afraid, Sire, that she has quoted the law on the books verbatim," the Councilor said after hesitating.

Dhar's sweat suddenly felt cold as he realized his life was forfeit. He couldn't do anything to save himself without the queen's consent, and Queen Tsorianya seemed intent on taking her legal claim to his life. Dhar exhaled as he closed his eyes. His body went limp, and his arms fell to his sides as he waited for the queen to take his life.

"It's your right to take it...he broke the law," said a voice inside Tsoria.

Tsoria cocked her head to the side with furrowed brows and a far-away look in an attempt to trace where the voice came from.

"He tried to kill you...they will never accept peace with Vol'aerai. Kill the king...kill everyone..." the voice said.

There was truth in their words. However, there was something sinister about the voice, leaving an unpleasant aftertaste in her mouth and a sick feeling in her stomach. Tsoria had ignored the feeling the night she accused Relvin of being a spy. This time she listened to her gut.

The feeling of his feet touching the ground caused Dhar to open his eyes. His knees almost buckled as his weight transferred to his legs, and the queen's hand retracted from his throat. The king stumbled back into his chair behind the negotiating table and caught his breath as he rubbed his neck.

Relvin withdrew his daggers from the general and let them retreat into his armor as he retreated to his place next to the queen. The crystal roots retreated from Tsoria's arm before her clothes reverted to the dress she had arrived in. A sweet, flowery smell returned to the air as she sat.

"Is it worth negotiating for your life now, King Dhar, or would you rather I decide for you?" Tsoria raised her hand to show a bell, formed from crystal root, swinging from side to side. "One last chance, Islatria's fate. It isn't yet too late," Tsoria said as she watched the king.

Dhar felt a bolt of lightning run down his spine as the words caused the memory of the poem from Isida's dream to flood back.

"Wait! You?" Dhar said as he pointed at Tsoria.

"Yes."

Dhar hit the table with his fist as he swore, which made the scribe jump in his seat but induced no visible reaction from Tsoria. "You have been playing with me this whole time!"

"If I were playing, we would be enjoying ourselves," Tsoria said. "These talks would have been conducted under more pleasant circumstances if you had come to talk when the enslavers delivered my message."

"What message?"

The bell disappeared as the roots were reabsorbed, and Tsoria rested her hand on her chair's armrests.

"Then they didn't tell you. That is unfortunate, but the situation remains unchanged. I anticipated their defiance and sent Queen Isida the dream, hoping she could convince you to talk before we were forced to spar on the battlefield. I may be young and a novice negotiator—as you realized—but make no mistake, your life is still on the line even though your neck is free from my hand. So, King Dhar, what is your life worth?"

"How am I to estimate that?"

"You could start by telling me how much gold, silver, gems, and other precious things you have stored away in your vaults. Would you give that up for your life?"

"So this is about money?" Dhar asked and shifted in his seat as Tsoria chuckled.

"We can pull precious metals or gems from the ground any time we want, and your version of wealth means nothing to us. How much does the average slave get sold for in your kingdom?"

"Thirty silver coins is the average," Dhar said.

"Is your life worth more than theirs?"

"Of course it is! I am the king. My life is more valuable than all my subjects combined."

"You still have much to learn about reigning over a kingdom, King Dhar," Tsoria said. "A subject's worth is not derived from their monarchs, but a monarch's worth depends on their subjects. You and I are only an empty vault. Our subjects are the precious gems."

King Dhar realized Isida was correct when she insisted the Vol'aerai were protecting themselves. Queen Tsorianya didn't value power or fortune; she valued her subjects over everything.

"What are your terms?" King Dhar asked.

"Firstly, the Nemoyid province must be turned over to the Vol'aerai. Your citizens who do not want to live with the Vol'aerai are free to leave for any other province with fair monetary compensation for what they leave behind to be paid by the Vol'aerai. Secondly, the freedom of all slaves within your kingdom who wish to join the Vol'aerai, their masters will be eligible for compensation from the royal coffers, and future enslavers who cross into Vol'aerai territory to capture our citizens or recapture previous slaves—who are now Vol'aerai citizens—will be executed on sight. Thirdly, non-slave citizens who wish to join the Vol'aerai will be welcomed but are ineligible for compensation for property or possessions left behind." Tsoria leaned forward in her chair. "Lastly, if anyone attempts to assassinate a Vol'aerai queen again, the treaty will be void, whether the assassin is from your kingdom or hired from another your entire realm will be taken by force. This last item is non-negotiable and will be enforced in perpetuity."

King Dhar squirmed under Tsoria's steadfast gaze while she said the last item. He was not accustomed to being on the receiving end of a stare that turned this young, petite woman into an ancient, unmovable tree towering over the table. His ego had gotten in the way, as Isida said. Dhar slumped in his chair because it felt like his kingdom was over since none of the terms solved his issue with the Tashtari.

"Dhar, I realize that the terms, as stipulated, skew in my favor, and you have not requested anything from me in return, perhaps because you are afraid—and you should be—the lives of your citizens are at stake, along with yours. However, I do not wish to be unreasonable. Now is your chance to request benefits for your kingdom." Tsoria went silent for several moments, waiting for the king to respond. "Perhaps something to do with the letter you sent to Lord Darrick, with your courier Morgon, who was under the protection of Relvin?"

King Dhar raised his head, and his mouth opened as he looked at Tsoria. "How did you know about that?"

"I was informed of the contents by the forest historians as I prepped for our negotiations. However, I won't divulge how they were privy to the contents. I won't allow the trees to be cut down and sold to the Tashtari as stipulated in your treaty."

"My reputation will mean nothing if I don't fulfill my trade agreement."

"I understand. I will help you negotiate a new treaty with the Tashtari and offer a conditional alliance to protect your kingdom if they don't accept. The forest borders will reopen for your citizens to hunt or gather within as soon as this treaty takes effect. The forest also offers its wisdom so everyone in your kingdom has a chance to thrive. You will not be forced to act on the advice or change your laws. Do we have a deal?"

Dhar stood and walked to the corner of the tent to confer with the councilor before sitting back in the chair. "I think these preliminary terms are acceptable. Many details need to be worked out, but if you are willing to come to Islatria in three weeks, we can work with my full staff of councilors to iron out the details and publicly sign the treaty."

"I will see you in a few weeks," Tsoria said with a smile.

Both monarchs stood and met at the side of the table to shake hands. The scribe pulled out two sheets of parchment and began to form his notes into official documents.

"Before we part ways today, there are two remaining items to resolve," Tsoria said. "The first is the exchange of prisoners. I have my champion back, so it is only fair I release the soldiers I took from your army."

"I saw you kill over four thousand troops, but I saw none taken prisoner," King Dhar said.

"To the contrary, what you witnessed was the capture, not the death of your troops. The roots that took them into the ground deposited them in holding areas back in the forest. I can assure you they were treated well. My healers treated any ailment of their bodies. Your soldiers had plenty to eat and drink, and they will be released when I exit this tent. The lead horses from your cavalry were the only casualties; they didn't heed my warning."

"So this was all a ruse to get me to sign a treaty?" Dhar asked.

"Yes and no. The Vol'aerai and the forest strive for peace, and I took great care to avoid killing anyone. But you have no idea how much pain the forest has been subjected to over the centuries, and I needed you to understand that we will no longer tolerate being trampled underfoot. I apologize for resorting to trickery, King Dhar, but I am glad that you fell for my trap—though you could have chosen to talk instead of trying to kill me—because I was not bluffing when I said you wouldn't see tomorrow if a treaty wasn't agreed upon. I was prepared to kill you and your entire army even though it would have pained me."

There was silence as King Dhar paused to contemplate how close he came to destroying his kingdom. "Queen Tsorianya, I recognize that this rift between our people has grown to a deep chasm, and this fragile bridge we have built will frighten many. However, I hope as we look into the void below and are confronted with our mistakes, we will rise above our past grievances and reinforce the bridge.

"That is also my wish, King Dhar."

"You said there were two agenda items. What was the second?"

"I would like to invite you to a feast tonight within my home village in honor of the preliminary treaty we have agreed upon and give you a chance to observe who the Vol'aerai are. You may bring whomever you wish. On my honor as Queen, your safety will be guaranteed, though you may bring any guards or weaponry you wish."

"I graciously accept your offer of hospitality, though we will bring no weapons. They were no help this morning, and they will only add to the tensions between us. How will I get to this village you mentioned?"

"A marked path through the forest will guide you to the village when it is time. I caution you not to stray from the designated area inside the forest without an escort. As you said, the bridge is still fragile."

"I have been pondering the attack that destroyed our catapults. What were the yellow clouds?"

"Tree pollen—"

"Pollen?" King Dhar asked.

Tsoria chuckled. "It was unnecessary, but it added to the mystery and confusion of what was happening beneath your feet." Tsoria stepped closer to Relvin and placed her hand in the crook of his arm. "King Dhar, I would like to introduce you to someone. I present my guard, champion, and husband, Relvin."

The helmet retreated from Relvin's head into his armor as he smiled.

"I knew it was you!" General Rashe said as he stepped forward, and they clasped each other's forearms.

"It's good to see you again, General Rashe," Relvin said, "and I'm thankful I wasn't forced to kill you today."

"You never cease to amaze me with your fighting skill, and it seems you've found an equally fierce wife. Though I must say, she's much better looking."

"She is, but don't make Daleah jealous," Relvin said. "I would hate to duel you on her behalf and make her raise your two sons alone."

"My wife will be glad as well. We have twin daughters now, and they are a handful."

"Congratulations! We will have to visit sometime."

"We look forward to it," Rashe said before Relvin released his forearm and turned his attention to the king. "My apologies, Your Majesty. Rashe taught me advanced combat techniques while I was a soldier of your army, and we got to know each other quite well."

"I saw great potential in you," Rashe said. "I hoped you would be my successor, but that was not in the cards."

"Doesn't switching sides and fighting against me make you a traitor?" Dhar asked.

"It does. However, a Vol'aerai queen would have been chosen to counter your treaty with the Tashtari regardless of which side I fought for. Given the power of the forest that you witnessed today, would my presence in your army have made any difference?"

The king paused to contemplate the hypothetical before extending his arm to Relvin, and they shook hands.

"We may never know. I'll have the record show that despite switching sides, you won't be branded as a traitor. Contrary to my reputation, I welcome this outcome over a prolonged bloody campaign."

"Our strategy was built around you being a reasonable man. I'm glad it paid off."

"I'll never hear the end of this from Queen Isida when I return. She was right. I should have attempted to negotiate first."

"If your majesties would seal both of these treaty copies, we can make this official," the councilor said as he placed two copies of the preliminary treaty on the table.

King Dhar pressed his ring into melted wax on each before Queen Tsoria sealed them with tiny crystal roots that grew from her ring and embedded themselves into the fibers of the paper in the shape of a tree.

As the monarchs and Relvin exited the tent with the treaty in hand, an opening in the forest appeared opposite the flagged path, and the soldiers plucked from Dhar's army emerged.

"As you can see, King Dhar, I keep my promises," Tsoria said. "We look forward to your presence on the other side of the bridge tonight."

The two doves flew from the tent peak and perched on Tsoria and Relvin's outside shoulders as they walked down the flagged path back to the Wispryn Weald.

"*You made it through your first political negotiation,*" Relvin said.

"*I never want to do that again. It was exhausting keeping up appearances for that long,*" Tsoria said.

"*But you stuck with it, I'm proud of you. How did Dhar look when you lifted him off the ground?*"

"*I had to bite my tongue to stop from laughing. The look on his face…*" Tsoria giggled. "*I shouldn't laugh. His shock turned to terror soon after. I don't think I've ever known what it feels like to be feared. I don't understand how anyone can enjoy that feeling.*"

"*What about the enslavers?*"

"*I felt hate, and defiance from them, not fear.*" Tsoria and Relvin smiled as they passed the first group of Dhar's returning soldiers. "*You didn't tell me about General Rashe before.*"

"*Not by name. He was the one who recommended me as a courier guard. I didn't expect to threaten his life.*"

"*I'm glad Dhar chose him as a guard, he seems like a good man,*" Tsoria said.

"*He is a good man,*" Relvin said.

"*I could tell you respect him. I hope he comes this evening so I can get to know him like you do.*"

"*Me too. I know you will like him.*"

They continued talking as they returned to the Wispryn Weald to prepare for the evening banquet.

CHAPTER 12

ALLIANCE

ON THE AGREED-UPON AFTERNOON three weeks after the battle, Tsoria and Relvin rode their horses across the northern bridge, passed through the first gatehouse, and followed the road east between towering walls. The three roads into Islatria were heavily fortified and designed to subject ground-based invaders to massive damage along the route to the main gates. An attack by boat would be met with projectiles from trebuchets and ballistae positions at each port near the three gates. If any gate were breached, the invaded section could be isolated using the secondary walls sectioning the city into three districts and an inner castle fortification where the wealthiest and most influential people lived. When Tsoria and Relvin reached the Dawn Gate, near the east port, four royal guards became their escorts, two in front and two behind, as they rode through the streets toward the castle keep.

While it was common for parades to attract crowds to greet visiting royalty, Tsoria was astonished by the sheer number of people lining the streets as they made their way through. People crowded the windows and balconies overlooking the main street and waved flags and streamers as the visiting Vol'aerai passed. Most seemed unsure if they should be excited after all the horror stories. Tsoria felt out of place as they rode down the street. She was used to being at the same level as her people, and riding through the streets and looking down at the people around her seemed self-aggrandizing even though she was a queen.

After surveying ahead, Tsoria fixed her eyes on a balcony overlooking the street. A child was squirming in his mother's arms and pulling himself over the railing. The young mother lost her grip on her son as she attempted to adjust her hold on him, and she watched in helpless anguish as he fell. Everyone turned to see what was happening when they heard the mother's shrill scream, but none had time to act on what was happening. The street below the boy burst open as roots pushed up to catch the child before impact. Tsoria dismounted her horse and approached the child while her hands and fingers articulated how the roots should move to place him on his feet. Tsoria checked the boy for injuries as the roots retreated, pulling the paving stones back into position as if they were never displaced. Relvin joined his wife on the street.

"That was scary but fun!" The boy said and laughed. "Thank you for catching me."

"You're welcome. I'm glad you are safe. However, don't lean so far next time. I won't always be around to catch you."

"Yes, miss..." The boy looked at the crown on her head. "Uhh, Queen?"

Tsoria laughed. "Queen Tsorianya. What's your name?"

"Jasper. Your dress smells beautiful."

"Thank you, Jasper, nice to meet you."

By then, the boy's mother had scrambled down the stairs, pushed her way through the crowd, and swept up Jasper in her arms. Tears streamed down her face, happy that her son had sustained no injuries from the heart-stopping fall.

"I can't thank you enough, Your Majesty," the mother said with a slight curtsy.

"You're welcome," Tsoria said with a smile. "Mind your mother, Jasper. You scared her half to death with that fall."

"Yes, Queen Tsorianya."

Tsoria and Relvin continued on foot for the rest of the journey, with the horses following behind. Word of the near accident spread through the crowd and energized the people. The cheers were loud and accompanied by enthusiastic flag-waving. A few children approached and gave Tsoria a bouquet, which made the escorts nervous, but she insisted they not interfere. Tsoria danced, talked, and played with the children as if she had known them all her life. Relvin lifted many children upon the horses to pretend to be royalty and wave at the crowd. This delayed their progress through the streets but was endearing, and by the time they reached the keep gates, they had quite the following of children trailing along.

King Dhar and Queen Isida were amused at the unexpected following the Vol'aerai dignitaries had attracted on their journey to the keep. After inquiring, they were informed by the guards of the events that had transpired earlier. Tsoria and Relvin dismissed the children and then turned their attention to the monarchs waiting within the keep's courtyard.

"Apologies for the—" Tsoria said, but the king raised a hand to signal her to stop.

"The guards have informed us of your deeds," Dhar said. "The purpose of our gathering is to save a future for our children, but sometimes it is more important to save them so they have a future. As it is said, 'Ink without action is meaningless.' Thank you for the reminder."

"A good reminder for us all," Tsoria said.

"Queen Tsorianya and Relvin, I would like you to meet Queen Isida," Dhar said as he gestured to his wife.

"It is a privilege to meet you, Your Majesty," Tsoria and Relvin said as they curtsied or bowed, respectively.

"The pleasure is mine," Isida said. "However, I am curious why Relvin is not addressed as king."

"The forest only appoints a queen," Relvin said.

"A matriarchy, interesting," Isida said.

"I am merely the chosen human representative of the forest. Appointing more than one forest speaker can confuse more than it helps," Tsoria said.

"Indeed," Isida said. "Well, now that we have been introduced, let us step inside to get out of this sun and enjoy refreshments before the afternoon activities. The legalities can wait for tomorrow after a night of rest. We have ensured that our best guest room is ready for you."

"Rest would be welcomed after a long journey, and your hospitality is appreciated, but I have one request regarding our lodgings if it does not offend you," Tsoria said as they walked towards the keep entrance.

"What is it?" Dhar said.

"I request we be allowed to grow a dwelling outside of the keep within its surrounding walls so that we may rest comfortably in an environment we are used to," Tsoria said.

"Grow a dwelling?" Isida asked. "Intriguing. I have no objection to your request."

"Nor do I," Dhar said. "I have seen how you live in the forest, but I haven't had the privilege of witnessing the process."

"May I suggest near the palace garden?" Isida said. "I think you will find it a most agreeable location. It is certainly a favorite of mine."

"That sounds like a lovely spot," Tsoria said.

A couple of attendants busied themselves around a small table in the middle of the foyer as the monarchs entered the front doors. One attendant took a pitcher and poured cups of cold hibiscus lavender tea, Queen Isida's favorite blend for hot summer days. The second attendant uncovered a platter containing an array of small strawberry lemon tarts and distributed them on cloth napkins. The monarchs and Relvin stood around the table and talked as they enjoyed the refreshments. The attendants stepped back but were ready if they were called to serve.

"Tsorianya, I can't get over how lovely your flower dress is," Isida said. "Are your clothes also grown?"

"Thank you. Yes, all our clothes are provided by the forest plants," Tsoria said.

"I suppose there is no need for a wardrobe to hold your clothes if they can be grown as required," Isida said.

"True, they are reclaimed when unneeded," Tsoria said.

"I would enjoy hearing more about your culture later," Isida said. "Perhaps you could grace me with your presence and resume this topic in my chambers while we prepare for the banquet tonight?"

"It would be a pleasure," Tsoria said.

When they finished the light refreshments and several polite topics, King Dhar led the group through the main attractions of the keep, detailing its history and highlighting the many accomplishments of his Taurille family lineage.

The tour of the keep culminated in a room that housed prized kingdom treasures marking noteworthy historical events. While the king talked about many items, Tsoria was drawn to a podium at the west side of the room brightly lit by the sun through a narrow window. Upon the stand lay what was left of a beautifully embellished book page that was burned around the edges and protected by a thin layer of wax. In the center of the page was an illustration of what appeared to be a crystal tree. A single word could be made out below the image: Myrkar.

"King Dhar, what is the significance of this?" Tsoria asked as she turned towards the king.

Dhar walked over to the podium and looked at the illustrated page.

"A fire destroyed the library many years back, and this page is the only surviving remnant of the book it came from. The only thing I know about it is that it chronicled a story of a disastrous trip across the Eris Sea," Dhar said. "There is a remote monastery of monks who would know more."

"Unfortunately, there isn't enough time to bring them here. I would have liked to hear the story," Tsoria said.

Queen Isida led them on a walk through the gardens, where Tsoria demonstrated how Vol'aerai dwellings were grown. Isida was so enamored with the beautiful natural look of it that she requested Tsoria replace the gazebo and other structures within the garden that had started to show their age over the years, something Tsoria was happy to do. After the garden tour, Dhar and Relvin split off to play games and participate in friendly duels while Isida and Tsoria retired to the temperate chambers of the Queen to relax and converse.

When the day's activities had concluded, King Dhar and Relvin were seated at the head table within the great hall. Everyone waited for the festivities to start, but even though it had become time, their queens hadn't yet arrived.

"Do you think we should send an attendant to check on them?" King Dhar leaned over to ask Relvin.

"I'm sure they are on their way. You know they are better at making an entrance than us men on occasions like this," Relvin said.

"Indeed, they are..." Dhar said and trailed off as the hall doors opened to reveal the two queens.

Everyone ceased all conversations and stood with King Dhar. Queen Isida and Tsorianya, enveloped by lavish floral dresses, walked over the threshold and made their way to the head table with all eyes captivated by every movement. The natural, sweet perfume of the flowers permeated the room and nearly made everyone forget why they were there, as if under a powerful enchantment. When the queens reached their positions at the table, King Dhar lost his tongue in Isida's alluring presence as if he were the infatuated young man he had been when they were first married.

"I...you...beautiful," Dhar said.

Isida blushed as she smiled. She turned to the room and took charge since Dhar was tongue-tied.

"We hope you enjoy the feast and entertainment this evening as we celebrate the beginning of a new partnership with the Vol'aerai, represented here by Queen Tsorianya and her husband, Relvin. Thank you for taking the time to join us tonight. Let the festivities begin!" Isida said before sitting.

Everyone took their seats and began conversations with their neighbors as if the spell on the room was suddenly broken, though, for several minutes, the prevailing topic was the queens' formalwear. Music, singing, and poetry readings entertained everyone as they enjoyed the food served to them and each other's company. Before the meal had finished, King Dhar led Isida to the floor to initiate the first dance they had participated in for years. The clouds over their marriage parted to remind the monarchs who they once were and could be again as they twirled and swayed to the music of their hearts late into the night.

Three days after their arrival, Tsoria and Relvin were in their dwelling by the garden. They stayed in bed until almost mid-morning since the official treaty had been signed in a large courtyard named Providence Square of central Islatria the day before. Tsoria was relieved to have made it through the exhausting process of crafting the treaty. Queen Isida seemed to sense when Tsoria required a break, making the process bearable for the young queen by pulling her away for light-hearted conversation during relaxing garden strolls or within Isida's chambers.

Tsoria and Relvin planned to spend time with General Rashe's family before they started their journey home the following day, but they were greeted by a messenger as they exited their dwelling.

"Morning, Queen Tsorianya, Relvin. King Dhar requests your presence this morning before you visit the general."

"Did he mention what he wished to discuss?" Tsoria asked.

"He gave no details. He only said to bring you to his council chambers," the messenger said.

"Lead the way," Tsoria said.

The messenger led them to the room where King Dhar was waiting.

"Queen Tsorianya and Relvin as requested, Sire," the messenger said after opening the door.

"Thank you," Dhar said.

Tsoria and Relvin entered, and the messenger closed the door as he left.

"Please, sit," Dhar said as he gestured to a couple of seats on the opposite side of the table.

King Dhar walked to one of the narrow north-facing windows of the room to look out as Tsoria and Relvin took a seat at the table. Neither spoke while they waited for Dhar to tell them why he had summoned them. After a few moments, Dhar turned to face them without sitting down.

"There is something I request you to do on your way home," Dhar said.

"What is it?" Tsoria asked.

"I want you to escort my messenger to Wardrich," Dhar said.

"Do you think Lord Darrick will defy the treaty?" Relvin asked.

"Yes, he does not take bad news well. I'm sure you have friends you wish to see again, Queen Tsorianya, and wish to ensure their safety. I see no better people to send than you two," Dhar said. "But before you go, how much do you know about him?"

"I heard stories and witnessed his cruelty, but I know little about his life," Tsoria said.

"His reputation is the only thing I know about him," Relvin said.

"As I assumed," Dhar said before facing the window. "Darrick and I grew up together."

"I wasn't aware he had friends," Tsoria said.

"I may be the last one he has," Dhar said as he turned back to face Tsoria and Relvin, "though I am unsure if a friend would ask what I will of you. Darrick was who others aspired to be when growing up. He was brave, strong, and kind. He was the only person unafraid to fight me without holding back, and still, the only one to knock me out. He was the reigning champion in boxing tournaments for years."

Dhar paused the story and stared off into a corner of the room for a while.

"What changed?" Tsoria asked, bringing Dhar back to the present.

"Darrick made it into the finals of the last tournament he participated in like all the others before. His opponent was smaller than Darrick and not as strong as he was. When it seemed like Darrick's victory was assured and his ego was the most inflated by the cheering crowd, the tables turned," Dhar said. "His rival was new that year, and no one knew how patient and calculating he was until Darrick had been beaten senseless."

"It must have been humiliating to be beaten like that," Relvin said.

"It was, or at least it would have been if he remembered the fight and how he lost," Dhar said.

"Was there any reason given for such a brutal attack?" Tsoria asked.

"The young man's older brother was pitted against Darrick in the tournament five years prior and died from his injuries two weeks after the fight."

"Revenge then," Relvin said.

"Sadly, yes," Dhar said as he sat at the table. "It was weeks before Darrick physically recovered from the beating, but he was never the same. I remained his friend when others abandoned him, but the friend I knew died that day."

"So the torment in Wardrich all these years has been because of your inability to deal with him?" Tsoria asked.

King Dhar rested his elbows on the table with his forehead leaning against clasped hands and exhaled as he closed his eyes for several moments. Dhar lowered his hands and lifted his head to look at Tsoria and Relvin.

"Yes. Whether or not anything could have been done to help him, I chose to exile him in the north. It was easier…It has been one of my biggest failures as a king. I want to believe he will see reason, that he is still in there, but I know he won't, and he isn't. If he attacks anyone, do whatever is necessary to stop him."

"Thank you for telling us his story," Tsoria said. "It doesn't undo Darrick's atrocities, but if he chooses to defy your orders, I will take no pleasure in his death. I will make it quick if he forces my hand and mourn who he never got to be. There has been enough suffering."

"Thank you, Queen Tsorianya. That is more than I could ask."

King Dhar stood and opened the door for Tsoria and Relvin to leave for General Rashe's house.

Queen Isida and Tsorianya sat in the garden's central gazebo, enjoying a private morning meal and chatting before Relvin and Tsoria set out on their journey home. The conversation was like the many others they had enjoyed during walks through the castle grounds, chatting about life, children, husbands, fashion, and anything else that parted them from their duties. However, there was only so long they could delay the homeward journey and the detour they would make along the way. The queens sipped tea during a lull in the conversation as they listened to birds sing and watched the bees buzz around the flowers.

"It was a morning much like this when I had the dream you sent to warn Dhar, and it still gives me the chills," Isida said.

"I would have sent the dream to Dhar, but you were the only receptive mind of influence I could connect to. If there was a possibility that the dream could stop the war from even happening, I had to try."

"Even I have trouble getting through to him sometimes," Isida said before sipping tea, "especially when it comes to war, but perhaps he will rethink that thanks to you."

"I apologize for troubling you with the dream."

"Please, think nothing of it. Dreams fade, but the mind never lets go of death. I have witnessed how killing affects my husband—no matter how justified—and he...we are both happier now. It's been years since he looked at me like…" Tsoria hung her head and looked down at the cup in her hand. "What is it?" Isida asked.

"I almost killed him," Tsoria said.

"That happens in war. He could have—"

"You don't understand. Dhar wasn't the problem. I almost chose to take his life without giving him the last chance that I promised to reconsider his options. I…" Tsoria sighed and finished her tea while watching the bees pollinating the flowers. "I have a feeling that this isn't over."

"If you think Dhar will retaliate, I—"

"No, that's not what I meant," Tsoria said as she turned to Isida and placed the cup onto its saucer on the table. "I haven't told anyone yet, but while holding Dhar in the air—"

Isida giggled at the thought.

"Apologies, continue," Isida said before sipping her tea.

"I felt a presence in the forest network, a voice that urged me not to trust Dhar, to kill him and everyone else. It nearly convinced me to believe the thoughts were my own, but the aftertaste of the words—"

"Sweet and then bitter like savamint?" Isida asked. Tsoria nodded as Isida put her cup down. "When Dhar returned, he told me of a similar experience in the tent."

"Similar? He—"

"Yes, he also heard a voice. Dhar was disturbed by how he was manipulated into attacking you, jeopardizing the decades of work his family has put into bringing peace and stability to the kingdom. He would have called for a recess to calm down if not for what it said."

Tsoria felt like her stomach was knotted as she thought about what Isida had said.

"So, one of my citizens wants to prevent peace between our nations," Tsoria said.

"Are you sure?" Isida asked.

"I suppose it could be one of the trees or animals, but what else could it be? I don't know of another group capable of speaking through the network like the Vol'aerai."

"Will your elders have an answer?"

"If they do, why wouldn't they warn me?" Tsoria asked.

"Maybe they thought there would be more time to prepare you, but it is possible they don't know," Isida said.

"Tsoria, sorry to interrupt, but everything is ready for our journey home. The messenger and I will wait in the courtyard," Relvin said.

"I will be there soon, my love." Tsoria sighed. "Thank you for listening, but our time together is nearing its end."

"You're welcome, Tsorianya. I don't often host guests as enjoyable to talk to as you. It has been a lovely morning in the garden."

"I enjoy your company as well, Isida. We will have to find more opportunities like this in the future."

"You are welcome in Islatria any time."

"Thank you, as are you in the Wispryn Weald, should you choose to visit."

Queen Isida and Tsorianya stood and walked together to the courtyard as two attendants stepped in to remove what was left behind.

CHAPTER 13
DEFIANCE

UKWARD WAS THE LARGEST CLAY processing town in the kingdom and was as pleasant a place as its name suggested. It was located near the western edge of the Ekbahn province, southeast of Paladin Lake. Tahira hummed beside the well as she operated the squeaky winch to pull the bucket from the depths. The sound of heavy steps moved through the square behind her, but Tahira ignored them to focus on her task. The footsteps stopped when another joined them at the other side.

"My Lord, we received this letter from King Dhar," the messenger said.

"What does he want now?" Damian said.

Tahira heard the crinkling of paper as the letter was opened and read aloud by the messenger to Lord Damian Carvell. She pretended not to listen to what was being said as she noisily pulled the bucket onto the edge of the well before pouring the water into the one she had brought to be filled.

"This is the last straw! I don't know how anyone can call him king after this," Damian said.

"What should be done, my Lord?"

"Burn it, and don't let anyone else know what it says."

"Yes, my Lord."

Tahira heard the messenger's quick steps retreat as she grabbed the handle of her bucket. She walked toward the mud pits without turning to see if Lord Damian suspected she had overheard the conversation. The sun beat upon Tahira's black hair as she made stops at each of the mud pits, disseminating water by ladle to each thirsty worker. She soon neared the pits where her friends Jestin and Sadon were mixing clay with her older sister Erza. Jestin was the oldest at nineteen, Sadon and Erza were seventeen, and Tahira was almost fifteen.

"You won't believe what I overheard," Tahira said with a cheery smile as they drank their share of water.

"What is it?" Erza asked.

"King Dhar signed a treaty with your people, Jestin!" Tahira said.

"How does that help? We are too far from the Wispryn Weald for them to rescue us," Jestin said.

"The treaty says any slave who wishes to join the Vol'aerai must be set free!" Tahira said.

"Where did you hear this?" Erza asked.

"I overheard a messenger delivering the news to Lord Damian while at the well," Tahira said. "You can go back home."

Jestin stopped walking in the mud.

"What about you? You are Kalumat. Your families are in the Heblana desert. I won't leave you here," Jestin said.

"The invitation is for any slave, not only Vol'aerai," Tahira said. "We can all leave together."

"None of you are going anywhere," Damian said.

Tahira turned to see Lord Damian approach the pits with guards. She hadn't fooled him like she had hoped.

"Dhar isn't my king," Damian said as he snatched Tahira's arm, causing her to drop the water bucket. "It is time you are taught the same lesson your sister learned for meddling in my affairs."

Damian dragged Tahira away from the pits as she struggled against his grip and looked back at her friends for help.

"Keep your hands off my sister!" Erza said.

Erza fought against the slippery earth that attempted to hold her back. Once free, Erza charged at Damian as mud flew off her feet and leaped at him before any guards could intervene. The collision of their bodies forced him to let go of Tahira as he was thrown off balance and fell to the ground.

"I won't let you take my sister!" Erza said as she leaped on top of the lord and pounded his face.

Two guards pulled Erza off their lord and secured her before she could strike him with a rock she had grabbed from the ground. Damien, bruised and bloodied by the attack, stood with the help of another guard and smiled after wiping the blood from his nose.

"Oh, I'm going to enjoy this, you filthy, mangy dog!" Damien said.

Tahira watched in horror as Damian drew back his fist and swung it at her sister. But before his fist contacted Erza's face, roots shot from the hard-packed ground, wrapped around his arms, and stopped his attack. The guards let go of Erza and drew their swords to cut the roots holding their lord, but their arms were bound before they could strike.

"Lord Damian Carvell, you have exploited these people for too long," Jestin said with unexpected authority as he stood on the bank of the clay pit he had been in. "Today, that ends."

Tahira ran into her sister's arms as they watched Jestin moving his arms like a conductor telling the roots what to do. Anyone who attempted to aid the captured men or to attack the four friends was bound and gathered together in a root cage grown to contain them.

"Does anyone else want to join their lord?" The few guards who weren't imprisoned placed their weapons on the ground and stepped back. "Wise choice. Do not prevent anyone from leaving this place or attempt to free those in the cage lest you want their fate. A representative of King Dhar will arrive in five days to pass judgment on those involved in this unlawful defiance of his treaty. Keep them alive until then."

Jestin walked to the clay pit where Sadon was and helped him step out. Tahira and Erza joined them before Jestin fainted as they embraced. Sadon lay Jestin on the ground as Tahira and Erza sat beside him.

"I'll be back with a cart," Sadon said as he ran off.

When Sadon returned with a donkey pulling a cart, the sisters climbed into the back and helped Sadon get Jestin aboard. Sadon climbed into the front seat and coaxed the donkey forward. Tahira shaded Jestin with her body as Erza cradled his head in her lap as the friends took the northern road away from Mukward. Two hours went by as they made steady progress north. They were in the middle of a conversation about what they would do for food when Tahira saw Jestin's eyes flutter open.

"He's awake!" Tahira said.

Erza embraced Jestin as soon as he sat upright while a few tears escaped her eyes. Sadon looked back and smiled before looking back at the road.

"Don't scare me like that," Erza said.

"I'm sorry. I didn't mean to worry you. Not everything was under my control," Jestin said.

"What happened back there? You didn't seem like the person we know," Sadon said over his shoulder.

"Because that wasn't me," Jestin said after Erza pulled back from his embrace.

"Then who was it?" Tahira asked.

"The Vol'aerai Queen, Tsorianya," Jestin said.

"Your friend Tsoria is a queen? When did that happen?" Sadon asked.

"I don't know," Jestin said.

"How could she control what you did or speak through you?" Erza asked.

"You remember what I told you about my people?" Jestin asked, continuing after his friends confirmed they remembered. "I never learned how to connect to the forest before, but in my desperation to help you, I must have figured it out."

"What did it feel like?" Tahira asked.

"It felt like going from being alone to having an entire army protecting me as Tsoria gave orders."

"So, the Queen took over your body and did that back at Mukward?" Erza asked.

"It was strange not having control over my body. She talked to me while it was happening and assured me I was never forgotten by anyone back home."

"Then we are headed to the Wispryn Weald?" Sadon asked.

"No. She wants me to ensure you get home. Go west. We'll use the nearest ferry to cross the river on our journey to the Heblana desert."

It was late afternoon, eight days after the official treaty was signed, and all the lords, ladies, freemen, and serfs from Lord Darrick's region of the Nemoyid province were gathered together in the great hall, murmuring amongst themselves. Cecelia stood with her ladies in the shadowy colonnades with a clear view of the front of the room. Lord Darrick sat on his throne, glaring at two hooded figures who had arrived that afternoon with the king's messenger, Colston.

"Did anyone get a peek at who those two are?" A lady asked.

"I heard even Lord Darrick doesn't know," another said.

"How were they let in?"

"Orders from His Majesty, even the guards were prevented from looking at them."

"How unusual…"

Cecelia overheard many speculative conversations as the crowd waited to be told why they had been summoned. She was also curious about the two figures and scrutinized their mannerisms for any hint of their identity. Cecelia knew one of them was a woman—possibly even royalty—based on size, build, and graceful gait. She guessed the other was a soldier or bodyguard to a princess because he was attentive to every movement around him. Whomever they were, Lord Darrick was agitated by their presence.

A sharp metallic clang of a halberd shaft pounding against the floor echoed from the back of the hall three times, signaling complete attendance, and Darrick nodded to Colston. The crowd fell silent as Colston stepped forward, turned to face the crowd, and projected his voice as he read from an unrolled scroll. Darrick seemed bored as the introduction was read, describing the king and his authority and the usual legalities. However, when Colston reached the substance of the proclamation, Darrick perked up.

"...announcing that King Dhar has brokered a treaty with the Vol'aerai after the most recent conflict in the Nemoyid province. The following announcements supersede any conflicting edicts: henceforth, Lord Darrick is relieved of his duties at Wardrich Castle—"

"What?" Lord Darrick asked as he exploded from the throne and headed toward the messenger.

The news surprised Cecelia, but her gaze was drawn to the tallest figure as he threw off his cloak and leaped between the messenger and Darrick. She instantly recognized the young man as Relvin, and murmurs rumbled through the great hall like a stampede. Relvin braced for a fight as daggers appeared from nowhere in his hands. Cecelia couldn't see Darrick's face, but his balled fists and huffing figure told her all she needed to know. Darrick backed away after several terrifying moments.

"Quiet everyone!" Colston commanded and waited for the crowd to settle down before continuing. "Furthermore, ownership of the castle and surrounding lands will be turned over to the Vol'aerai. Overseeing this transfer is Tsorianya," Cecelia pivoted her gaze to the second figure, eager to confirm her ears didn't deceive her. "Queen of the Vol'aerai, and her husband, Relvin."

The second hooded figure gracefully removed their cloak. Cecelia gasped with the crowd as Tsoria's dress bloomed and filled the room with a sweet scent while a crown grew upon her head. Tsoria walked toward the throne and stepped onto the first step of the throne platform before Darrick turned around to see what the fuss was all about. Cecelia's joy turned to terror as she saw the look on Darrick's face. She knew what was about to happen and wanted to tell Tsoria to run.

"Any attempt to stop this—" Colston said.

"I paid for you, whore. I will do what I please with you!" Derrick said as he lunged at Tsoria.

It looked like Tsoria had frozen in fear when she stopped ascending the steps and turned to face Lord Darrick. Tsoria's left arm appeared to get darker starting from the shoulder down but Cecelia didn't get a good look.

"I wouldn't do that, Darrick," Relvin said.

Lord Darrick didn't seem to hear Relvin. Cecelia held her breath, unsure of what to expect. When Darrick was about to strike, Tsoria shot out her left arm and broke his thick neck with one swift movement.

The crowd drew back and sharply inhaled as Darrick's lifeless body fell to the floor with a thud. Cecelia almost fainted from the relief she felt. The women around her kept her standing and assured her she wasn't dreaming; Darrick had been killed before their eyes.

"May you find solace in death as we do in life," Tsoria said as she turned away from Darrick, approached the throne, and sat.

Cecelia caught a glint of light from Tsoria's cheek as Colston sighed and turned away from the scene.

"What you saw demonstrates what could happen if you defy the king's order. I can skip over the part relating to his next posting..." He paused to find his place in the document. "Those who do not wish to live with the Vol'aerai will be given two months to vacate the Nemoyid province with their belongings. Slaves will be granted unconditional freedom if they decide to live with the Vol'aerai. Fair compensation for losses will be calculated on a case-by-case basis. This concludes the king's proclamation." Colston lowered his arms and rolled up the scroll before addressing the crowd one last time. "Tomorrow, Queen Tsorianya and I will be available to answer questions and ensure a smooth transition."

Colston gestured to Tsoria as he backed a couple of paces away. Tsoria stood and surveyed those gathered in the room before speaking.

"I regret that you had to witness death on this day. King Dhar and I hoped force would be unnecessary, but Darrick chose to end his future as you are called to decide yours. I don't wish to harm anyone and won't force you to live with the Vol'aerai," Tsoria gestured with open palms to the crowd, "but you are all invited to join us. Many of you watched me grow up here. I know your families have worked these lands, passing them from father to son for generations. I invite you to continue your legacy and build a better future for your children." Tsoria descended the steps until she was on the same level as the people. "I know more than many how frightening it is to be forced from your home to start a new life…and I will understand if you choose not to stay. I hope you can set aside your assumptions before deciding. You may all return home and discuss the situation with your family."

The crowd filtered out of the hall, discussing everything that had occurred as several guards hauled off Lord Darrick's body to be prepared for burial.

"My little Tsoria, you've returned!" Cecelia said as she emerged from the shadows.

Tsoria turned, and her face lit up as she ran toward Cecelia with open arms, squealing in delight.

"Cecelia, I have missed you," Tsoria said as they parted after their long embrace, and she surveyed all the ladies surrounding them, "I have missed all of you. We have so much to talk about."

Tsoria hugged each of the ladies and chatted with them, shedding plenty of happy tears. Tsoria searched the group of ladies before turning back to Cecelia.

"Where—" Tsoria said.

"Raven is no longer with us, Tsoria," Cecelia said with a heavy heart. "She was Darrick's last victim four nights after you left."

Cecelia wrapped Tsoria in her arms again and mourned as the other ladies gathered around.

"Now, where is that husband of yours?" Cecelia said after they dried their tears.

Tsoria smiled and grasped Cecelia's hand as she led the women to where Relvin talked with Colston.

"Relvin, I wish to introduce you to Cecelia," Tsoria said as Relvin was wrapped in Cecelia's arms before she finished her sentence, "the woman who made this all possible."

"Thank you for taking care of my little Tsoria. You've brought joy back to this old maid," Cecelia said.

"You're welcome," Relvin said, and after parting, "I am honored to meet you in person, Cecelia. Tsoria told me many wonderful things about you. Perhaps we could get better acquainted during the evening meal."

"Oh, as long as you don't try charming me. I might be tempted to steal a handsome gentleman like you away from Tsoria. I don't see that going well for me after seeing what happened to Darrick," Cecelia said. Everyone in the group laughed and shuffled off to the Flower Garden.

Relvin and Tsoria entertained the ladies with stories about their escape from the castle and the events leading up to the present. While the evening meal was served to them within the chambers, the topic changed to life within the forest and attracted the attention of the castle staff, who had a lot of questions about their future and what their life would be like should they join the Vol'aerai.

Cecelia rested well that night, knowing that Darrick could no longer harm any of her ladies and they weren't required to fulfill the pleasures of anyone.

King Dhar had wondered if the treaty had fractured his kingdom beyond repair in the weeks following its signing. His court was filled with far more cases than ever before. Councilors roamed the provinces, hearing cases and deciding them on precedent, but he was given daily communications on issues he needed to address. Queen Tsorianya sent representatives to become part of his legal teams in every province, speeding up their communication of pressing matters. Since they could tap into the forest network for advice and talk with each other without delay, he could give immediate feedback on cases. He soon concluded that his kingdom was not fractured because of the treaty; it had broken long before. The treaty was the first real fix to the cracks that had been covered up or ignored.

"Your Majesty, our livelihood is ruined because of your treaty with the Vol'aerai," Fasik said.

King Dhar had heard these words numerous times over the past weeks, and each time, a solution was found for the business in question to continue. However, for the enslavers, the case he was now presiding over, the treaty had destroyed their ability to make a living. The number of slaves leaving the kingdom for the Wispryn Weald left a labor deficit before the busiest harvest months. Landowners became desperate to steal workers and slaves from others, causing more than a few legal fights in the courts. Duke Westin was instrumental in forming a solution after transforming most of the Oundar province in the years before the treaty. Labor coalitions were formed between landowners for workers to roam to where they were needed and be paid fair wages. Despite the shift in thinking required and the work it took to change gears, the collective health and happiness of the kingdom increased because of the treaty, and King Dhar couldn't bring himself to be sad at the destruction of one exploitive business.

"There is high demand in many trades right now," Dhar said.

"To what trade do our skills apply, Sire?" Teivel asked.

"Food is always in demand. How about hunting?" Dhar asked.

"We have expenses that hunting would not provide for," Jorvel said.

"Have you tried learning a new trade?" Dhar asked. "There is a huge opportunity in the pottery industry in the Ekbahn province and the wineries in Etamis and Myrine."

Some of the enslavers seemed receptive to King Dhar's suggestions, but the seven lead enslavers closest to the throne pressed on.

"You suggest we labor in the muck and stain our hands with grapes, Sire? We demand something that pays as well or better than our previous occupation," Leiden said.

"You demand?" Dhar asked, not believing what he had heard.

Fasik heard the king's incredulous tone and attempted to backtrack.

"Your Most Royal Majesty, pardon his poor choice of words—" Fasik said with a slight bow and open arms to the side.

"Don't try to use flattery to weasel your way out of this. His words were not a mistake. I tolerated your kind before because slavery was ingrained in society, and I failed to see a way to eliminate it. You dirtied your hands for years and had no qualms about it, and here you are making demands from me?"

"You ruined us! It is your responsibility!" Fasik said, dropping all niceties.

"Get out of my court!" Dhar said.

The guards at the base of the throne platform stepped forward to push the enslavers out. Most bowed and started towards the entrance, distancing themselves from those in front who stayed a little longer.

"You will regret this," Fasik said as he pointed his finger toward the king.

"Not throwing you in the stocks for your insolence is the only thing I might regret. Get out before I change my mind!"

Fasik jerked his arms away from the guards when they grabbed them to force him out before turning to leave. The guards followed behind to ensure he complied with Dhar's orders.

CHAPTER 14
MIGRATION

K ARAH LOOKED AT THE MIGRANTS encircling the fire as they listened to the soft voice of a young woman singing at dusk. She pondered the months of wandering east to Regent Lake, north to the heart of Jaxier, west to Lone Isle Lake, and then south to spend their last coins for a ferry across the river to the Oundar province. Every town was as unwelcoming as Islatria, and Karah was losing hope when she ran across one of the first ragtag groups traveling to the Wispryn Weald. They shared their food, stories, and hope for more…a better future.

"Mother," Shadir said, stirring in her arms to look up as the song ended, "will those Voler…people accept us?"

Karah wished she could assure her son he had nothing to worry about, but he had voiced the question everyone was replaying in their mind. She looked at Shadir and smiled despite the voice inside sowing doubts about their promises.

"I hope so. We have to try—"

"It's…every town doesn't like us. What makes them hate us? Is it because I'm hurt?"

"Please don't think that," Karah said as she kissed her son's forehead. "None of this is your fault."

Karah massaged her son's injured leg as a tear rolled down her face and smiled when Shadir wiped it away with one of his little fingers. She was proud of how Shadir had braved the long journey despite struggling to walk with his crutch. A few people in the group were kind enough to give him cart rides when he got tired.

"I don't know why they—" Karah said.

"It's because they are confronted with who they are inside when they see you," a male voice said.

Karah looked around for who had spoken in the dim light and watched a young man approach. He had joined the group that day, but they hadn't met yet.

"I apologize if I am intruding on a private conversation. My name is Jeki. May I join you?"

Karah gestured to the ground next to her.

"Thank you," Jeki said as he sat.

"Are you going to the Wispryn Weald as well?" Karah asked.

"Yes, I have looked forward to this for many years." Jeki looked at the fire with a faraway look as a smile lingered on his lips before he returned his attention to Karah and Shadir. "What are your names?"

"I'm Karah, and this is my son Shadir."

"I'm glad to meet you," Jeki said as he smiled and waved at the boy.

Shadir returned a shy wave and rested his head against his mother.

"What did you mean—" Karah said.

"I noticed your son struggling to walk earlier today. May I see his leg?" Jeki asked.

"What do you want?" Karah rotated her body away as she hugged her son but kept an eye on Jeki. "We don't have anything to trade."

"I'm a healer. Perhaps I can do something other surgeons couldn't."

"We couldn't afford one," Karah said, her eyes welling with tears.

"Ahh…I understand. I still wish to help."

Karah held her son close, skeptical that anyone could help him this long after the injury, but she wanted to see him run and play with other children. She turned toward the kind-looking young man.

"Can you help him?" Karah asked with a quivering voice.

"Yes. I ask for nothing except an opportunity to ease both of your suffering."

Karah relaxed her embrace and directed her son to show his leg to Jeki. The young man rolled up Shadir's pant leg, exposing the deformed limb. Jeki ran his hands over where the leg had been broken, feeling the bones beneath that were not stitched together correctly.

"Shadir," Jeki said as he looked up from the injury, "what I'm about to do will hurt, but I know you are a brave boy. Can you keep your leg still for me?"

Shadir smiled at being called brave and nodded.

"You will feel a pinch soon." Jeki ran his hand beneath the leg, causing Shadir to wince. "The people who look at you and show their disgust or hate can't help themselves. You remind them of their empty soul."

The young man's hands grasped both sides of the bone and shifted it without warning. Tears ran down the boy's cheeks from the pain as a sharp yell escaped his lips, drawing the attention of everyone around the fire.

"The worst is over, Shadir. You are doing well. Breathe..." Jeki said and waited until Shadir calmed down before continuing the treatment. "They try to fill their soul with more possessions, fame, power, or anything else they have acquired, thinking it will give them an edge when they finish the race," Shadir grimaced several times as Jeki worked his hands and fingers along the injured leg, applying pressure as if he were molding clay, "but if life doesn't let you cross the finish line with a body, why would it let you leave with anything else your soul can't hold?"

Jeki closed his eyes as his hands surrounded Shadir's leg where the break was.

"It feels like my leg has a fever, Mother," Shadir said.

"Almost finished…" Jeki said.

The crackling of the fire and the chirping field crickets were the only sounds while Karah waited. She felt Shadir relax in her arms moments before Jeki opened his eyes and let go of her son's leg.

"I can assure you that there is no need to fear being accepted by the Vol'aerai," Jeki said and smiled at Shadir. "You are a good, brave boy."

Shadir reached down and felt his leg.

"It doesn't hurt anymore," Shadir said.

"Go ahead and walk on it," Jeki said.

"Mother, my leg is…" Shadir cautiously stood. "Jeki made my leg better!"

Shadir beamed while he spread his arms and ran around in the firelight and between the people watching him as he whooped and hollered in delight. Several other kids joined in his merriment. Tears rolled down Karah's cheeks as she laughed at seeing her son running for the first time since the accident.

"Thank you, thank you, thank you!" Karah said as she threw her arms around Jeki's neck. "How could I ever repay you for what you have done for my boy?"

"The joy on your face and your son's face is more than enough," Jeki said after they parted.

"No surgeon could ever do that. Are you a magician?" Karah asked.

Jeki laughed.

"No. I merely used the gift of healing granted to me by the forest to help your son," Jeki said.

The crowd around the fire grew as more people from camp gathered to see what the excitement was all about. They had seen Shadir struggle with walking before and were amazed after being told what had happened moments before.

"You…you're one of them?" Karah said to Jeki with sudden clarity.

"Yes, I'm Vol'aerai."

The people gasped before asking questions at the same time.

"Please, not all at once," Jeki said with a smile as he stood and walked toward the fire so he could be seen and heard by everyone. "No doubt you have heard many tales about the Vol'aerai, but we are no different than you. Let me tell you my story, and then I'll answer your questions."

Jeki told how he had lived in the Wispryn Weald and been taken as a child. Many of the crowd could relate to the hardships endured as he told tales of what his master, Duke Westin, was like and how he was treated.

"Five years into my servitude, when I was fifteen, the Duke's daughter became ill. He loved his daughter and spent a fortune on doctors, medicines, and herbs in the hopes of healing her, but nothing they did worked. Some of the 'cures' made it worse. The sicker she became, the meaner he was."

"Did she die?" A concerned child asked and looked embarrassed as the crowd turned towards him after his outburst.

"She lived," Jeki said with a chuckle. "Duke Westin was a hard master, but I couldn't let his daughter suffer anymore. I snuck into her room and called on the forest to heal her. When she opened her eyes and smiled, I knew it was the right choice."

Jeki explained to the people what aliuscerai was after someone asked if he always had the healing gift. The children were excited when he told them they also could learn to talk to the animals.

"The Duke realized that if it weren't for a slave—the lowest of the low in his opinion at the time—his daughter would have died. He treated me more like a son than a slave afterward, and his whole world shifted little by little. His business became more profitable when he treated his serfs better, giving them rest days and tending to their health and wellness."

Jeki explained that he stayed to work for Duke Westin and helped him reconcile with his workers until the Vol'aerai treaty. He paused to look around at the faces lit by the fire.

"The stories you have heard about the Vol'aerai come from a place of misunderstanding and fear, and although I don't know the reasons for that fear, we have no desire to harm anyone. This treaty with King Dhar brings Vol'aerai, like me, home and provides an opportunity for all of you. We want you to thrive and we're happy you have accepted the invitation. Are there any questions?"

Jeki answered as many questions as he could, talking late into the night. He finished with two stories for the kids before the crowd dispersed to sleep.

As Karah lay beside her son that night and thought about everything that had happened that day, she no longer had any doubts about her decision.

A little over three weeks had passed, and Wardrich resembled a construction site more than a castle. Only one-third of the people residing within or around the castle grounds left for the southern provinces, and the castle walls reminded the people who stayed of unpleasant memories, even without Darrick. After the last family opting to migrate south had left, those that remained voted to disassemble the castle. The orchards, gardens, and fields were left intact. A new Vol'aerai village sprung up in its place, and Cecelia was appointed as the elder. Lellia and other Vol'aerai visited to help transition the people into their new life as the castle was torn down.

The preconceived ideas and tales about the Vol'aerai lingered in the peoples' minds, causing more than a few misunderstandings, but each day, the work brought them closer together. Everyone soon found a way to begin their new life as the Vol'aerai guided roots to disassemble the castle and loaded the stones and beams onto carts to be sent as construction materials for those who migrated south. Older children and farmers helped gather ingredients, cooks made the meals and distributed water to the workers, and mothers and elderly took care of and played with the children. Lellia spent her time talking with Cecelia and coaching her in her new role as an elder. Each day, more of the castle grounds were cleared, and Vol'aerai buildings were grown into place.

Before the sun rose on the first day after the village was complete, a special meal was prepared, and Queen Tsorianya raised her cup to welcome the people as Vol'aerai and dedicate them to the forest. As everyone watched the sunrise for the first time in the new village, the forest spread around and embraced it as its own.

"Look, Kelin," Myrna said as she pointed to a collection of structures blending into the trees ahead as the cart bumped along the uneven forest floor. "We are home."

Her two-year-old son, Kelin, looked in the direction she was pointing and copied her gesture before turning his gaze to his mother, who held him in her arms as the cart creaked and groaned.

"Home?" Kelin asked.

"Yes, that is our new home."

"Hungry," Kelin said as he pointed to his mouth.

"I know you are hungry, Kelin. We will eat soon."

Myrna was glad that their journey was nearing its end. They had started migrating late in the two-month period and caught up with one of the last caravans heading north. She was thankful that her husband Harlan was able to buy a cart because taking care of a toddler and walking in the late stages of pregnancy would've been prohibitive. A couple of travelers they had offered a ride to dangled their legs off the back of the cart along with the few possessions and supplies they had for their northward journey. Harlan stopped the cart as they arrived at the edge of the village and hopped off before going around to help his visibly pregnant wife down after being handed their son.

The older couple they had lent a ride to got off the back of the cart and approached. "Thank you for making this journey easier for us," the older gentleman said to Harlan and Myrna as he steadied his wife beside him.

"You're welcome. I'm sure we'll see each other around here often," Harlan said.

Unsure what to do or where to go, Harlan and Myrna looked around when a young man approached.

"Welcome! We are happy you have decided to make the Wispryn Weald your new home. My name is Jeki, and I can show you to your dwelling."

"Where is the stable?" Harlan asked.

"Everywhere," Jeki said. "We let the horses roam where they wish and call them as needed. I'll help you unharness the horse and set it free."

Harlan and Jeki loosed the straps securing the harness, and before it walked off into the woods, the horse paused to nuzzle Harlan's chest.

"The mare thanks you for being kinder than its previous owner and wishes your family a long, happy life," Jeki said.

"You can talk with them?" Myrna asked.

"Yes, and in time, you may learn to as well."

Jeki showed them where the main amenities were in the village before leading them through the center to a dwelling in the north where they could settle in.

"When ready, you can explore and mingle around your new home," Jeki said.

"Where can I prepare food for my son?" Myrna asked.

"The village center is where we prepare our meals, and the evening meal will be ready in about an hour, but those preparing the food will have something for your son."

After thanking Jeki for his help, Myrna headed to the village center with Kelin in her arms. Harlan headed back to the cart to bring the few possessions they owned into their new home. Small groups of migrants continued entering the village, and Harlan helped them unload and carry their belongings into their dwellings. Myrna and Kelin had already finished eating by the time Harlan joined them at the table, and while he ate, a young woman sat down across from them to converse.

"Welcome to the Wispryn Weald, and thank you for helping the others settle in. I am Tsorianya."

"Queen Tsorianya?" Myrna asked.

"There is no need for formalities," Tsoria said, "I am as much a servant as I am queen. What are your names?"

"I'm Myrna. My husband is Harlan Warner and our son is named Kelin."

Kelin cooed and was mesmerized as a butterfly fluttered above the table. Those nearby smiled at his wonderment.

"I hope the journey wasn't too taxing," Tsoria said.

"Without our cart and the people we met along the way, I couldn't have done it," Myrna said.

"I imagine traveling with a two-year-old while pregnant is tough."

"We almost waited until the birth of our second child, but our adoptive parents convinced us to take the chance," Myrna said.

"Are your real parents—" Tsoria asked.

"Oh, no. Both our parents are alive, but they don't want anything to do with us."

"I'm sorry. That must have been difficult," Tsoria said.

"It was tough leaving Drianfir without our families' support," Harlan said, "but we found refuge in Khuraja—"

"What a coincidence! My husband Relvin grew up in Khuraja," Tsoria said.

Myrna and Harlan exchanged silent glances before turning back to Tsoria.

"Relvin...Moriss?" Myrna asked.

"You know him?" Tsoria asked.

"Yeah...I...met Relvin before you knew him," Myrna said, looking around uncomfortably.

"He didn't tell me about you," Tsoria said.

"Relvin never knew my name, and it's not a story for the table," Myrna said before pausing to look at her husband as he put his arm around her waist. "He is a good man, though he learned some things the hard way. Even if he never tells you the story, he and his family are why I am here."

"Something we have in common," Tsoria said.

Harlan finished his meal before taking Kelin from his wife to give her arms a break.

"While we were in Khuraja, we learned that Myrna was pregnant with our second child," Harlan said. "Soon after, King Dhar called for soldiers to fight the Vol'aerai, and I was forced to be part of the army."

"The weeks he was gone were difficult," Myrna said.

"I can imagine," Tsoria said.

"I was afraid I would have to raise two kids alone," Myrna said, "but Relvin's family supported me during that time. I don't know how Relvin's mother knew Harlan was safe, but her conviction kept my hope alive."

"I'm glad Myrna had support while I was gone," Harlan said. "I was one of the soldiers caught in the yellow clouds."

"You are the first of those soldiers I have met," Tsoria said. "I hope you weren't traumatized."

"Like the other soldiers that were pulled underground, I thought I was dead," Harlan said. "Learning that we had become prisoners didn't alleviate our fears. We imagined the horrible ways we would be tortured or used as sacrifices…"

While the adults listened to Harlan's story, the children played games or made friends with the curious wildlife. Kelin interjected several times and smiled when he was given attention for his efforts.

"While we squabbled amongst ourselves, the cages retreated into the ground. We thought it was a trick and didn't move at first, but tables with chairs emerged from the ground, food and water were brought, and our captors asked us to join them for a meal without hesitation even though we were armed."

"My people would've been protected if anything had happened," Tsoria said.

"Many of us saw the wolves watching every move we made from the woods," Harlan said, passing Kelin back to Myrna because he was reaching for her. "How we were treated behind enemy lines made a lasting impression on me and many others. When the treaty was official, Relvin's parents persuaded us to take a leap of faith and make a new life in the Wispryn Weald."

"And now we are here," Myrna said.

"Well, I am glad you are here. Thank you for telling your story," Tsoria said. "It's unfortunate my husband is busy in another village, but I can tell him later."

"May I make a request?" Myrna asked.

"Yes," Tsoria said.

"I want to meet Relvin, but please don't tell him I'm here until his parents arrive."

"When will that be?"

"Soon."

"I promise," Tsoria said. "It was a pleasure to meet your family, but I should welcome more newcomers before the light fades. Have a lovely evening!"

"You as well, Queen Tsorianya!"

After Tsoria stood and walked away from the table, Harlan and Myrna started conversations with several other families they hadn't yet met.

The small group struggled as they traveled west across the Heblana desert with the hot sun beating upon them. Their parched throats and cracking lips begged for water, but their water skins ran dry a day earlier when they had to abandon most of what they brought. Every dune they climbed hid another behind, making it impossible to confirm if they were going in a straight line or not. Hour after hour, they trudged on, hoping one of the mirages taunting their sanity wouldn't be a fantasy.

After the confrontation with the king, more than half of the enslavers left the group to learn new trades. The seven remaining men, Fasik, Teivel, Leidon, Lyrkin, Jorvel, Dormin, and Nezara, decided to seek their fortunes in the Kalumat nation. They were shading their eyes from the setting sun when one of them spotted what appeared to be a large patch of vegetation jutting from the sandy ocean ahead. With renewed spirits, they adjusted their heading and plodded on. The group was stumbling through rows of date palms and desert brush an hour after the stars peeked out of the night sky. With loud shouts and laughter, they plunged headfirst into a large pool of water they found soon after. Once their thirst was quenched, they lay on the pool's bank and fell asleep.

The seven enslavers woke at the edge of the oasis to the bright mid-morning sun shining in their faces. After sitting up and glancing around, they noticed two Kalumat soldiers armed with scimitars standing in the shade of a nearby palm tree.

"Good morning, travelers," one of the soldiers said. "If you have crossed the dunes with ill intent—"

"We have information for the Malikan," Fasik said. "We are unarmed, though you are welcome to check."

"There is no need, we have checked," the soldier said. "The Malikan will see you in his tent. Follow us."

The seven men followed the Kalumat guards to a large tent and entered. A mature man with dark hair and a beard greeted them with a smile as they entered.

"Come in, my friends. I am Farouq Majidd, Malikan of the Kalumat."

"Thank you for your hospitality, Malikan," Fasik said. "We have come from the Islatrian kingdom and wish to offer our services to the Kalumat."

"Fortune favors you. Few make such a long journey without perishing in the hot sun. Let us sit to enjoy ourselves before we talk business." Farouq gestured to a low table with cushions on the floor around it. "Have a seat."

The Kalumat leader sat at one side of the table and clapped his hands. Jestin entered the tent with a tray of goat's milk. He served a cup to each guest before whispering in Farouq's ear, who nodded. Tahira entered with platters of dates for everyone.

"Help yourself, my friends. I'm sure you are famished, and the dates are especially plump this year. Later, we will have a big feast," Farouq said as Jestin and Tahira exited the tent.

Farouq chatted with the enslavers about small matters while they enjoyed the food in front of them. When they were finished, the Kalumat leader wiped his hands on a wet towel.

"Tell me, what news do you bring from Islatria?" Farouq asked.

"King Dhar has signed a treaty with the Vol'aerai of the Wispryn Weald," Fasik said, "but this has caused many to question his strength and is fracturing his empire. If you act now, we can help you take advantage of the chaos and leave this barren wasteland for prosperous lands to the east."

"Your proposal would make me a legend among my people. My ancestors were exiled to the Heblana desert to die as punishment for crimes long forgotten. Long have we dreamed of returning to the lands of our forefathers to claim what should have been ours. What services are you offering the Kalumat?"

"We know where all the secret entrances are for each city, allowing you to take over the Yashir province from the inside. We also know which trade routes to disrupt to cause the most damage to commerce. Once you control the Yashir province, Ekbahn can be persuaded to be an ally as they have no love for the king."

"We have been building up to a large attack for years, and this information you are willing to provide would help our cause," Farouq said, detecting a glint in Fasik's eyes as he glanced at the others. "However, there is a matter to resolve first."

"I'm sure we can develop an acceptable solution to any issue," Leidon said.

"I'm encouraged by your enthusiasm," Farouq said with a smile. "The problem is that someone has taken the purity of my eldest daughter, and if not for the bravery of her and her friends, my youngest would've had the same fate."

"That is terrible news. Whoever is responsible should be punished," Teivel said.

"I'm pleased you think so because that is where I need your help." Farouq snapped his fingers, and seven guards entered the tent, taking positions behind each slaver.

"Malikan, I hope you aren't accusing us of this crime against your family. We never defiled your daughter," Fasik said.

"You speak the truth," Farouq said. "The man who did attack her is beyond my reach and facing judgment for a different crime..."

The enslavers relaxed.

"I'm glad because false accusations would jeopardize our partnership," Fasik said.

Farouq continued after his pause, "However, you and your kind are ultimately responsible."

"What do you mean?" The enslavers asked together growing nervous.

"I know what you are," Farouq said. "That young man who served you drinks earlier is my eldest daughter's betrothed. He informed me that this mark on your forearms—what you described as a tattoo of brotherhood—was given to you by the Vol'aerai queen for kidnapping their children."

"He is lying! He has never met us before. How could he know anything about us?" Fasik asked.

"I have known him for less than a moon, but helping my daughters return home tells me as much about his character as your offer does about you. I trust my daughters, and they vouched for him," Farouq said as he removed the pit from the date in his hand with a small dagger. "They told me he is one of the children you stole from the Vol'aerai twelve years ago."

Farouq popped the pitted date into his mouth and chewed while he watched the enslavers look at each other. Their wide panicked eyes confirmed what he had been told.

"We beg of you, have mercy!" Fasik said.

Farouq stabbed the dagger blade into the table, and the guards slit each slaver's throat. He watched blood spray the table as the enslavers clutched their necks in a vain attempt to save their life.

"I have mercy, but not for you," Farouq said as the last breath gurgled from their slit throats.

"What should we do with them?" The guards asked.

"Drag their bodies downwind for the vultures," Farouq said. "I don't want their stench to ruin Erza's wedding."

CHAPTER 15
RELIEVED

TSORIA LAY BESIDE HER HUSBAND on a rare lazy morning as they discussed the last two months of events in her parents' village. The time had passed quickly for them, and the constant traveling, village dedications, and political matters they dealt with sapped their energy. There was never enough sleep, but the return of Tsoria's captured friends, Jeki, Briel, and Aleya, brought rest for many aching hearts and joyous celebrations. Each recited stories for days around the evening fires. They found solace in one another when they shared their trauma, but it was their humorous tales that were the easiest to recall years later. Jestin's parents heard the stories later because they traveled to the Kalumat nation to visit their son and act as delegates for the Vol'aerai after the wedding celebrations concluded.

"If anyone knew what it was like to be a nation's ruler, no one would envy any royalty," Tsoria said.

"True. Most people envy the glory, power, and riches instead of the responsibility."

"Responsibility I would gladly give to someone else so I could relax."

"Well, if last night wasn't relaxing enough, I could be persuaded to extend the intimacy longer."

Tsoria chuckled and kissed Relvin.

"Talking with you and enjoying this quiet morning is the intimacy I crave right now."

Relvin traced the contours of Tsoria's body like he had done many times before, relishing how her soft skin felt in his hands while Tsoria studied his face.

"What are you thinking about?" Tsoria asked after a couple of minutes.

"Nothing in particular," Relvin said.

"You aren't getting off that easy."

"What do you mean?"

"There are times you look at me, and I can tell you are thinking only about me. But there are times you are thinking about something else, and you never tell me what it is."

"It's in the past and nothing for you to worry about," Relvin said, trying to end the conversation.

"I promise everything will stay private if that is your concern."

"Now you are using my words?"

Tsoria giggled. "Caught that, did you? You tend to steer around the subject whenever I ask, so this time, I'm not letting you leave until you tell me."

"I don't feel like this…" Relvin sighed as Tsoria waited for him to continue. "Do you remember when I told you why I left the army?"

Tsoria nodded.

"You were afraid you had become a once-decent man. Is that what this is about?"

Relvin looked away.

"You are a decent man, Relvin, a good man."

"How can I be when I never got to apologize? I never made things right, and I'm not sure I can. I don't know her name or if she still lives in the same town." A few tears escaped Relvin's eyes as he pulled away to lie on his back and look up. "It is the not knowing, the inability to resolve this issue that makes me feel underserving of what we have. She deserved better than what she was subjected to."

Tsoria wanted to ease his mind by telling him she had met the woman he was referring to, but she wasn't about to break her promise to Myrna. Tsoria rested an arm on Relvin's chest as she looked down into his eyes.

"You are not the person you were then, and perhaps you have made up for your mistakes but are not giving yourself the credit you deserve."

"Even if I have, the fear on her face still haunts me, and the whispers in my head won't let me forget what I was party to."

"Whispers?" Tsoria asked with concern.

"Yeah, a voice that speaks inside, but it feels cold and slimy as if pulling me into the darkness."

"I know of that voice. I don't know where it's from, but it's not you. I sense that whatever you were party to in the past has been forgiven."

"I wish I knew for sure..."

Tsoria rested her head on Relvin's chest and wrapped her arms around him.

"Until you do, if you need a reminder that you are not a monster, ask me, and I will gladly tell your doubts to leave you alone. Your heart is mine to know. Even if you doubt it, you are a good man."

"Thank you for believing in me even when I can't, my love."

"You're welcome. This is what marriage is for, right? Sometimes it is easy, other times it's hard, but through it all, we have each other to lean on as we navigate life."

They lay together in silence, holding on to each other for several minutes before Tsoria took a deep breath and then repositioned herself to lay on her side facing her husband.

"I don't want this to end, Relvin," Tsoria said before he turned to face her.

"Then let it not end. No emergency or person needs our attention right now." Relvin leaned in to kiss his wife, but she pulled back before their lips met.

"I am afraid that is not quite true," Tsoria said.

Footsteps stopped outside their dwelling, and one of the villagers called out to them. "I apologize for disturbing you, Queen Tsorianya."

"It's fine. I will be out soon," Tsoria said.

"There is a family that arrived from one of the southern provinces not long ago requesting Relvin's presence," the villager said.

Tsoria lay back down on the bed and smiled at Relvin. "Lucky you."

"I'll be right out, "Relvin said before getting out of bed to be dressed by the forest.

Relvin leaned down to kiss Tsoria.

"Give me a few more moments to rest," Tsoria said.

Tsoria lay her head down as the door withdrew to let Relvin out before regrowing. She knew who was asking to see her husband and was glad they had arrived to put his mind at ease.

Relvin exited the doorway and was greeted by the bright sunlight of mid-morning. He joined the villager a short distance away, who took him to the village center. A middle-aged couple stood as Relvin approached after interrupting their conversation.

"Since you wouldn't come to see us, we came to see you, my son," his father said as he hugged Relvin and clapped him on the back before letting go.

"Mother, Father, how did you know where to go to find me?" Relvin asked before embracing his mother.

"I always know where you are, Relvin," his mother said before stepping back to get a good look at her son. "It is good to see that you are well-fed and healthy. We have a lot to talk about."

"We certainly do. Are you here to visit or stay?"

"We are moving here. Fayla and Varial came as well," his mother said as she looked around but didn't see her daughters anywhere. "Well, they're around here somewhere. They're getting to that age where they would rather be around those their age than their parents."

"Your brothers decided to stay behind with their wives and run the business. We thought a change of pace would be good for…" his father said before stopping when Tsoria grabbed the crook of Relvin's arm. "Who might this be? Did you get married and not invite us to the wedding?"

Relvin smiled.

"Yes, I suppose I did, but to be fair, it was a spur-of-the-moment decision, and the ceremony was…" Relvin glanced at his wife. "…intimate. Tsoria, these are my parents, Gregory and Daisie. Father, Mother, this is my love and Queen of the Vol'aerai."

"Apologies, Your Majesty, we didn't know," Relvin's parents said as they scrambled to bow or courtesy in respect.

The formality of the greeting brought a smile to her face as Tsoria let go of Relvin's arm and stepped towards them.

"There is no need to be formal here, especially since we are family. I'm glad to meet you," she said as she embraced them.

"How did you charm your way into the heart of a queen, Relvin?" Gregory asked.

"When we met, she was not a queen. It all started after a long journey to Wardrich Castle…"

Relvin recounted the story with help from Tsoria as they all sat together around the table. Fayla and Varial joined before the midday meal and asked so many questions that Relvin had to start over from the beginning. While his sisters listened to the story, Relvin's parents helped the villagers finish the meal preparations and distribute the food, even though they were told not to trouble themselves. The rest of the afternoon was a variable mix of storytelling, touring the village, introductions, and daily village activities.

When the evening meal had been eaten and the tables cleared, Relvin's mother pulled him aside for a private stroll through the woods instead of joining the others for stories and songs around the fire.

"How do you like it here, Mother?" Relvin asked.

"It feels like the home I've always wanted," Daisie said.

"You always were most content when you were in your garden. Though small, every farmer was jealous of it."

She chuckled. "They were always trying to figure out my secret for the healthiest and best-producing plants in the area. They never did find out and never will now that I'm gone."

"Will you not tell anyone?" Relvin asked.

"I keep no secrets from your father, and you know the answer."

"I don't recall you telling me."

"You live here after sending me messages through the plants for years, and you still don't know?" His mother said through the forest network.

"You can...when?" Relvin asked as he stopped walking.

Daisie turned to look at her son and smiled. "Since the day I met your father. What we told everyone about that day wasn't the entire story."

"You met in a field—"

"Yes, that part was true, but it is what happened in the field we left out."

"Did someone try to attack you?" Relvin asked.

"Nothing like that," Daisie said and chuckled before turning to resume their walk. "When I touched the barley plants, I felt sadness because they were all sickly, but I also felt their desire to give their short life to fulfill their purpose."

"It must have been strange to feel a plant's emotion."

"At first...but it made sense after thinking about it. We strive to have purpose and meaning for our existence. Why shouldn't the plants also strive for purpose?"

"That hadn't occurred to me," Relvin said.

They stopped to watch some twinkling fireflies before continuing their walk.

"Back in the field, I sang my favorite song for when I feel sad. I didn't think it would do anything except cheer me up, but I imagined the plants growing strong roots and leaves that would reach to the sky. By the time I finished the song, every plant was mature and loaded with the plumpest heads of grain anyone had seen far ahead of harvest time."

"The yield must have surprised the field caretakers."

"They harvested more from that field than the closest five fields combined. No one could explain why their field did so well that year compared to everyone else," Daisie said.

"Did no one see what happened?" Relvin asked.

"Your father did but couldn't explain why a song would have any effect on plants. When I fainted after, he ran to my side and held me until I woke. When I asked why he didn't fetch a surgeon, he said, 'Your enchanting beauty compelled me to stay at your side.'" Daisie giggled at the memory. "He began negotiations with my father for marriage that evening."

"What you experienced is called aliuscerai."

"Oh? I had wondered if it had a name," Daisie said with a glance at her son, "but I suppose there is much I will learn now that I'm here."

"With your experience, you will learn quickly," Relvin said, pushing aside some branches for his mother.

"I thought your father would think I was crazy when I told him about my abilities, but he never questioned it after seeing what happened in the field."

"I thought leaving messages for you through the plants made me a crazy at first, but I…" Relvin's voice cracked as he stopped walking. "I messed up, Mother, and I needed to feel close to you."

"I could feel you struggling with something when you came to see us," Daisie said as she turned to face her son and hugged him before stepping back, "but it didn't feel like the right time to ask."

"I was ashamed, afraid you would see me differently if you knew."

"Relvin, my son," Daisie said as she reached to touch his face and look into his eyes, "I see you as I always have. You are my son regardless of your faults."

Relvin put his hand over his mother's before pulling her hand down as he turned away, looking into the distance.

Relvin started his story from his early training days even though he had told his parents many details before. He recalled how his skills had attracted the attention of General Rashe early on and how he was placed in an advanced platoon years earlier than normal.

"We became like family; we trusted each other, and had each other's backs. But after the Suraddin Uprising everything changed. Only five of us made it out alive without debilitating injuries."

Daisie listened without judgment as Relvin told of the many times he had gotten drunk to cope with the aftermath of the battle, making poor decisions in his inebriated state. General Rashe stepped in to help Relvin learn better ways to cope and after several months Relvin rejoined his friends on patrols.

"Looking back, I should have noticed the signs, the mysterious detours coinciding with times that people were found murdered, robbed, or raped in every town we were sent to patrol." Relvin paused as a stag walked nearby, pausing to stare at Relvin and Daisie for a few moments before going deeper into the woods. "A year before I left the army, we were investigating a rash of crimes in Drianfir. My friends told me they had a lead and stationed me at one end of an alley to prevent anyone from running away while they entered from the other end. I waited…then I heard her screams." Relvin shuttered as he recalled the memories. "I abandoned my post and ran to investigate…my colleagues stopped me from getting close but there was no mistaking what had happened. Her disheveled clothes, tears, and terror on her face are etched in my memory." Relvin wiped tears from his eyes. "The group we had been tasked to find was the one I had been part of for years. I trusted them, but they used me to help them get away with their crimes."

Daisie lay her hand on Relvin's shoulder while a lone bird sang a melancholy tune. She waited for Relvin to regain his composure.

"I tried to distance myself from them and report their actions, but they turned against me and framed me for a crime I didn't commit. General Rashe believed me, but it wasn't enough without witnesses. So I asked for a military trial-by-combat, which forbids proxy fighters, and said I would battle all four of my accusers at the same time." Relvin stared off into the woods as fireflies flew around them. "I don't remember the fight but was told it was the bloodiest and most vicious in history. Everyone moved aside as I left the arena, afraid they might be my next victim."

"Not everyone stepped back in fear that day," Daisie said as she walked among the fireflies.

Relvin stared at his mother in bewilderment. "What do you mean?"

"Think back…"

Relvin paused to think, staring at the ground before he raised his head and looked at his mother with mouth agape. "She was there!"

"Yes, Myrna saw the fight."

"Myrna? Wait, how did—"

"She came to the house a little over three years after your trial looking for you, and she told me her side of the story…"

Almost two years before migrating to the Wispryn Weald, Myrna knocked on the door of the humble home she had been directed to in Khuraja and paced as she waited for an answer. A warm breeze coming from the desert tussled her long brown hair. The little bundle in her arms squirmed a little, and she peeked under the blanket to check on her baby, who had fallen asleep not long after she nursed him.

"Don't worry, little one," Myrna said as she stroked one of his little fat cheeks and smiled.

The door creaked open, and a kind-looking middle-aged woman came into view.

"How can I help you?" the woman asked.

"Pardon me, madam," Myrna said. "I was looking for Relvin Moriss and was told this is where I might find him. Am I in the wrong place?"

"Relvin travels for work and hasn't been here for some time. I'm his mother, Daisie. Is there anything I can help you with?"

"I was hoping to speak with him, but perhaps it is better this way. Could you give him a message for me the next time you see him?"

"I would be glad to."

"My name is Myrna Werner." Myrna sighed. "He won't know me by name."

"I'm afraid to ask, but is that Relvin's baby?" Daisie asked.

"Oh, no, no. This little bundle is my husband's child." Myrna looked down at her baby and smiled with a sparkle in her eyes. "But he wouldn't be here if your son hadn't intervened."

"Come in and rest while you tell me how you know my son and what you wish him to know."

Daisie moved out of the doorway, and Myrna stepped in to take the seat offered at the kitchen table. Relvin's mother disappeared for a few minutes and returned with a padded basket she set on a bench beside the table.

"Thank you, my arms need a rest," Myrna said as she carefully lay her son inside the basket.

"I know that feeling. My five children wore my arms out until I couldn't hold them," Daisie said, "but now I miss those days."

"I am enjoying the time while I can."

"Would you like some water?"

"Yes, please, if it is not too much trouble."

Daisie found a clean cup and poured some well water from a pitcher for Myrna.

"Your son is cute," Daisie said as she set the water in front of Myrna and sat across the table. "What is his name?"

"Thank you," Myrna said before she took a drink. "His name is Kelin, and if I hadn't gone through the worst evening of my life—the night I met your son—I wouldn't have met my husband."

Daisie looked worried at Myrna's statement but didn't say what was on her mind.

"Four and a half years ago," Myrna said, "I was walking home alone through the streets of Drianfir, struggling with a large basket from the market. A guard offered to carry it and ensure I made it home. He was charming, easy to talk with, and purposefully distracting me from realizing the danger I was in. Before I could escape, I was surrounded and—"

Kelin stirred in the basket and fussed a little, but Myrna calmed him back to sleep before she continued the story.

"I knew I couldn't stop them, but I fought anyway." Myrna closed her eyes and a few tears rolled down her cheeks. "Relvin showed up after the first soldier raped me…before anyone else had a turn. The way they talked, I knew he was in their group, but his face…the others looked at me like I was a piece of meat, Relvin was horrified when he saw me. While they were occupied with Relvin, I managed to stumble out of the alley and back home before I passed out."

Daisie slipped a hand below Myrna's and placed her other hand above. There was no need for words, Daisie's teary eyes said everything Myrna needed to hear. With a deep breath, Myrna continued.

"When I woke the next morning, I thought the worst was over, but nothing prepared me for what came after. My parents were ashamed of me, like what happened was at my invitation. My betrothed spit in my face and left when told I was no longer chaste. I was afraid to close my eyes to sleep. I hardly left the house because the townsfolk gave me dirty looks and called me whore, adulterer, dirty, harlot, and succubus.

The insults stabbed at my heart but the worst was an awful voice that wouldn't stop saying, 'You are worthless…no one wants you…no one will fight for you…end it all…' When I couldn't take it anymore I walked to the bridge outside the main gate to throw myself off."

"What stopped you?" Daisie asked.

Myrna took a drink from the cup and smiled.

"I met my husband, Harlan, on the bridge that day. We didn't speak but his presence deterred me from jumping and I returned home. I tried several more times to jump, but it didn't matter which day or hour I tried to jump, he was there, a lighthouse in the storm. I was angry at him for always being there the first time we spoke, and that is where our courtship began."

Myrna laughed, and Daisie joined her, waking Kelin in the process.

"May I?" Daisie asked, gesturing to Kelin.

"Yes," Myrna said.

Daisie picked Kelin up from the basket and rocked him until he stopped fussing.

"I miss this," Daisie said as Kelin stared back with his big brown eyes and yawned.

Daisie fawned over the baby for some time before returning him to Myrna.

"It was another six moons before I saw Relvin again, Myrna said, continuing her story. "Harlan and I found ourselves on the edge of an area set up for a trial by combat in the middle of the main square. Before I saw who was in the arena, I recognized their voices and my heart started pounding. Harlan began to guide me away when he noticed me panicking; that's when I saw Relvin among them. My rapist and his friends from the alley taunted and circled him like vultures."

"Four at the same time?"

Myrna nodded. "I didn't think he had a chance, but I have never seen anyone move faster than Relvin did when the fight began. He was fearless, a ferocious whirlwind of blades, feet, and fists. When Relvin finished tearing them apart, he stretched his arms to each side in vindication with blood dripping off his dagger blades and uttered the loudest, pained roar I had ever heard."

"My son…" Daisie trailed off as she cried.

"Relvin didn't recognize or hear me when he walked past without waiting for the verdict, absolving him of all charges. Your son fought to clear his name that day, but it felt like he was fighting for everyone harmed by those men." Myrna looked Daisie in the eyes and clutched her hand. "The voice that almost killed me was wrong. Harlan wanted me. Relvin fought for me. I am worth it. I hope to be as proud of my son as you should be of Relvin."

"…As you walked past her that day, Myrna said: 'Thank you, go in peace,'" Daisie said, ending the story.

Daisie touched her son's face and looked into his eyes while the evening light twinkled off the tears flowing down his cheeks.

"Myrna wants you to know the memories of that night no longer paralyze her with fear or cause her shame, though the pain isn't gone. It will be a long road to recovery, but you helped her get there. Her husband Harlan is a good, honest, and loving man. Their first child, Kelin, is a little over two years old and their second child is on the way."

Relvin grasped his mother's hands caressing his face.

"Thank you for telling me, Mother. It means a lot to me."

"We are proud of you, son. Don't let your past or the thought of what could have been, weigh you down. Saving everyone is great, but that doesn't make saving one person any less important."

Relvin embraced his mother as her words settled in his mind, and relief came to his heart. After some time, they loosened their hold on each other and stepped back to dry their tears.

"Now, when do I get grandchildren?" Daisie asked.

Relvin laughed at the question, clearing the tense air from the previous conversation. "Well, I don't have an answer to that question yet, but perhaps now that you are here we can have a fírha'achíd."

"What's that?" Daisie asked.

"A Vol'aerai celebration of marriage."

"Ahh…your father and I would enjoy that."

On their way back to the village center, they discussed various other lively topics before joining the rest of the villagers around the evening campfire.

CHAPTER 16
PROMISE

AT HIS TEMPORARY TREE NURSERY on the eastern coast, Gafre and Terril looked at the result of their project bobbing with the gentle swells of the bay waters.

"Do you think she will notice?" Gafre asked.

"It's hard to miss," Terril said.

"Perhaps she will be blind," Gafre said turning to his apprentice.

"Even a blind queen will be able to sense this tangle of roots isn't the boat she asked for," Terril said gesturing towards the three joined trees.

"You're right. Only one thing left to do—" Gafre said.

"Apologize when the queen arrives?"

"Your plan is better. We wouldn't get far if we ran."

"Not to mention, she would still be able to find us if we did."

"First project from a queen and I fail," Gafre said sighing. "Perhaps my expectations were too high."

With nothing more to do that could be done in time, he sat on the sand with his apprentice, waiting for the queen's arrival. Gafre had expected to create three separate ships of different configurations from the seedlings. Instead, the roots of each reached for each other as they grew and entangled themselves with the largest tree in the center. They were a floating island at best.

Three riders dismounted their horses behind them on the beach about half an hour later. Gafre and Terril stood and turned to greet them.

"Greetings, Queen Tsorianya," Gafre said before gesturing towards his apprentice. "This is Terril, and he has helped me with the project you requested."

"A pleasure to meet you both in person," Tsoria said, then gestured to her companions. "My husband Relvin and my sister Eviara have come with me to see the results."

"We developed three trees that contain the requested qualities, but I am afraid that we have been unable to form them into a boat."

"Well, every problem has a solution. Have you been able to connect to the trees?"

"Yes, but both Terril and I have been unable to talk with them. We get bits and pieces but not full thoughts."

Tsoria waded to the entangled trees and hoisted herself onto the woven roots. The trees were not much taller than Tsoria when she stood and the long fern-like leaf fronds swayed with the wind. She closed her eyes as she touched the trunk of the center tree. After half an hour, she returned to shore.

"It is as you said."

"So it is a failure—"

"I wouldn't say that. I felt an aloneness, a longing to figure out what they are...they are like children discovering the world for the first time."

"Most trees have discovered themselves by now."

"But most trees have others like them or close enough that they have been guided in their growth. These three have each other, but none know more than the others. The many voices of the forest are overwhelming and even scaring them. This is a wrinkle in our plan, but I am sure it will work itself out."

"Could I try talking with them?" Eviara asked.

"Sure. It could be good practice," Tsoria said.

Eviara ran out into the lapping waves and pulled herself onto the root mass as her sister had done earlier. Those on shore watched as she touched each of the three trees and rested her head on them for a few minutes before sitting down with her back to the center tree and closing her eyes.

Like most Vol'aerai, Eviara had never been on a boat. The gentle movement of the roots beneath her felt strange, at first. But as she let herself relax, the day's warmth and rocking awakened a primal feeling she knew from long before she knew anything other than her body's needs. She almost drifted to sleep as she let that feeling take over.

"What is this warmth…" A trio of voices said in the stillness of her mind, *"…from the creature lying on us?"*

"Am I dreaming?" Eviara asked. *"Is anyone there?"*

"Did it hear us? I don't know…too many voices…too noisy," the trio said.

"Focus on the feeling, ignore everything else," Eviara said, excited at hearing trees speaking for the first time.

"It heard. What is it?" The trio said.

"I'm Eviara, a human."

"Eviara? Human? We are…What are we?" The trio asked.

Eviara sensed sadness from the trio of trees and tried to reassure them, *"Don't be sad…You are the first trees of your kind. There is much for you to learn but I came to help."*

"We would like that," the trio said.

"Let us begin with your name…" Eviara said.

Eviara and the trees talked as the hours passed. Their questions were never-ending. Many Eviara couldn't answer, but she taught them what she knew, and their friendship and trust grew along with their knowledge.

"Relvin, could you call Eviara to eat?" Tsoria said as she put the final touches on the food.

Relvin turned and walked to the shore when a delighted laugh from Eviara reached everyone's ears. What they saw as they all ran out onto the beach put a smile on their faces. The root island where Eviara stood was sailing around the shallow water of the cove in whatever direction Eviara moved her arms. It looked like the trees had learned to reposition their branches and leaves to catch the breeze in a way that would propel them. They watched for several minutes before Relvin whistled to get Eviara's attention and motioned for her to return to shore. Eviara turned the tree island back to shore and ran through the shallow water to join the others.

"I can talk to the trees!" Eviara said with a beaming smile.

"It looked like you were having a lot of fun out there," Relvin said.

"I was. The hollarck trees are playful and eager to learn more as they grow."

"Hollarck trees?" Gafre said.

"When I told them my name they were sad at not knowing what they were. I helped them pick a name and understand their purpose," Tsoria said.

"I'll make a note of that," Gafre said.

Tsoria noticed lacy root bracers on Eviara's forearms and asked, "Did those come from the trees?"

"Yeah," Tsoria said, lifting her arms for the others to inspect them. "With them, I can direct them in whatever direction I wish to explore. They are excited to travel and see what is out there."

"Looks like we have a captain," Relvin said. "Now we need a ship."

"After we eat, we can help my sister shape the trees into a ship. We have much to accomplish before tomorrow and more on the way to meet King Dhar south of here," Tsoria said.

Three days later, on a warm autumn day, the fishermen of Karnell port were cleaning and mending their nets after the morning catch as gulls fought over scraps and warned rivals away from their territory. Karnell had been a sleepy town in Karn Bay located between the Etnamis and Nemoyid provinces on the kingdom's eastern coast. However, several weeks after the treaty, families began arriving by boat and land from the south and the Vol'aerai from the west. The sleepy little town of Karnell awoke as families established themselves and transformed it into a thriving Vol'aerai community.

While most of the previous occupants had abandoned the port, the fishermen stayed to protect what had been passed on for generations. Royalty seemed to have largely forgotten the town even existed, or at least never deemed it worthy of visiting, which suited these old-timers. The less meddling rulers did, the happier they were. The fishermen were content with the Vol'aerai because they seemed more interested in letting them live their lives than controlling them. So, on the day when King Dhar sailed into port, they warily watched as his flagship, Magnus Releon, was moored.

King Dhar disembarked once the ship was secure and was accompanied by two guards and Captain Brent Harkis. The town elder approached to greet them.

"Welcome to Karnell, King Dhar. I am Elder Kaled. I hope the journey was pleasant," Kaled said with a slight bow. "Please let me know if you require anything while you are here so I may make arrangements."

"Thank you for your hospitality, elder Kaled. The seas were calm, and the winds were fair, making our journey faster than anticipated. I presume Queen Tsorianya has not arrived?"

"She is on her way, but it may be another couple of hours before she arrives."

"While we wait, perhaps my men can be shown where to replenish the water barrels and forage for fresh food for the journey," Brent said.

"I will have some villagers show them where to find everything required. We have prepared refreshments for you and your men in the village center while we wait for the queen's arrival."

"Lead the way," Dhar said.

The dock bustled with activity after Kaled led Dhar and his entourage to the village center. Large wooden barrels were hauled up from the ship's hold by net and pulleys and deposited on the dock below, where sailors waited to cart them off to be filled with fresh water. The groups responsible for gathering food were led to the nearby fruit trees and fields for vegetables to supplement the salted meats and hard-tack they would be subsisting on during their journey. Once everyone returned to the Magnus Releon, stowed the food and water below deck, and had a chance to enjoy some refreshments, the ship carrying Queen Tsorianya made its way into port.

King Dhar anticipated Queen Tsorianya's arrival but had not expected her to arrive by boat. He wondered how the ship had even made it this far as it came close enough to inspect. The vessel looked like it had been washed out to sea before construction finished. The ship's frame was exposed, and the hull cladding wouldn't have kept the water from washing over the sides if there had been rough seas. King Dhar greeted Tsoria when she stepped onto the dock after the Vol'aerai vessel was moored across from the Magnus Releon.

"I didn't think the Vol'aerai possessed ships," Dhar said.

"We didn't until now," Tsoria said. "I intend to present this ship as an alternative to the trade agreement."

"Will this vessel make it to the islands?" Dhar asked. "It seems like it would sink with any large wave."

"I understand your concerns, King Dhar, but have faith. It has only been two days since we started forming the trees into a ship."

"Two days?" Dhar asked in surprise.

"I wanted a completed vessel to show you before we set sail, but we ran into a few issues that delayed our progress. It will be completed before we get to the Tashtari."

"It normally takes eighteen months to build the ships the Tashtari want to construct. Growing one in under a year is impressive already."

"To be fair, we are cheating by accelerating the growth, but the process is demanding."

"As a matter of principle, I don't condone cheating, but in this case, please continue."

"Would you and Captain Brent be interested in hearing about the design?" Tsoria asked. "Any feedback you might have to improve the ship's value to the Tashtari would be helpful."

"Please, lead the way," Dhar said.

"After you, the captain of our humble vessel awaits your presence onboard and will give you the tour."

King Dhar called for Captain Brent to join them before they boarded the Vol'aerai ship. Eviara stepped forward from the main mast she had been leaning on to greet the guests.

"Your Majesty, Captain, welcome aboard the Priter Elorai. I'm Eviara and it is a privilege to give you a tour of this ship."

The shock of having a preteen captain was apparent on the faces of the two guests, but Captain Brent was the first to recover and treat Eviara as an equal by title.

"Captain Eviara, thank you for having us aboard your vessel," Brent said. "Before we are shown the ship's qualities, may I ask what the meaning of the name is?"

"Priter Elorai has two meanings depending on how it is pronounced: First Three Explorers or Spirited Explorers. I prefer the latter meaning," Eviara said.

"A fitting ship name. Please lead the way around your fine vessel," Brent said.

"Thank you, Captain. I'm still learning nautical terms and would appreciate any corrections during the tour. The Priter Elorai is a living vessel, and as you can see, it is still growing, but the ship will be a large caravel when we reach the Tashtari islands. The hull, masts, and sails are grown from three hollarck trees," Eviara said.

"I've never heard of hollarck trees," Dhar said.

"These three are the only hollarck trees in existence. Queen Tsori-anya, my sister, commissioned our best plant specialist, Gafre, to create them four months ago. They were designed to thrive in seawater and are stronger than white oak."

"Four months?" Dhar asked, turning to Tsoria. "That would mean you had them created for this purpose before the enslavers told me about you."

"I needed to be ready for every outcome," Tsoria said.

"Impressive forethought," Dhar said, returning his attention to Eviara. "Apologies, Captain, please continue."

"The main mast is male, and the fore and…uh…I forgot the term for the aft mast."

"Mizzen mast," Brent said.

"Right." Eviara chuckled. "The fore and mizzen masts are female. We are standing on the lower deck, which is still being formed," Eviara said as she led the group aftward. "Here we have the galley and scullery."

Captain Brent was surprised to see a stone oven in the galley suspended by roots with a clay-lined vent for the smoke.

"I've never seen a full oven on a ship before. How do you keep the fire under control or the food from spilling?" Brent asked.

"The roots adjust the oven position to ensure nothing spills and fire doesn't escape. If an issue does arise, there is sand and plenty of water to snuff anything out." Eviara drew their attention to a container of fresh water grown into the wall near the galley door. "The trees absorb seawater, filter it, and keep this container filled."

"Leaving no need for water barrels," Brent said.

"Correct," Eviara said. "There will be water containers fore and aft on the upper decks."

"What are these protrusions?" Brent asked as he inspected the trunk of the Mizzen mast.

"Salt polyps and mushrooms. The trees exude excess salt into the polyps which can be removed for use. The mushrooms help the trees filter the seawater and extract the salt. They are also edible." The group walked forward, where they were shown two private latrines. "Waste drops to a hidden but vented area below where the trees mix and compost it. There is a second section under the galley where kitchen scrap and upper cabin latrine waste are composted," Eviara said.

"I did not expect anything like this," Dhar said.

"There are separate fore and aft cargo holds," Eviara said.

"I don't see any ropes, capstans, or pulleys. How is heavy cargo supposed to be moved or the sails adjusted?" Brent asked.

"We thought you would have that question," Eviara said. "I will show you."

Eviara reached out with her hands, and roots grew around each person, lifting them from the lower deck and depositing them back on the dock. They watched the roots fling the young captain close to the top of the main mast as she laughed in delight. Thin vine-like branches grew from the mast to catch and secure Eviara. All three trees unfurled their long fern-like leaves that interlocked like barbs of a feather, showing what it looked like under full sail to the agape King, Captain, and Magnus Releon crew, who watched from the railing. Eviara jumped from the branch she was standing on, did a flip midair, and was caught by roots and deposited on her feet near the others on the dock.

"Do you think the Priter Elorai will suffice to convince the Tashtari to renegotiate when finished?" Eviara asked.

"I think there is a good chance they will be as impressed as we are once it is complete," Dhar said before going silent as he rubbed his beard.

"I sense there is more to that statement," Tsoria said.

"My whole plan is derailed—I mean that in a good way—I anticipated negotiating for days while coming up with acceptable alternatives."

"If this will be a problem—"

"This might work out better," Dhar said snapping his fingers as his face lit up. "We should arrive before the main event of their Aquana festival if we leave tomorrow morning. I suggest we petition King Arion to allow us to enter the two-day race around the island."

"Allowing us to demonstrate our solution instead of only talking about it," Tsoria said.

"Exactly," Dhar said.

"Will I be ready to race against more knowledgeable captains?" Eviara asked.

"It will be a five-day journey to the Tashtari Islands," Brent said, "My first mate can captain the Magnus Releon while I teach you."

"Good idea," Dhar said.

"Captain Brent, would you give me a tour of the Magnus Releon?" Eviara asked.

"Certainly," Brent said as he led Eviara across the dock to his vessel.

Tsoria and Relvin followed Dhar to discuss the plan in more detail before the evening meal.

In the morning, while final preparations were made for the journey across the Sardus Sea, Grryffan and Frrynner strolled into Karnell. Those new to living in the Wispryn Weald had grown accustomed to the prevalence of wildlife, but predators were still regarded with fear. The people warily monitored the wolves as they strolled through the town. Frightened parents grabbed their children and headed for the nearest building for safety. A few men attempted to scare the wolves away but weren't successful at changing their course. A toddler who hadn't learned how dangerous animals could be managed to escape everyone's gaze during the panic until he ran into the open as fast as his unsteady legs could carry him. The toddler threw its arms around Frrynner and happily cooed.

"Fuffy goggy," the child said as he buried his face and hands in Frrynner's fur.

To everyone's surprise, the female wolf was gentle and kept him on his feet whenever he stumbled. The boy's mother was apprehensive and amazed as Frrynner nudged her son to return. The wolf bowed her head when she stopped before the mother, who reached out to pull the boy into her arms.

"Thank you," the mother said.

Tsoria approached the small crowd with a smile before kneeling to pet Frrynner.

"This is Frrynner, and she says that you're welcome. She could tell by your scent that you were the boy's mother," Tsoria said. "Frrynner is fierce, but she is a gentle soul around children, and knows how hard keeping them safe can be. Neither she nor her mate Grryffan will harm anyone here."

"There is much to get used to here," the mother said.

"Yes. This is an adjustment for everyone," Tsoria said, "but we will be patient with you as the forest is with us. The alphas hope they didn't frighten anyone too much. Excuse me while I attend to the matter they wish to discuss."

As Tsoria rose and walked away with the wolves by her side, the townsfolk relaxed and continued their morning activities.

The alphas conversed with Queen Tsorianya as they walked with her toward the forest edge.

"*Alpha Tsorianya, since the end of Voletia's reign, all alphas have sworn an oath to fulfill a sacred duty when the time is right, but no alpha has been summoned to fulfill this oath until now,*" Grryffan said.

"*There is someone who wishes to meet you, and we are here to lead you to them,*" Frrynner said.

"*We are about to leave for the Tashtari Islands. I should be there to negotiate the new trade agreement,*" Tsoria said and stopped walking to look at the wolves. "*Can't this wait until we return?*"

"*Leave the Tashtari to King Dhar, Relvin, and Eviara. Your task is more important,*" Grryffan said as he and his mate turned around, facing Tsoria.

"*May I ask what this task is and who I'm supposed to meet?*" Tsoria asked.

"*You may, alpha Tsorianya, but we have strict instructions not to reveal the answer. They will introduce themselves when you see them,*" Frrynner said.

"*I was hoping to accompany my sister on this voyage,*" Tsoria said, sighing, "*but you are right. Relvin and Eviara know what needs to be done. As soon as I let Relvin know the plan has changed, I will follow you to where I'm needed.*"

"*There is a horse for you at the forest's edge,*" Grryffan said.

Tsoria watched the alphas walk to the trees before she turned toward the port. "*Relvin, I won't be meeting the Tashtari.*"

"*I thought the plan was for you to go?*" Relvin asked.

"*The alphas have come to lead me somewhere and won't say why, but they say it is more important.*"

"*I see. Then you should go. I will explain to King Dhar and make sure Eviara is safe,*" Relvin said.

"*Thank you. I'll see you when you return,*" Tsoria said.

"*I look forward to it. I love you,*" Relvin said.

"*I love you,*" Tsoria said.

Tsoria mounted the horse waiting for her in the forest and started the journey to the destination only the wolves knew.

CHAPTER 17
VOYAGE

T WO HOURS AFTER SUNRISE, the Magnus Releon sailed out of Karn Bay. The Priter Elorai followed behind with Eviara, Relvin, and Captain Brent on board. Captain Brent had learned a lot about Eviara during the conversation with her the previous evening and looked forward to the challenge of teaching her. He couldn't pass on the opportunity to challenge himself and allow his first mate to gain experience being a captain without his supervision.

Adapting his knowledge to such an unconventional vessel required Captain Brent to adjust how he taught. He spent a decade moving up the ladder from scrubbing the deck to captain. However, there were only five days to condense his extensive knowledge into essential lessons, turning Eviara into a captain. It was a lot to ask of anyone to learn, but he found that Eviara and the Priter Elorai were more than up to the task. He learned to recognize what every creak and groan of his ship meant, but she and the Priter Elorai had a trust and connection he could never have with his crew or vessel. She felt the stresses the ship experienced, the wind speed and direction, the waves against the hull, and the currents, allowing her to make snap decisions and refinements to sail and rudder configurations faster than any top crew could. She wasn't afraid to push the limits, challenge the captain's wisdom, or make mistakes and grow from them.

Captain Brent was impressed by the growth of the Priter Elorai and Eviara each day. He had taught many about currents, storms, celestial navigation, sailing against the wind, and many other skills, but none had ever learned as fast as his current pupil. He took every opportunity to test her to ensure she hadn't forgotten what he had taught. By the time the Priter Elorai sailed ahead of the Magnus Releon between the fortifications at the mouth of Bulwark Bay, Captain Brent was confident Eviara would hold her own in the race despite her limited experience.

The Aquana Festival was the most anticipated annual event in the Tashtari Islands and spanned an entire week. It marked the anniversary of their split from what is now the Islatrian Kingdom and the beginning of their independence. Since Dashran was the first settlement and capital of the islands, it attracted the largest crowds and was the most decorated of all the cities. Tashtari flag streamers—green islands in the middle, a blue sea bottom half, and a golden yellow sky top half—spanned the streets between the yellow, cream, or white walls of the buildings that lined them. Every domed roof was a shade of blue or green, matching the doors and windows. Civic buildings were easy to recognize by the purest white, royal blue, and gold. Each of the seven islands sponsored a day of celebration and organized the day's events: parades, dances, songs, duels, gifts, and regional delicacies. The main island, where Dashran was, sponsored the closing ceremonies on the last festival day.

It was already the fourth day of the festival as the two visiting ships sailed into the Dashran harbor. The Magnus Releon was known to the Tashtari from past negotiations, but the leading Vol'aerai ship with its green peacock-like sails and unique design was what caught everyone's attention. However, even though many speculated about the reason for their arrival, most weren't concerned as long as the visitors weren't there to disrupt the festivities or cause trouble. King Dhar and Relvin disembarked when both ships were moored and King Arion Marín's official, Lucas, approached with a company of guards sent to meet them at the dock.

"King Dhar, I extend King Arion's greetings and an invitation to join the festivities. Your visit is unexpected, which leads me to conclude you are not here to deliver the first shipment," Lucas said.

"I apologize for not sending word beforehand. There has been a complication to the treaty that Relvin, a Vol'aerai delegate, and I wish to discuss with King Arion," Dhar said.

"You have come in the middle of our Aquana Festival. All political matters are postponed until after it has finished."

"I understand, but we came to ask for permission to demonstrate our solution to the problem. The political talks can be postponed at His Majesty's convenience. Our request should not take him away from the festivities long."

"Very well. I'll lead you to the palace. If King Arion doesn't grant you an audience, you will wait until after the festival."

"Thank you," King Dhar said.

The first four guards turned to lead the way through the busy streets. Lucas, King Dhar, and Relvin followed behind in single file, with guards flanking and trailing after. They threaded their way through dancing crowds, admiring the musical prowess of performing artists. Their noses were accosted by the delicious aromas billowing from open doors with queues waiting to taste each chef's festival delicacies. After leaving the crowded lower city, they hiked the winding road up the mountainside lined with terraced homes and gardens.

Toward the end of the path, they meandered through seven terraced gardens with gravity-fed fountains that represented the seven Tashtari islands, Lucas explained as they passed through them. King Dhar and Relvin were told to wait in the palace atrium entrance while

Lucas left to talk to King Arion. The skylight provided ample lighting for the central planter and revealed the colorful mosaics decorating the walls and floor while they waited.

Lucas returned within a few minutes and motioned them to enter the throne room. King Dhar and Relvin entered the oval room and stopped before the platform where King Arion sat beside the queen's empty throne. The backs of their thrones were made from paired halves of a giant blue mussel native to the waters around the islands from which the blue color for their roofs and dyes came. Relvin bowed his head.

"King Dhar, I hear you have come to show a solution to a problem," Arion said.

"Yes, Your Majesty. I apologize for the inconvenience of our arrival and assure you that the problem has been resolved," Dhar said.

"If the problem is resolved, why do you come to me?"

"The problem was diplomatic and involved the lumber source for the trade agreement. I will not get into details for brevity. I have brought Relvin, a Vol'aerai, to explain the solution we are asking you to consider."

"Please, continue," Arion said as he gestured to Relvin.

"Your Majesty," Relvin said. "Tsorianya, Queen of the Vol'aerai, sends her greetings but regrettably couldn't attend. I am sure you have seen or been briefed about the Vol'aerai ship moored in the harbor, the solution we have come to present. The Vol'aerai are willing to provide trees that can be grown into ships to meet your needs."

"Grown? That is possible?"

"Yes, Sire. The three trees that make up the ship were designed to be grown into ships. The Priter Elorai is the first of its kind. The Vol'aerai wish to provide these trees to you as an alternative to the agreed-upon lumber and to train captains to talk to them."

"How can anyone talk to the trees?" Arion asked.

"I understand your skepticism. I wasn't born Vol'aerai. King Dhar can verify that I was a soldier in his army, but I learned what the Vol'aerai have. May I demonstrate?"

"Please," Arion said.

Relvin stretched out his left hand, and the roots of his bracer grew a walking stick. The Tashtari monarch watched in fascination as the walking stick changed into a shield before the roots receded into his bracer.

"It may seem like a magic trick, Sire, but my connection to nature allows me to tell the plants what I need. You can learn as well. With your permission, let us demonstrate what is possible by letting the Priter Elorai compete in the race."

"I will allow it," Arion said, "but any changes to the trade agreement will be discussed after the festival."

"Of course. Thank you, King Arion. We will inform Captain Eviara of your decision," Dhar said.

Eviara looked out over Dashran from her position towards the top of the main mast as she waited for Relvin and King Dhar to return. The crowds filling the streets below moved like water around the buildings as islands jutting from the depths. Gulls flew overhead and called out to each other as they hunted for fish or food scraps to steal. Families and friends enjoyed private outings away from the crowds on boats of all sizes dancing upon the bay waters.

Back at the dock below, the Magnus Releon crew was busy inspecting ropes, cleaning the deck, and ensuring every ship piece was in perfect working order. Captain Brent had disembarked from the Priter Elorai after parting words with Eviara and resumed command of his ship soon after King Dhar and Relvin left. A young man inspecting moorings and cargo on the docks caught Eviara's attention. His efforts seemed lackluster as he made his way closer to the two ships. After dawdling at a pile of nets near the Priter Elorai, he scrambled up the ship hull and headed aftward to the captain's quarters.

"Hello, who do we have here?" Eviara said to herself as she dropped to the deck without a sound with the help of the trees.

The young man was not in the cabin for long before he stepped out into the sun of the main deck, where roots curled around his feet, preventing him from snooping any further. Eviara stepped into view from behind the main mast as the man tried to free himself from the roots' grip.

"Who are you? What are you doing aboard my ship?" Eviara asked.

The man looked perplexed when he saw Eviara.

"It can't be…Tsoria? It's me, Corin. How have you not aged?"

It was Eviara's turn to look confused, but she quickly recovered.

"I am Eviara, Captain of the Priter Elorai. I ask again, what are you doing aboard my ship? And how do you know my sister?"

"Ah, sister, now it makes sense. You look almost the same as Tsoria looked twelve years ago."

"You were one of her friends?" Corin nodded. "Are you trying to escape?"

"No. I'm the first mate of King Arion's flagship, Aurora, and I am married to its Captain's youngest daughter."

"Then you are here as a spy."

"Yes, but I haven't come to sabotage. I volunteered to scout it because this vessel couldn't be anything but Vol'aerai design. My life may be here now, but the forest is still my home."

"I understand. If Tsoria was here, she would have loved to see you again and would want you to know that the rest of your friends are well. Jeki, Briel, and Aleya have returned to the Wispryn Weald. Jestin is married to a daughter of the Kalumat Malikan. Tsoria is the Vol'aerai Queen."

Eviara motioned for the Priter Elorai to release Corin.

"I'm relieved to hear they are doing well."

"Would you like a tour before the race?"

"It would be best if I'm as surprised as everyone else about the capabilities of the Priter Elorai. I don't want to sabotage your chances, but I will follow my captain's orders once the race starts. I wish you the best of luck in the race." Corin headed to the starboard side to debark but turned to Eviara again. "You haven't sailed the waters around these islands, have you?"

"No, why?" Eviara asked.

"There is someone you should meet. Expect a guest that knows these waters better than any their age before sunrise."

"How do I know they won't be here to sabotage us?"

"It's in their best interest to win so they can prove their father wrong, and it's in my best interest not to be caught helping them rebel. You will understand why when you meet. I will see you after the race."

Corin climbed over the side, dropped to the dock below, and headed back to the Aurora, leaving Eviara to ponder who she would meet.

Tikka stood on the balcony of her room, watching the sun paint the clouds in shades of red as it set. She closed her eyes and stretched her arms to the side as her black hair flew like a flag in the sea breeze. She pretended she was on the bow of a ship sailing the vast uncharted waters. She heard the friendly chatter of dolphins instead of the festival below as they raced to the world's edge. She didn't notice when the door of her room opened, letting her lady-in-waiting, Safia, enter.

"No amount of pretending will bring you any closer to the sea, Your Highness," Safia said, startling Tikka from her daydream.

"Why must I be punished for being a princess?" Tikka asked as she turned around.

"As next in line for the crown, you have a duty to your people. Only a male heir can free you from this obligation," Safia said.

"I hope for a brother every day."

"Even if you weren't royalty, you are eleven and unable to choose your path."

"Why are you here, Safia? It's not time for bed."

"A letter has come for you from Lady Mina," Safia said.

"What does it say?" Tikka said as she entered her room.

Safia opened the letter and read the contents.

"It's an invitation to spend the last festival days with her. Shall I pack some things for you?"

"No need, we wear the same size garb. I will walk there before it gets too dark. You may go Safia."

"Let me know if you need anything before you leave, Your Highness."

Safia put the letter on Tikka's desk and exited the room. The princess flopped onto her bed and lay there for a few minutes, contemplating the destiny she didn't want. The oldest male heir inherited the throne regardless of birth order by law, but due to several miscarriages, she remained an only child. Since her mother's latest pregnancy was reaching full term, Tikka was hopeful for a brother to free her from the shackles that bound her. The waiting made her antsy. If she couldn't be on the sea, being away from the palace was better than nothing.

Tikka got up and strolled to her desk to freshen up before leaving. A peculiar symbol in the corner of Mina's letter caught her attention. She brought out her pen and sat at her desk. A smile spread across her lips after deciphering the coded message within the letter. Tikka set the letter ablaze and tossed it into the fireplace before heading to her friend Mina's house.

People milled about in the streets after late-night meals as Tikka made her way to the docks. She danced to the music and skipped around, like many other children staying awake late on festival days. At the edge of the crowds, she slipped away into the shadowy docks. Barrels, nets, and piles of rope provided hiding places to dodge detection as she snuck her way to the Priter Elorai, the only ship with a captain who wouldn't recognize her.

Tikka climbed the side of the Priter Elorai and peeked over the railing. She was surprised to find no crew keeping watch as she scrambled onto the deck. An unwavering warm glow invited her down a short hall towards the doorway of what Tikka assumed was the captain's quarters. After crossing the threshold into the room, she stared in awe at how different it was from the ships she knew. Tikka walked around, inspecting everything inside since the room seemed empty. The light came from several glowing mushrooms. The walls were smooth bark wood instead of hewn planks like the ships she knew. The bed, table, and chairs were grown from the decking as if enchanted. As she finished her tour of the room, she was startled by the presence of a girl her age watching her from the doorway.

"What do you think?" Eviara asked.

"I have never seen any vessel built—" Tikka said.

"Grown, not built. It's a Vol'aerai ship."

"It's amazing…Oh, where are my manners? Please excuse my intrusion. I'm Princess Tikka. Are you the captain's daughter?"

Eviara smiled as she walked into the room and sat at the table.

"Ahh…Princess. You are the navigator Corin sent?"

"Yes."

"I'm Eviara, Captain of the Priter Elorai."

"You are the captain? You look the same age as me."

"I'm almost eleven…"

"You are younger…" Tikka said as she joined Eviara at the table and pouted. "It's not fair. I hate being a princess; I'm not allowed to have fun. All I do is train all day to be queen."

"Sorry, I wouldn't know what that is like. The Vol'aerai don't have royalty. Well, my sister is the queen—which makes me a princess, I suppose—but it is rare for us to have a queen."

"Tell me about the Vol'aerai. I don't remember any mention of them in my studies."

Tikka was fascinated by the tales Eviara told about the Vol'aerai. The ability to talk with the plants and animals seemed like living in a magical fairytale. Tikka didn't think her tales were as grand in comparison but Eviara found equal delight in the princess's attempts to ditch her royal duties to do as she wished. The excitement of making a new friend kept them awake talking and giggling even after they lay beside each other on the bed intending to fall asleep. They slept in the end.

In the morning, Tikka woke to the delicious smell that made her mouth water. She sat up and stretched her limbs as Eviara walked in with a fresh loaf of bread and placed it on the table next to the platter of grilled fish fillets atop mushrooms and onions already there.

"Morning, Tikka, I hope you slept well," Eviara said.

Tikka felt the ship sway without mooring lines stopping its movement.

"Are we at sea?" Tikka asked.

"I didn't want anyone to stop us if they recognized you." Eviara sat down and motioned for Tikka to join her. "Did you sleep well?"

"Like a rock," Tikka said, stretching her limbs as she stood and walked to the table.

Tikka sat and the two of them enjoyed the food before them as they chatted. After they had finished, the girls walked to the ship's bow, the cool salty air flowing through their hair. Tikka looked around and saw no competitors behind them.

"I wanted a challenge," Eviara said with a twinkle in her eyes, turning her back to the railing as she faced Tikka. "Ready to show them what we can do?"

"Do you have to ask?"

"Thought so," Eviara said as she stretched out her arms.

The Priter Elorai unfurled more leaves from its branches and meshed them together. Tikka could feel the ship cut through the waves and the bow spray reached higher as they picked up speed. Soon they were making modest gains on their nearest competitor.

The first day went by without much excitement as they sailed around the southern side of the main island. Tikka told Eviara what each island they saw was known for, and each time they passed a competitor she would tell Eviara about their captain or the vessel they commanded. They expected to be in the middle position by the next morning, but Tikka was worried it would not be enough.

"I don't think we can overtake the Aurora before the narrow northern passage," Tikka said as they ate the evening meal together.

"Can we pass them after?" Eviara asked.

"It's possible…"

Eviara waited for Tikka to continue but grew impatient after swallowing the food in her mouth. "But?" Eviara asked.

"Captain Diego Monito commands the Aurora—"

"Corin's captain."

Tikka nodded before taking a bite of bread. "He is…competitive, and his crew is the best. I know he isn't pushing the Aurora to the limit."

"And if we don't pass him by the narrows we might never pass him," Eviara said, Tikka nodded in reply. "Any suggestions?"

"One…but it's dangerous for a large vessel like the Priter Elorai even in the best conditions."

"Tell me."

"Have anything to draw with?" Tikka asked, looking around.

"Use your finger on the table," Eviara said, clearing the dishes."

Tikka hesitated but as she drew the rough outlines of each Tashtari Island, the table morphed to create a map where her fingers touched, eliciting a giggle before she spoke.

"The race is around the center island, Malor," Tikka said as she traced the path, "but between the eastern island, Asín, and Malor is a rocky reef. Only small boats venture through there."

"The larger ships go around," Eviara said.

"It's a longer route, but it's safer. Tomorrow morning at high tide there is one path through the reef that should be deep enough."

"You think we can take that route?"

"It's risky but possible," Tikka said, looking at Eviara.

"Possible is all we need," Eviara said.

Tikka joined Eviara at the bow of the Priter Elorai on the morning of the second race day and peered into the mists hovering over the surface.

"Good. The mists aren't too thick," Tikka said. "I should be able to guide us through."

"Ready?" Eviara asked.

"Always," Tikka said.

The Priter Elorai lifted Tikka to a position on the foremast for a better view to call out directions to Eviara as they headed for the rocky reef.

Corin stood on the quarterdeck with Captain Diego as they rounded the northeastern corner of Asín Island. The mists had burned off and the positions of their competitor's ships were being called out from the crow's nest.

"The Vol'aerai ship?" Diego asked after not hearing it mentioned.

"Unknown, Captain," the barrelman shouted back.

"Where could they have disappeared? Surely they didn't give up," Diego said.

"I'm sure they will turn up soon, Captain," Corin said.

A shout from the crow's nest brought his attention back to the Aurora's deck, "Ship ahead!"

"Vol'aerai?" Diego shouted back.

"Aye, Captain," the barrelman said.

Corin followed Captain Diego to the ship's bow and watched the Priter Elorai exit the rocky reef waters off the port bow ahead of the Aurora.

"Their ship looks intact. That captain is reckless, attempting that passage without prior experience," Diego said.

"Her navigator is the reckless one," Corin said before he could stop his thoughts from becoming words.

Diego looked over and saw Corin try to hide his smile as he watched the Vol'aerai vessel take the lead position ahead. "*She's* on that ship?"

"I never said the navigator was—"

"Don't play dumb with me, Corin. I knew you hadn't told me everything when you returned from scouting that ship. You arranged this, didn't you?"

Corin was having too much fun to be able to lie to his captain convincingly so he said nothing which was confirmation enough for Diego. The captain sighed as he leaned on the railing beside Corin while watching the Vol'aerai ship

"I know, there will be hell to pay," Corin said. "I never thought Tikka would advise Captain Eviara to take the reef route."

Diego chuckled. "As my son-in-law, I won't tell the king you were involved, but if he finds out, I won't come to your aid."

"I wouldn't expect you to," Corin said.

After a long pause filled with the calls of gulls and the spray of water as the Aurora split the seas, Diego spoke, "I admit, it was worth seeing what that vessel and her captain could do. I'm impressed..."

"You always were happier when challenged."

"We grow when challenged. I'll discipline you later, but the race isn't over." Diego stood and turned with a determination Corin hadn't seen in a long time. "Push her to the limit."

"Aye, captain."

The Aurora's deck became a flurry of activity as Captain Diego barked orders while returning to his position on the quarterdeck. The crew sprung into action before Corin repeated the orders while trailing behind the Captain. Crew morale was high earlier when the Aurora was in the lead, but a worthy challenge brought out their best.

CHAPTER 18
PORTENT

ON THE FINAL MORNING OF THE FESTIVAL, after an intense second day of racing, the Priter Elorai sailed into Bulwark Bay a full boat length ahead of the Aurora. The sharp clang of bells rang over the waters as the news was spread. Eviara and Tikka hollered and danced on deck as they celebrated their win.

The Priter Elorai retracted most of its leaves, slowing their pace through the bay. The Aurora caught up on their port side and matched their speed. Captain Diego smiled as he bowed to the girls, and his crew lining Aurora's starboard side followed suit. The Aurora slowed to follow behind the Priter Elorai as they returned to port.

A cheering crowd welcomed them into port as the remaining competitors neared the opening of the bay. Eviara and Tikka beamed as they waved back, but as their vessel was brought alongside the dock, the princess stopped waving, and her smile faded.

"What is it, Tikka?" Eviara asked.

"With the fun I had on the ship, I forgot that my father is the first to greet the winner," Tikka said.

Eviara saw King Arion standing beside his guards with a pleasant smile alongside King Dhar and Relvin.

"He doesn't look angry," Eviara said as she turned to Tikka.

"He will stick to the traditions in front of the people, but once we get to the palace, he will show it."

"Then keep up appearances for the people as long as he does."

Eviara and Tikka disembarked from the Priter Elorai when it was moored and were enwreathed in flower necklaces. King Arion greeted the girls before starting the procession through the streets with his guards, retracing their ancestors' path. Eviara and Tikka waved to the people behind a herald that announced their win to the cheering crowd. King Dhar and Relvin followed close behind.

The smiling faces and cheering from the people didn't distract Tikka from her thoughts as each step brought her closer to the palace. She tried to think of the words she would use to apologize but knew nothing she said would spare her from punishment. Tikka felt Eviara squeeze her hand and smiled back to thank her for being there.

When the group entered the palace atrium, Tikka said, "Father, let me explain—"

King Arion whirled around and stepped towards Tikka with anger.

"Explain what? That you defied me again? That you used Lady Mina as cover for your disrespect of the Tashtari traditions?" King Arion asked.

"I'm sorry—"

"You have once again done what I expressly forbade you from doing…this time using a foreign captain who didn't know any better." Arion walked around with animated gestures as he continued berating the princess. "You are heir to the throne and have obligations to the kingdom whether you like it or not! If I can't keep my house in order, how do you think that makes me appear to the people?"

Tikka tried several times to get a word in to explain but was cut off each time. The chastising would have continued had it not been for the interruption of a displeased midwife barreling towards the king.

"Stop this at once," Camila said to King Arion.

"I give the—"

"I don't care," Camila said as she cut Arion off. "You are throwing the palace harmony out of balance and causing complications for the queen. Stop talking if you want any chance at having a healthy baby."

Camila, the royal midwife, adhered to traditional birthing practices like most Tashtari midwives and was superstitious about the environment into which a baby is born. The birthing room decorations were chosen with great care. Oil lamps lit the room because the sunlight was too bright. Wardrobes, cabinets, and drawers remained open to symbolize an open womb. No hair or clothing was allowed to have knots or braids. Conversations could never be louder than normal voices, and arguments or conflicts couldn't be within the building where the birthing chambers were. A small crowd was present to ensure no changeling was swapped for true royal heirs, but no male was allowed in. It was believed that a deviation from these traditions could cause complications or deformities in the child being born.

"I—"

"Not one word, Your Majesty," Camila said as she stuck a finger in the King's face.

Tikka had never seen her father afraid of anyone before, but there was something more to the terror in his eyes than the woman berating him, something Tikka didn't yet understand. King Arion pressed his lips together, complying with the midwife's orders. Camila was mid-turn in her effort to return to the birthing chamber when she spied Princess Tikka and Eviara and inspected them.

"The birthing chambers aren't for children, but I have tried all the traditional ways to undo the harm already caused. Princess Tikka, follow me and bring your friend."

King Arion opened his mouth and raised a hand, but a sharp look from the midwife changed his mind. Camila hurried Tikka and Eviara away, leaving the men to wait for her return.

Relvin watched as King Arion wrung his hands while he paced. It hadn't been an hour, but Relvin assumed it felt like an eternity to the expectant father. King Dhar tried to calm and console Arion, but none dared raise their voice above a whisper to avoid the midwife's ire.

Camila and Eviara's footsteps echoed down the hall from the direction of the birthing chamber, drawing Relvin and Dhar's attention. Arion didn't notice until they were ten paces from his position. The fear on his face subsided a little when they curtsied before him with calm faces, a sign that they brought good news.

"Her Majesty has birthed a prince," Eviara said. "Queen Zaria and Prince Mateo are well."

Tears fell from King Arion's eyes as relief washed over his face, and he dared to breathe again.

"A son…I have a son," Arion said with a smile.

"In all my years as a midwife," Camila said. "I've never seen anyone survive the labor complications the Queen had. They both would have died had it not been for Eviara's unconventional help."

Eviara attempted to downplay her role in saving them, but before she could say much, King Arion took Eviara's hand and bowed his head to kiss it.

"Thank you, Lady Eviara," Arion said. "I owe you a debt for saving their lives."

Eviara blushed from the attention before speaking, "Her Majesty will need rest but is eager to introduce you to your son. Camila will lead the way."

"I insist you all dine with us tonight as our honored guests," Arion said. "There is much to celebrate. A new life begins as the Aquana festival ends."

Dhar was the first to talk as they watched Camila lead Arion away, "If winning the race wasn't enough to bring him to the table, saving the queen and prince certainly is." Dhar turned to face Relvin and Eviara.

"Let's enjoy the last festival day before we dine with King Arion this evening."

The sun was still high overhead when King Dhar, Relvin, and Eviara arrived at the town below, and the festival showed no signs of stopping. The news of Prince Mateo's birth had already spread to the people and seemed to invigorate their celebrations. Babies born during the Aquana festival were a good omen to the Tashtari, and the prince's birth was a sign of good things to come.

Despite the crowds, the streets weren't difficult to navigate. They bought local delicacies from various vendors and ate them while listening to nearby musicians. Several times they were pulled into dances at squares they loitered in. None of them knew the steps, but their deficiencies didn't prevent anyone from enjoying the revelry.

Dhar eventually led them to a large plaza near the docks where the best musicians took turns performing on a stage in the center. Crowds stood around the stage, dancing and singing along with the music. Several busy restaurants with outdoor seating lined the edges. A commotion at the southern edge of the square drew their attention. Corin was beckoning them to join him at one of the tables.

"Your hair makes you stand out in this crowd," Corin said to Eviara as they got close.

"Yeah, I've gotten curious looks all day. Must not be many redheads in Dashran," Eviara said.

"None that I know in the Tashtari Islands. Come, join us. We just sat down," Corin said.

King Dhar, Eviara, and Relvin followed Corin to the table his family sat at. Corin's wife, Adeline, and his in-laws, Captain Diego and Lucía, stood to greet the three visitors before they sat at the table. Corin got the attention of an attendant and requested a specialty dish for everyone after they ordered drinks.

"This year's race was the best in years," Diego said. "Thanks for that Eviara

"It was a struggle to compete with your experience. I don't think I would've won without Tikka," Eviara said.

"Well you pushed my crew to use every trick of the trade," Diego said. "Speaking of Tikka, I haven't decided on Corin's punishment for sending her to you."

"Whatever it is, it was worth it," Corin said, lifting his cup in a salute to Eviara before taking a drink.

"Family and friends are everything to Vol'aerai," Eviara said.

"I learned that the hard way," Dhar said before drinking from his cup, "...don't anger their queen."

"Oh? That sounds like a tale worth hearing. Please go on, Your Majesty," Diego said, leaning forward.

Dhar told the story of how he learned of the Vol'aerai. Partway through the retelling, the server came with platters of sweetened mint rice topped with various diced fruits. The rest of the story came between bites of food, while Relvin and Eviara interjected details throughout the story.

"Sounds like I missed a lot back home," Corin said after the story ended.

"Well, it has been twelve years." Eviara nearly shoveled another spoonful into her mouth but cocked her head to the side as she looked up. "Corin, how did you get here? The Tashtari don't seem to rely on slavery."

"I was sold to a lord in Bruen province who put me to work in a mine. Most of the workers were there to pay off debts, however, slaves were given the most dangerous jobs." Corin described many of the hardships he had to endure and the horrors he saw during his years as a slave. "One day a kind old man pushed me out of the way of falling rocks, losing his life in the process. In the chaotic aftermath, I escaped and wandered to a port where I stowed away on the Aurora—"

"It took my crew two days before we caught this overworked half-starved kid stealing our food in the cargo hold," Diego said as he motioned to Corin with his cup, his drink sloshing over the side. "We were already at sea by then and weren't being pursued so we kept going."

"I was put to work and became one of the crew—"

"And part of the family," Adeline said as she rested her head on his shoulder.

"Why couldn't you pick some other—" Diego said.

"Be nice!" Adeline said, scolding her father.

"I'm teasing," Diego said, chuckling.

"It's fine, Adie," Corin said, before kissing her forehead. "He lost to an eleven-year-old today, he's still sore—"

"I thanked Eviara for the challenge, didn't I?" Diego asked, looking around for confirmation on the faces around him.

Relvin smiled as the friendly banter continued between the family members. He wished Tsoria was there. Their conversations through the forest network during the trip weren't a substitute for being together. Relvin wondered if she had dealt with whatever the wolves had summoned her for. Tears rolled down his cheeks as a sudden unexplained wave of grief washed over him. A small hand clutched his hand and he looked over to see his sadness mirrored in Eviara's eyes.

"Tsoria…" They said in unison.

Lucía was the first to notice that something was wrong. "Are you alright? Was it something we said?"

Relvin raised his hand and shook his head.

"Tsoria's in trouble isn't she?" Corin asked. "I can feel it, though not as strong as you."

"Tsoria is grieving," Eviara said, wiping her tears away, "though we don't know why."

"Please excuse us," Relvin said before they stood. "We'll return soon."

King Dhar remained with Diego and his family while Relvin and Eviara retreated to the Priter Elorai for privacy.

Before the evening banquet, the square where Relvin and Eviara had spent the afternoon was reconfigured. The center stage was set up with a large table and chairs with cushions before being surrounded by blue and white curtains, blocking the view inside. Streamers were hung between the stage and the surrounding buildings. A carriage pulled up to the stage and King Arion and his family ducked inside with their entourage. Guards were posted at each corner looking out as the square was filled with tables radiating from the center stage and torches were set up between them. Men distributed wine barrels around the perimeter as food carts were brought to each surrounding building for cooks to prepare.

Relvin and Eviara approached the center tent and spoke with one of the guards outside who ducked inside briefly before parting the curtains for them to enter.

"What did you wish to discuss?" Arion asked after a brief greeting, motioning for them to sit.

"King Arion, I'm afraid we must cut our visit short," Relvin said. "Queen Tsorianya wishes us to return home."

"Such unfortunate news," Arion said.

"What about the banquet?" Zaria asked, laying on a divan with ladies-in-waiting fussing over her post-birth care.

"We will stay tonight, tomorrow morning we will return home. The plan was to stay for several more days to discuss the treaty terms, but perhaps it is best not to rush into this so soon after the birth of your son," Relvin said.

"When will you return?" Arion asked.

"I don't have an answer for you presently, but the queen is committed to resolving this matter," Relvin said.

"I don't doubt it. You've proven yourself a friend to the Tashtari already," Arion said before looking at Eviara who looked down and fidgeted with her hands. "What do you wish to say, Lady Eviara?"

"I apologize for helping Tikka disobey you, Your Majesty," Eviara said.

"Father, she didn't—" Tikka said.

"I did know," Eviara said, giving Tikka a sharp look before returning her attention to Arion. "She boarded the Priter Elorai the night before the race. We discussed many things including her reasons for disobeying you," Eviara said.

"I appreciate the honesty," Arion said glancing at Tikka, "but an heir to the throne has a duty—"

"I am not asking for Tikka to go without punishment," Eviara said.

"Oh? You wish to propose a solution?" Arion asked.

"With Mateo's birth, the throne is no longer her destiny, but if he doesn't survive, Tikka will still inherit the throne," Eviara said.

"Making her brother's care Tikka's priority," Zaria said, reaching into the bassinet beside her to caress one of his little cheeks as he slept.

"Yes," Eviara said.

"A fair punishment," Arion said, locking eyes with Tikka who replied with a nod.

"There is another reason," Eviara said. "Hollarck trees require attention and care—like a baby—and it is easier for them to connect to younger people during their early growth."

"I see. Mateo's care is also training," Arion said.

"Giving her an incentive and reward for being faithful to her task," Eviara said with a wink at Tikka.

"You thought this out more than I anticipated," Arion said.

"I cannot take all the credit. My sister helped earlier this afternoon," Eviara said.

The conversation turned to more pleasant topics as they waited for the banquet to be ready. King Dhar joined them before people started claiming seats at the tables outside. With how noisy everyone was

Eviara wondered why Mateo didn't wake up, and Queen Zaria showed her how babies were bundled with special padding to cover their ears during noisy functions.

A sharp clang of metal rang out from each corner of the stage as the guards pounded their spears against the ground three times slowly. The crowd quieted before the third strike. King Arion stood and helped his wife to her feet as she held the prince. The attendants pulled the curtains aside and tied them to the posts with white ropes.

"We gather tonight for the closing ceremony of the Aquana Festival," Arion said. "We honor those who have won the race today." Eviara and Tikka stood and waved at the crowd before retaking their seats. "We celebrate the anniversary of Tashtari. And we welcome the birth of Mateo, heir to the throne." The crowd stood and chanted the prince's name until Arion raised his hand so they would be silent. "Let the closing ceremonies begin!"

The tables buzzed with conversation as musicians, illusionists, poets, and dancers took turns regaling everyone with their talents. Relvin and Eviara enjoyed the company and the entertainment but were eager for the morning when they would begin their journey to reunite with Tsoria.

CHAPTER 19
CANDOR

JUST OVER A WEEK LATER, the Priter Elorai undulated with the sea swells in the north two days west of the dead zone around Dragonhead Island. Below the deck, Tsoria made small talk as she shared the morning meal with Relvin and Eviara. The previous day, Relvin and Eviara had picked her up from the north shore and recounted everything that transpired during their journey to and on the Tashtari Islands. Tsoria could tell they wished to know about her journey but neither Relvin nor Eviara asked.

As they finished their morning meal, Tsoria spoke, "I appreciate you not pressing me for answers about what I went through while you were in Dashran. I needed the time to recharge after my experience."

"The experience must have been draining," Relvin said.

Tsoria nodded.

"In more than one way," Tsoria said, taking a breath, "but I'm ready to tell you about what I learned and why we are not returning home yet. While you were paraded through the streets of Dashran after the race, I was…"

Tsoria and the Alphas hiked up the steep trail winding up the tallest mountain at the source of the Wyre River. Tsoria felt the effects of the altitude as she walked between the two wolves; Grryffan took the lead. A week had passed since they started their journey, and Tsoria was forced to take the last section on foot as the trail had become too difficult for the horse to continue. The crunch of the soil beneath her boots and the subsequent occasional clattering of rocks cascading down the mountainside contrasted with the quiet plodding of the wolves' paws before and behind.

Hour after hour, they trudged on until, a little after noon, Grryffan disappeared around a bend in the trail. When Tsoria caught up with him, she found herself in a small clearing with a circle of scraggly-looking pine trees. Tsoria entered the band of trees after the wolves, who bowed their heads towards an aged woman standing outside the entrance of a large Vol'aerai dwelling. The woman's white hair waved in the cold mountain breeze that flowed down from the snow-covered peaks.

"Welcome, Tsorianya. I have waited many years for someone like you to visit me."

"I thought I knew all the Vol'aerai elders. I wasn't aware that one lived up here in the mountains," Tsoria said.

"I may be old, but I'm not an elder."

"May I ask who you are and why the alpha wolves have brought me to you?"

"You may, but conversations like that are better suited in comfortable settings. Follow me inside where it is warm," the woman said as she turned and gestured to her dwelling with her right arm.

"Thank you." Tsoria walked forward a few paces before noticing a ring on the woman's left hand, which appeared identical to hers. "You're a queen, aren't you?"

The woman smiled.

"So you noticed the ring? We have much to discuss."

The woman led Tsoria and the two wolves into her dwelling, where a central fire cast its warmth and light around the large room, chunks of meat danced in boiling water within a small stone caldron suspended above, and a covered stone pot was nestled among the coals of the fire. A couple of chairs grew from the ground near the fire with a table between them as the woman walked to a small adjoining storage room in the back of the dwelling next to a couple of other openings leading to a bed chamber and latrine.

"Make yourselves comfortable," the woman said as she returned with an armful of potatoes, parsnips, carrots, garlic, and onions.

The wolves lay next to the fire and rested with their eyes closed while Tsoria sat at the table where the woman set the vegetables down. A couple of cutting boards were brought to the table, and both women grew knives from crystal root and started peeling and chopping the vegetables for the stew.

"You are the first visitors to my home since I banished myself to this remote location…many years ago. Stories are told of me in the villages below, but none encompass the whole truth of history. Let's start at the very beginning. My name is Voletia, the first queen."

Tsoria nearly cut herself when her hand slipped from shock as she looked up from the potato she was peeling.

"You're the…? But that would make you…" Tsoria tried to come up with the age of the first queen but gave up counting. "How?"

"All in due time, young one. As I said, we have much to discuss. I presume the elders told you of my younger years when I learned to talk with the forest and animals within?" Tsoria nodded. "However, not everything in our history is recollected in its entirety. You know about the crystal tree, right?"

Tsoria nodded and spoke before Voletia could continue the story, "Do you know the name Myrkar?"

Voletia stopped cutting the onion she was working on and looked at Tsoria, surprised.

"How did you learn of that name?"

"When King Dhar showed us around the castle, there was a room with a burnt, illustrated book page depicting a crystal tree with the word Myrkar underneath."

"Did Dhar tell you anything about it?"

"I asked, but he didn't know why it was kept."

"I suspected as such. Sadly, history has been lost to the ravaging of time because of my decisions. Today, I will tell you everything that has never been passed down."

Voletia resumed the task of slicing and dicing the vegetables on the table.

"Before the first people walked this world, two crystal trees dwelled here. I don't know how they came to be or if there was ever a time that they weren't here, but they were known as Mykel and Myrkar. Like the old trees, they roamed freely and worked the soil until life began to take hold. Over time, a change began in Myrkar. While they both worked the soil, Mykel brought life to the world, and Myrkar was…an apprentice, for lack of a better word. Instead of inspiring Myrkar, seeing Mykel create brought the poison of jealousy, distrust, anger, and hate. The toxin was imperceptible at first, but it festered and grew until it permeated throughout its heartwood and took over. Mykel promised to heal the heartwood rot and pleaded with him for an unknown number of centuries, but eventually was forced to banish Myrkar and the trees and creatures who were also poisoned to a remote location for the good of the world's development. With Myrkar banished, our world developed for quite some time, during which humans came to be."

Voletia picked up the diced vegetables and dumped them into the caldron of boiling water before walking to the storage room again. After returning, she stirred several spices into the stew, tasted it, and stirred in more. She pulled the covered stone pot from the coals and removed the lid, releasing the smell of freshly baked bread into the room. After removing the loaf and setting it aside to cool, she sat back down to continue the story.

"In time, I was born and, as you know, was appointed as the first queen of the forest. Unlike you, I was a child at the time, but you are a child at heart, and much like you, I was unsure of myself and the reason for my appointment. When I had grown, I married a man known as Lorca, raised three children, and lived happily for decades. You should have seen us in the beginning when we were all so new to the abilities granted by the forest. We were like children mesmerized by the simplest things."

Voletia smiled and giggled as she thought back, and her eyes sparkled as she seemed to be watching a replay of those days within the firelight. Then her smile faded, and the light in her eyes dimmed again.

"What happened?" Tsoria asked.

"Myrkar," Voletia said as she turned from the fire to look at Tsoria. "Myrkar might have been banished but he was also waiting, watching, and whispering. It's easy to sway, manipulate, or exploit humans if you know where to push. Myrkar became a master of disguise, infiltrating the tiniest of cracks in each person, twisting their desires, and using their fears to control them and grow stronger while destroying the world. Contrary to what you may have been told, the people of the south did not turn against us because their minds were closed to the forest's voice. They were turned against us because they listened to Myrkar's poisonous voice—"

"The voice that tastes like savamint," Tsoria said.

"You are familiar with it," Voletia said. "Good."

"I thought it was my thoughts, my desires."

"A master of disguise, as I said."

Voletia arose to visit the storage room once again and returned with a couple of dishes with diced raw rabbit upon them. After placing the meat next to Grryffan and Frrynner, she grew some bowls and dished up the stew for Tsoria and herself. Slices of bread were cut off as desired and dipped in stew or eaten plain. Although Tsoria tried not to rush her meal, it didn't take long before she finished her stew.

"Feel free to have more. There is plenty," Voletia said.

"My stomach seems like a bottomless pit lately," Tsoria said as she sliced off another slab of bread after refilling her bowl with stew. "I don't know what is wrong."

Voletia flashed a smile after studying the young queen. "Nothing is wrong, Tsoria."

"But what is making me so hungry? This is not like me."

"Perhaps not, but you aren't the only one who needs food."

Tsoria looked puzzled.

"I don't understand."

"There is still plenty to tell you. Perhaps you will figure out the reason as you listen." Voletia stood to place a few logs on the dying fire before sitting back down to continue. "Now, where was I?"

"Myrkar, human fears, savamint…"

"Ahh, yes. I hadn't learned about Myrkar, even after fifty years as queen, which made it impossible to tackle the real problem. During that time, relations between the people to the south and the forest degraded more and more. In an attempt to heal relations, Lorca and representatives from the Vol'aerai and tribes of the south set out on a sea voyage to search out new lands, thinking that if they worked together on the venture, they might find common ground upon which peace could be formed. I thought it was a good plan, even though I stayed behind, and it seemed to work as intended for a few months, but no one was prepared for what was to come."

Tsoria finished her second helping of stew and pushed away the bowl.

"Anything more, my dear?" Voletia asked.

"I have eaten more than enough, thank you. It was delicious," Tsoria said.

"Good. You will need the energy."

"What changed to derail months of good relations between everyone?"

Voletia looked at the fire again and took a deep breath.

"After exploring what is now the Tashtari islands to the east and the lands to the west, their journey took them north. They were intrigued to find an island surrounded by tall rocky protrusions at regular intervals. Birds didn't fly past the rocky pillars, and fish swam around it—which should have been enough warning to steer clear of the area—but they were spurred on by a natural curiosity to explore. I felt something was wrong when they crossed between the pillars but couldn't contact Lorca to assuage my fears." Voletia's voice faltered and she wiped away tears. "Hours passed before I collapsed in agony as I experienced what felt like daggers stabbing my heart. I knew at that moment that Lorca was dead—"

The story was interrupted by Voletia's inability to hold in her emotions any longer. Her face contorted with grief, and large tears fell upon her lap as she wept. Tsoria reached out to comfort Voletia as the first queen clutched her chest as if she were experiencing pain. The alpha wolves walked to Voletia's side and laid their front paws on her lap. After some time, Voletia straightened up, wiped away her tears, and breathed deeply.

"I'm sorry," Voletia said.

"No need to apologize," Tsoria said.

"It has been many years since I let myself feel the pain of the loss I felt then. I still miss him dearly."

"I can't imagine—"

"I hope you never experience what I felt that day…"

Voletia looked at Grryffan and Frrynner and reached to stroke their heads. When she stopped petting them, they lay on either side of her chair, and then she looked at Tsoria.

"…but I know you will. If you love anything, you will feel the pain of losing it. The night you watched Relvin get attacked by dogs, you got a taste of how it feels, and I knew then why the forest wanted to crown you queen."

"The alphas mentioned someone—"

"It was me. I prompted Relvin's horse to take the northern path to reach you days earlier. I had the vine in Wardrich burrow into the wall to dislodge the grate. I led the horse to carry you both to the nearest village before Relvin bled out. I have watched you both for a long time."

"Why would you be so interested in us?"

Voletia smiled at Tsoria before looking back at the fire but said nothing.

"What happened after the island?"

"When the ship returned to Islatria, only two of the thirty men who had stepped onto the island disembarked, and they were shaken from what had occurred. A formal inquiry was held, which spiraled into accusations of trickery, treachery, and traitorous actions by my husband Lorca and the other Vol'aerai. Nothing I said would persuade them to look at the facts in a different light, and I was forced to make a quick exit before I was subjected to the murderous intent of those demanding retribution."

"What happened on the island to cause them to think Lorca and the Vol'aerai betrayed them?"

"According to the two who managed to escape to tell the story..."

Jerwin stepped from the rowboat to join the rest of the men on the island's shore. The sharp rocks lining the narrow cove had seemed ominous to him as they sailed between them, and the dead trees and silence enforced the terrible foreboding. The black beach sand crunched underfoot as he joined the other men who had arrived before him.

"Men, I know this island gives us all weird feelings, but take heart, for we will not be here for more than a day," Captain Frennik said. "You have worked together admirably on this historic journey, and tomorrow, we head for home."

Jerwin could not wait to see his wife and children again and joined the other men, cheering at the good news. He was glad to be in the last group of men with his friend Marlin to converse as they trekked through the forest.

"Do you think a fire or volcano killed everything on the island?" Marlin asked.

"No, the trees are dark, but they don't look burnt," Jerwin said.

Jerwin broke a small branch off from one of the trees as they passed it. Instead of snapping like a dried twig, it bent before breaking.

"Look at this, Marlin."

Marlin took the branch from his friend and inspected the heartwood.

"They look dead, but they aren't."

They inspected the next tree much closer and noticed tiny malformed red-brown leaves and dark sap seeping from the bark. The trees were sickly and twisted but alive.

"Perhaps there is something in the soil that is poisoning them," Jerwin said.

"What could affect the entire island, though?"

When they looked around, they noticed they had fallen some distance behind the group and quickened their pace to catch up. A couple of hours after noon, they reached a clearing where an enormous tree unaffected by the sickness grew. Its leaves sparkled in the sun, and at the base of it was a large throne made from woven roots or branches.

Lorca and the other Vol'aerai seemed happy to see the crystal tree and approached with open arms, which made everyone else in the group feel at ease and venture forth. Jerwin and Marlin watched as Lorca stood still for a few minutes, approached the throne, and sat down.

"Come, my friends, let us sit down and take our ease for tonight at this spot," Lorca said.

Tables and chairs grew in the clearing as Lorca raised his hands, and the men happily sat down to rest their legs. The men carrying food started distributing it among the tables, and almost everyone forgot their troubles and relaxed. However, Jerwin was barely touching his food, and Marlin took notice.

"Jerwin, what's wrong?" Marlin asked as he chewed the food in his mouth.

"Have you noticed? The Vol'aerai haven't moved from where they were before everyone sat down."

Marlin followed his friend's gaze toward the crystal tree. Lorca was still on the throne, and the other Vol'aerai were standing on either side of him. None were eating, which suddenly made Marlin lose his appetite.

"Do you think they poisoned the food?" Marlin asked.

"I don't think so, but something doesn't feel right. I didn't want to say but they've acted differently since we crossed between the pillars," Jerwin said.

"We all feel—"

"Not like them."

Jerwin watched as Lorca twitched and grimaced like he was in pain before closing his eyes. When his eyes opened, they no longer sparkled and were cold and dead. Lorca started speaking but with a voice that sent shivers down Jerwin's spine.

"I have enjoyed this journey with all of you, but it has ended. Now that you have eaten, it is time for me to eat. Witness the power of Myrkar!"

The Vol'aerai on either side of the throne reached out with their hands and roots shot from the ground to impale the captain and leaders from the other tribes. Their bodies contorted in agony as they rapidly aged to the horror of all present. Their bodies were cast aside after releasing their last breath. A cruel smile spread across Lorca's face.

"Mmm, your lives are intoxicating. Who will be my next meal?"

Jerwin and Marlin were the first to run for the shore after seeing what happened to their captain. Lorca's cruel laugh and the screams of their companions echoed around them as they ran.

"This is my domain! Run all you want. Your fear is so delicious!" A voice said inside their heads.

Jerwin and Marlin tripped on roots or rocks in their haste and were scratched many times by branches as they ran, but they only stopped long enough to help each other back on their feet. The fresh memory of their captain's life being sucked out of him and the occasional scream from subsequent victims spurred them to keep running. When they broke free from the forest, they pushed a row boat into the water and jumped in.

The friends strained at the oars, arriving at the closest of the three ships that had brought them to the island faster than it seemed. Jerwin and Marlin scrambled aboard where they were met by the first mate, Dorin, who questioned them about the reason for their early return.

"Pull up anchor, and with all haste, let us fly from this cursed island," Jerwin said, panting after the strenuous rowing.

"We will wait for the captain before—" Dorin said.

"The captain is dead! You are now the captain," Marlin said. "If you wait, we all die!"

"Calm yourself, men. What is the—"

Terrified shouts came from the direction of the shore. Everyone turned to watch as two other rowboats that had managed to escape were being pulled to land by roots. The men jumped into the water to swim the remaining distance but didn't get far before they were hauled back. Before Dorin started shouting orders, his men had cut the anchor loose, hoisted the sails, and signaled the other ships to retreat.

"I know my husband, and he wouldn't do what they said he did. Those two men spoke the truth of what they saw, but their conclusion was wrong."

"What do you think happened?" Tsoria asked.

"Since the Vol'aerai are aware of the crystal tree here, I believe Lorca and the others were lulled into a false sense of security around Myrkar, and with its poisonous silver tongue, they weren't given a chance to see their error. Before they suspected anything, Myrkar grew his roots deep within them and used them as puppets. Lorca and the other Vol'aerai were dead as soon as he sat on the throne, and once they were under his control, there was nothing to stop Myrkar from ravaging the others."

"That is what started all the wars?"

"Yes, but I made a mistake that cemented the fear of the Vol'aerai in their minds forever. Before the Vol'aerai started fleeing north, there was an attack on one of our villages. An angry mob slaughtered everyone including one of my sons and his three children. When I saw their bodies, I wailed in anguish until I could cry no more. Men, women, and children were murdered for the simple crime of being Vol'aerai, and something broke inside me. I needed a way to handle all the pain and anger I felt inside and that's when Myrkar found his way into my mind."

Voletia's chin quivered as she looked into the flames and Tsoria waited for her to continue.

"I tracked down the mob that had killed our people and used the same power that Myrkar used on the island to suck the life from the people. I made the parents watch as their children grew old and lifeless in front of them before they experienced the same fate. I still remember every face," Voletia reached towards the fire like she was caressing the face of someone before her, "every soul I extinguished. I enacted my justice on those who hurt us, and it was sweet at the moment, but it was revenge, not justice. The bitterness was still there, the pain was greater than ever, and the guilt tore me apart, but my life was extended beyond normal years by the life I stole."

Tsoria contemplated what Voletia told her for several minutes. The Islatrian fear of the Vol'aerai finally made sense to Tsoria, and she realized how easily Myrkar's poisonous voice could have brought her the same fate.

"You are right, our history isn't as pleasant and peaceful as we are taught," Tsoria said.

Voletia nodded before turning away from the fire to look at Tsoria.

"I exiled myself to the mountains out of guilt and fear to prevent myself from hurting more people. I hibernate in a crystal root pod and experience world events as lucid dreams most years. I'm woken whenever a new queen is appointed so I can pass my knowledge on…"

Voletia looked at Frrynner as her eyes watered. Frrynner sat up and placed a paw on Voletia's lap. Voletia sighed and closed her eyes.

"You've brought me here for more than history, haven't you?" Tsoria asked.

Voletia opened her eyes as she turned to face Tsoria. "I don't trust myself to finish the task given to me but hesitate to pass it on. The training could kill you if you fail. Do you want to continue?"

Chapter 20
ANGUISH

"WHAT HAPPENED?" EVIARA ASKED when Tsoria was silent for some time without continuing her story.

Tsoria looked up from her long stare into the cup she clasped and continued the story. "Voletia spent her remaining time training me for the task that she failed, and when it concluded Voletia passed away. I buried her surrounded by the only companions she had for centuries, the circle of ancient trees where I trained."

"That wasn't all, was it?" Relvin asked Tsoria privately as she finished the water in her cup.

Tsoria looked at her husband and shook her head. After reading each other's eyes, Relvin nodded and sighed.

"I trust you. I don't need to know yet," Relvin said.

"Thank you," Tsoria said.

"That was when we felt your sadness," Eviara said after putting the pieces together.

"Yes," Tsoria said turning to her sister. "Witnessing her last breath hit me harder than I thought it would after less than half a day."

"I wish I got to meet her," Eviara said, pouting as she propped her chin up in her hands with elbows on the table.

Tsoria smiled as she reached across the table to lift Eviara's chin before speaking, "Voletia would have wanted to meet you too had she the time."

"What are we sailing towards?" Relvin asked.

"Dragonhead Island to change the world's fate," Tsoria said.

"That sounds ominous," Relvin said. "Myrkar could've changed—"

"Based on what has happened in the kingdom over the years and the voice I heard while negotiating with King Dhar, I would expect that Myrkar is even more entrenched in his ways."

"What do you expect us to encounter on the island?" Eviara asked.

"Once we cross into the dead zone around the island, we will be cut off from everyone. Myrkar will use our isolation to his advantage and might attempt to get us to give up or turn against each other. We can count on Myrkar to let us experience each other's pain to convince us to give up."

"What is the plan?" Relvin asked.

"Before we enter the mouth of the Dragonhead Island cove, Relvin and I will depart in a rowboat to confront Myrkar. Eviara, I need you on the Priter Elorai outside the cove."

Tsoria reached up to her neck, detached a woven grass string with Voletia's ring as a pendant, and handed it to Eviara.

"I need you to drop this ring into the sea when you feel my signal, but no sooner."

"What signal will I be waiting for if we can't talk with each other?" Eviara asked.

"I will be in extreme pain," Tsoria said.

"Will your life be in danger?" Relvin asked.

Tsoria reached across the table to take Relvin's hand and locked eyes with him.

"More than you know, my love."

Eviara reached out to place her hand on top of theirs.

"We will do this together as a family," Eviara said.

"Yes, we will," Relvin said.

"Relvin, could you teach me to fight?" Tsoria asked.

"I can teach you some basic moves, but…" Tsoria waited as Relvin stared at their clasped hands before he pulled away. "Follow me. I have an idea."

Tsoria followed Relvin up the stairs with Eviara close behind. Relvin pulled Tsoria into a dance position once they were on the main deck.

"What does this have to do with fighting?" Tsoria asked as they began to dance.

"Knowing how your partner moves and reading their signals is as important in dance as in fighting."

Tsoria was still getting used to the ship's movement and stepped on Relvin's foot when the ship rocked to one side. He adjusted his stance to prevent them from falling.

"A battle is chaotic and fluid. When things go wrong, adjust to compensate and keep going."

The more they danced, the better Tsoria became at reading Relvin's movements, even when she couldn't see where he was. When Relvin was satisfied with her progress he taught her basic fighting moves before they practiced with the Priter Elorai attacking them. Every other activity aboard the ship turned into a lesson as he tested her awareness without warning. Although she couldn't match Relvin's experience or skill in such a short time, he was an excellent teacher and she became comfortable using the tools of war.

Tsoria stood at the boat's bow and watched as the rocky pillars of the dead zone boundary came closer. She shivered as her fear and isolation grew, though the sea spray and wind sapping her body heat didn't help. She tried to push her worries from her head, but the feelings traveled to the pit of her stomach and made her nauseated. Tsoria felt like her scared nine-year-old self again, huddling with her friends the first night in the cart as they were dragged farther from home. A familial warmth embraced her like Cecelia's arms on Tsoria's first night at Wardrich as she whimpered in bed. This time, Relvin held her close and kissed her neck.

"You are not alone," Relvin said in her ear. "No matter how you feel, I will be by your side, my queen."

Tsoria melted in his arms as she turned her head to kiss him.

"Thank you, my love. I needed that reminder."

"You're welcome."

Tsoria basked in Relvin's warmth as the boat rose and fell with each swell.

"Relvin, I don't know if I will succeed. I may not be powerful enough, but there is one thing you must promise to do if we are to have any chance."

"What?"

"Be the man I fell in love with. No matter what happens, don't fight out of anger, hate, selfishness, or revenge. Fight to protect, to save, for love."

"My life is yours, as always."

Tsoria kissed Relvin again as Eviara joined them.

"We will pass the boundary soon," Eviara said.

The trio held each other as they crossed the boundary into the dead zone. They felt a sudden emptiness around them as their connection to the forest was severed, and their skin prickled as if prodded with thousands of needles. Tsoria was the first of the trio to perceive the twinge of a headache as they approached the island, but they all were experiencing one by the time the Priter Elorai took a position before the cove entrance.

Tsoria and Relvin walked to the starboard side amidships and descended to a boat, grown to take them ashore. The roots tethering the rowboat to the ship pushed it away from the side of the Priter Elorai before detaching. The rowboat grew four oars from its hull and rowed the couple into the cove under the queen's guidance. Sharp rocky protrusions threatened to tear at the boat if the intruders drifted too far to either side while they passed into the mouth of the cove. Tsoria and Relvin stepped out after the bottom of the vessel ran aground on the black sandy shores that half hid the weathered skeletons of abandoned rowboats from centuries past. They were ten paces from the trees when the queen pressed her fingers at her temples and stumbled with her eyes closed. Relvin caught her before she fell.

"Are you alright, Tsoria?" Relvin asked.

"Yes," Tsoria said after a few moments and straightened her stance. "There is so much anger, hate, and pain in these trees. I feel it worsening my headache, but I'm fine now."

"Are you sure?"

"I have set up a block in my mind to filter it out. The pain is manageable now."

"Good, because retreat isn't an option," Relvin said as he pointed toward the rowboat.

Tsoria turned to where her husband pointed and watched as roots attacked their boat and pulled it into the sand, sucking any life and nutrients from it.

"If the boats from long ago had been alive, nobody would have escaped to tell us what happened," Tsoria said.

They walked through an opening in the forest ahead that invited them to continue on their quest. Their footsteps seemed deafening in the quiet surroundings. The breeze whistled and moaned through the tree branches as if in pain. Hours after arriving on the island, they arrived at their destination, a clearing with Myrkar in the center.

"*Queen Tsorianya, what a surprise,*" Myrkar said. "*I'm sure you are tired from your journey to see me. Come, sit on the throne, and rest your weary legs.*"

"*I haven't come to rest, Myrkar,*" Tsoria said.

"*I'm flattered you know my name. You are the first queen to visit me since this world was created, and I was starting to think I was forgotten.*"

The throne is your right by appointment, a courtesy I don't reserve for everyone."

"Was Queen Voletia's husband Lorca one of those special few the throne was reserved for?" Tsoria asked.

"You surprise me again. I thought history had died with the first queen over a millennia ago."

"History isn't as dead as you might think," Tsoria said, feeling the atmosphere around them grow more oppressive as Myrkar went quiet for a moment.

"Since you have declined my offer, I'm inclined to ask, what is the purpose of your visit?"

"I'm extending the courtesy of asking you to leave this world alone," Tsoria said.

"You are asking me to give up my position as ruler and protector of this world to you? Why should I?"

"Because you aren't the ruler of this world, Mykel is."

"Mykel, ruler?" Myrkar scoffed. "Mykel's power over this world wanes more as I gain influence. No one has heard him speak in centuries. You might as well join me because he can't protect you."

It was true. Tsoria hadn't heard Mykel speak, but she had felt his presence on enough occasions to know he was there. Tsoria could still feel Mykel's subtle, patient, and unwavering strength within the ring on her left hand despite being cut off from the forest and his direct influence.

"Poison weakens the body, but with a cure and enough time, it can be eliminated," Tsoria said.

"And you are here to eliminate me?" Myrkar asked.

"I'm here to administer the cure."

"And if I refuse?"

Crystal roots grew from Tsoria and Relvin's wedding rings to envelop them in armor.

"Refusing my courtesy would be unwise," Tsoria said.

"You think that you two can defeat me?" Myrkar asked.

"*We bet our lives. Are you willing to bet yours?*" Relvin said as a battle axe grew in each hand.

"*Then continuing this conversation is pointless,*" Myrkar said.

The twisted and sickly trees creaked and groaned as they moved to erase the path that led Tsoria and Relvin to Myrkar. Tsoria closed her eyes and removed the block she had set up in her mind. The angry and pained voices of the trees flooded back, but for her to feel where all the roots were, she needed to open herself to everything.

Relvin sprung into action as the first attack came from behind them from the twisted forest. Myrkar using his pawns first was what Relvin had expected as he swung his axes at each root that threatened the queen. The inability to connect to Tsoria through the network was a hindrance but not detrimental to their movements since the dance training during their journey. Relvin and Tsoria moved not as individuals, but as one complete person while they fought to protect each other.

"*You entertain me, Relvin,*" Myrkar said. "*I wonder how long you can keep this up?*"

Relvin ignored Myrkar and concentrated on the myriad of attacks to repel.

"*What makes you fight so hard for each other?*"

Relvin continued to ignore Myrkar.

"*I can offer you more wealth than you can dream of if you help me remove Mykel from power.*"

"*With Tsoria, I'm already wealthier than I deserve,*" Relvin said.

Relvin swung Tsoria around, pulling her from harm's way as he used a backhanded axe swing to cut at the roots.

"*I can see you are a man of strength. I can give you the strength to overpower any foe,*" Myrkar said.

"*Strength is useless against the enemy inside,*" Relvin said.

A barrage of roots from either side of them tested Relvin and Tsoria as they ferociously fought them off and dodged as best as they could.

"You act as if you and Tsorianya are equals, but isn't it unfair that she is queen and you're only her guard? I would make you a king and give you the power to rule the land," Myrkar said.

"I'm the king of her heart. What more do I need?"

"You may be king of her heart now, but will that always be the case? I know your wife is keeping secrets from you."

"She has a good reason," Relvin said.

Relvin could feel his limbs tiring as had happened during the battle with King Dhar, but this time it occurred much sooner than normal. Relvin deduced that though the crystal armor enhanced his strength his stamina was drained by being in the twisted forest of the island. Separation from the forest network was doing more than preventing communication between them.

"Yes, she knows you can't protect her—like the night you failed to prevent the attack on Myrna—and you are a monster of rage—like when you killed the men who did it."

"That might have worked on me before but not anymore."

"Perhaps not," Myrkar said. *"I can't detect the guilt about that night you used to carry with you. But what about before then? I know how many women were defiled under your watch, how many people were murdered, and those—"*

"Enough! I don't care what you have to say! Knowing won't undo what has been done, nor will I betray Tsoria," Relvin said.

Relvin refocused all his energy on defending Tsoria, ignoring multiple other attempts Myrkar made to get under his skin.

"Since you have refused to help me, I will show you how powerless you are to stop what is coming. Watch and despair."

A tangle of roots sprung up at the edge of Relvin's vision. He only had enough time to cross his axes in front of him like a shield as they pushed him some distance away from Tsoria before retreating into the ground.

Eviara waited at the stern of the Priter Elorai, facing the cove opening with Voletia's ring clasped in her right hand. She could feel Relvin and Tsoria's rising anxiety as they fought. She could tell they were having a difficult time. She worried that she had missed her sister's signal with every minute that passed.

"The fight isn't going well. We should rescue Queen Tsorianya," a voice like the Priter Elorai said.

"I'm not here to rescue them," Eviara said.

"I know, but perhaps you could have a more important role. You might even be the hero, Eviara."

"My role is important," Eviara said but paused. *"You aren't the Priter Elorai. Get out of my head, Myrkar!"*

"How did you figure it out?" Myrkar asked, dropping the act.

"Why would I tell you that?"

"Hmm, defiant like your sister," Myrkar said. *"I know you are part of this. Why else would she have you wait out here? What are you hiding from me?"*

Eviara focused on the water below to avoid thinking about the ring in her hand.

"Get out of my head!" Eviara said.

"It doesn't matter," Myrkar said. *"There is nothing you can do to change the outcome of this fight. You will all have time to regret acting against me as you die."*

"I have grown tired of playing with you," Myrkar said to Relvin and Tsoria. *"It is time I clear the last obstacle to my ascension as the rightful ruler of this world."*

Tsoria turned to Relvin and said, "Be the man I love."

Relvin nodded, picking up the signal she sent for him to be ready for the endgame, whatever it was.

"How touching," Myrkar said mockingly. *"Now for you to feel real strength and die!"*

Crystal roots shot from the ground toward them. Relvin reformed the weapon in his right hand into a large shield as he ran to protect Tsoria from the attack, but he was too far away to reach her in time.

"Tsoria!" Relvin said.

True to Tsoria's prediction, Myrkar allowed the pain she felt as the crystal roots tore into her flesh to be experienced by them all. Relvin stopped in his tracks, fell to his knees, and leaned on the shield, short of breath like he had been kicked in the chest by a horse. Somehow, Tsoria was still standing, though she clutched her stomach as she mouthed the words "I love you" to Relvin.

Tsoria rapidly aged before Relvin's eyes, and he didn't understand why she didn't do anything to stop Myrkar's attack. He couldn't save her, he didn't have the strength and she didn't have the time…but perhaps he could give her the time she needed. He trusted there was a way to turn this all around even if he never saw the result, and poured his desires into one final act.

"My life is yours, my queen!" Relvin said as he lifted his left hand toward Tsoria.

Roots shot from Relvin's wedding ring toward his wife and embedded into the skin of her arm. He could feel his body weaken as his life drained before Myrkar's roots impacted his shield and tore it apart.

"You should have killed me first, Myrkar," Relvin said with a smile despite doubting he had done enough.

Eviara threw up over the side of the ship as a wave of extreme pain emanating from her sister cascaded over her body and overwhelmed her nerves. Eviara gritted her teeth as she fought to draw air into her lungs and override her desire to curl into a ball. Her grip on the ring in her hand tightened, causing it to dig into her flesh and draw blood.

"I will not fail you, sister," Eviara said, but she still had difficulty releasing it.

"*We will help, little captain,*" the Priter Elorai said.

The bracer on her arm grew around her fingers like a glove and pried her fist open, allowing the ring to fall to the waters below. Eviara collapsed to the deck as the Priter Elorai did everything possible to ease her suffering.

"*All this time and training to defeat me, and this is all you can do?*" Myrkar asked. "*You are weak, pathetic creatures destined to fail, all because you can't sacrifice anyone. Love is a figment of the imagination. Love makes you weak and vulnerable.*"

The pain from Myrkar's roots extracting the life from her overwhelmed Tsoria's body, but her physical pain was not what hurt the most. Voletia had warned her that she would feel the pain of loss, but nothing she had been through dulled the pain she experienced as she watched her husband die giving everything he had to her. Tsoria was proud of the man Relvin had remained until the end, but it broke her heart seeing him go to such extremes to keep her alive.

"*May my life be enough. It was my honor to serve you, my queen. I love you, Tsorianya…*" Relvin said as he breathed his last.

"*I love you, Relvin, my king,*" Tsoria said, closing her eyes.

Without the forest to assure her everything would work out, Tsoria clung to the feeling of Relvin's warmth embracing her one last time. Tears fell from her eyes, but she didn't have the luxury of mourning his death at that moment. Her husband's death would be in vain if she were distracted from what she had set out to accomplish. While she still felt him, Tsoria pushed everything else away. She pushed past the pain overwhelming her nerves, the sound of her beating heart, and the rush of air filling her lungs. She searched the depths of her being for what had gotten her through Voletia's training…

CHAPTER 21
REBIRTH

ORE THAN A WEEK EARLIER, Voletia rose from her chair and walked outside. The wolves followed her to the door but turned to look at Tsoria when she didn't get up to follow.

"It is time to train, Alpha Tsorianya," Grryffan said.

"Am I ready?" Tsoria asked.

"Are you willing to be?"

"Yes."

"Then you are ready," Grryffan said.

"We will be nearby while you train, guiding you as much as possible, but some things you must figure out on your own," Frrynner said.

Tsoria left her chair and followed the wolves out of the warm dwelling interior into the cold mountain air. Voletia stood at the far side of the ancient circle, waiting for Tsoria to enter. The Alphas stopped at the edge of the clearing.

"I must confess, I have wanted to meet you for a long time," Voletia said, "but I didn't want you to be appointed queen. I only wanted to get you away from Wardrich."

"You didn't want me to be queen?" Tsoria asked.

"I wanted to spare you the pain of what's to come after and me the pain of putting you through what I must," Voletia said.

"Why?"

"I will tell you…if you survive. This is your last chance to change your mind."

Voletia's clothes transformed into full crystal armor as soon as Tsoria reached the edge of the clearing. Tsoria, a little frightened by what Voletia said, hesitated to enter as the once kind queen, the symbol of the Vol'aerai, was poised for all-out war.

"*Breathe, Alpha Tsorianya. Everything you need is inside, beside, and around you,*" Frrynner said.

"*When you step into the ring, watch her eyes, her movements, and be ready for anything,*" Grryffan said.

Tsoria felt the heavy weight of the future on her shoulders as she stepped forward. However, as her clothes became crystal armor, she breathed and cleared her mind of everything except what was in front of her because the present was the only thing she had room to worry about. When Tsoria was within the circle of trees, a crystal root cage grew around the perimeter, blocking any escape and preventing the alphas from joining the fight.

"The rules are simple," Voletia said, "neither of us has control over any plants except those forming our armor until one of us wins."

"How do I win?" Tsoria asked.

"Survive," Voletia said as a sword and shield grew into her hands.

Voletia initiated her attack without waiting for Tsoria to be ready. Tsoria barely had time to create a shield to deflect the attack as she stepped to the side, but as she did, Voletia was already moving in for her next attack. Voletia's shield slammed into Tsoria's helmet, which threw the young queen against the root cage, and she fell to the ground.

"If this is all you can do, you will never win!" Voletia said.

Tsoria scrambled to her feet and grew a sword to complement the shield, but there was little she could do except defend as Voletia rained down blow after blow upon her. The first queen moved like an energetic teenager despite her incredible age. Voletia's attacks were precise, and she allowed almost no time for recovery. Tsoria fell to the ground time after time, wondering if this was what it was like on the other side of Relvin's blades.

"Who do you think you are? Queen of the Vol'aerai?" Voletia asked. "You are only a scared weakling. I am the true queen!"

Tsoria wondered if she had made a mistake taking on Voletia. Relvin should be the one to fight, not her. Although she had watched him, Relvin had not taught her how to use the sword or shield she wielded. She would have been dead already if not for the crystal armor, but even it was being damaged by each blow and was repairing itself often. Voletia's sword struck Tsoria's shield hard, and she felt the force transfer to her arm as she stumbled back several paces.

"I am stronger..." said Voletia. Tsoria was struck several times in rapid succession. "...I am faster..." Tsoria took several more blows from Voletia's attacks and found herself on the ground again. "...and there can only be one queen of the forest! I'm the only one worthy of being queen!"

"Breathe, Tsorianya..." Frrynner said.

"What is she trying to do?" Grryffan asked.

"She is trying to kill me, and the way it is going, she will," Tsoria said as she was kicked hard by Voletia.

"What is Voletia trying to do?" Grryffan asked.

Tsoria wondered why she was being asked the same question, but the slight change in wording made her remember the purpose of the training as she continued to take a beating.

"You let your sister get kidnapped. You couldn't even kill King Dhar to save the Vol'aerai! You are weak and pathetic! You should have stayed in Wardrich to be Darrick's whore because that is all you are good for!" Voletia said.

"She is trying to provoke me!" Tsoria said.

"Why?" Grryffan asked.

Tsoria thought back to when Voletia told her about the massacre of the villages. Voletia's anger while taking revenge and the reason Grryffan gave her for why she was appointed queen flooded back to her.

"She knew I could never win with conventional battle. This was never about knowing combat and being a fair fight."

"Go on..." Grryffan prompted.

"She wants me to give in to despair or hate and let my anger take over..."

Between attacks, Tsoria caught glimpses of Voletia's eyes in the light of the cage and saw nothing but pain and sadness. Every taunt and blow she hit Tsoria with caused tears to fall.

"No...that's not it. Myrkar wants that. Voletia wants the exact opposite. If I kill her in hate, I make the same mistake she did."

"Exactly! Brace yourself for the real lesson."

Tsoria got up with determination and dusted herself off. Voletia stepped back and let her sword and shield dissolve away.

"It is now time for you to die so I can take my rightful place on the throne," Voletia said.

Voletia thrust her hands out, and numerous crystal roots burst forth from her armor toward Tsoria. The young queen had enough time to bring her shield in front of her body before taking the full force of the attack. Searing pain from every puncture of her flesh overloaded Tsoria's senses. Her body grew older and weaker as Voletia siphoned off Tsoria's life. She wondered why the pain was limited to her arms and legs. As she checked her body, she realized that all of her armor had retreated from everywhere except the most vital areas of her body and was most thickly layered where she had brought the shield in front, which she clutched with her hands. The roots had embedded into the armor but had not fully pierced the heavy layering that protected her torso.

"I'm pregnant!" Tsoria said, surprised that it had taken her this long to figure out what her body had known.

Tsoria had no time to delight in the revelation as her life continued to be drained by her baby, fighting to live, and by Voletia, fighting to kill. She wasn't sure if there was anything she could do, but she knew a decision needed to be made. Save herself or protect the child inside. She took a deep breath to calm herself.

"Hey, little one. I am your mother, and I look forward to meeting you," Tsoria said.

Tsoria's instincts kicked into overdrive, and she used all that remained to keep her baby alive. Like a siphon between two buckets of water, she felt the flow of life reverse course and pass from Voletia towards that which she loved. The return of life started slow but soon was a torrent. The youth and vigor of her body returned, and the overflow of life pulled from Voletia spilled over into the ancient trees around them, down the mountain slopes to the valleys, bringing rejuvenation.

"How do I stop it? I don't want to kill you, Voletia."

Voletia's helmet retreated. She looked calm and happy despite the drain of her life.

"The process can't be stopped. It is my life or yours. Far too many were unable to fulfill their potential because of me," Voletia said. "This was always going to be my penance for what I had done."

"No! There is still more I can learn from you."

"Dear child, there isn't a reason for me to stay around anymore. You have learned all I have to teach. You have all the tools you need to defeat Myrkar."

"I'm not ready…" Tsoria said as tears fell from her eyes.

"Yes, you are. You chose to save what you loved instead of yourself. Hate, anger, selfishness, and revenge corrupt the soul and strengthen Myrkar. Love is the only way you will win."

Tsoria's wounds healed as each crystal root retracted from her one at a time.

"Please, let me save you!"

"My time has come, my dear, but before it passes, I will tell you why I didn't want you to be queen. I didn't want to burden you with this monumental task because you are my descendant. I wish we had more time to get to know each other, but I am happy to have met you. You have brought me peace. I love you…"

The last roots left Tsoria's body as Voletia breathed her last and collapsed to the ground. The crystal cage around them retreated as Tsoria rushed to Voletia's side and held her close to her chest. Tears cascaded from Tsoria's eyes at the loss of her ancestor, whom she had only known for a few hours but who had left such an impression on her. A sudden and immense wave of sadness flooded the forest as the wolves howled at the sky, and Tsoria wailed.

Amid the noise of her screaming nerves, the heartbreak from losing her husband, and the assault of Myrkar urging her to give up, Tsoria wasn't fighting alone. She longed for Relvin's embrace, but at the moment, feeling her child's heartbeat was all she needed to give her the strength to keep going. Tsoria fought for each breath as she opened her eyes after reversing the flow of life as she had learned in her training. A barely perceptible but familiar feeling grew in the back of her mind as the warmth of the forest came back. A crystal root from Voletia's ring had made it to her without Myrkar detecting it.

"One last struggle, little one. Mother will protect you again, my little Willow," Tsoria said.

Tsoria's pain subsided to a manageable level, and her breathing became easy as her heartbeat and the baby's slowed.

"*Hahahahaha! I told you love makes you vulnerable. You might have protected your child from my attack but haven't saved them. I'm draining the life from you as we speak, and when you die, your baby dies,*" Myrkar said.

"*You're right. Love does make me vulnerable—*"

"*What was that? I couldn't hear you after admitting that I was right.*"

"But love doesn't make me weak," Tsoria said.

"Your husband is dead, you are dying along with your child, and then your sister is next. How is love anything but weakness?"

Tsoria felt her body rejuvenate as her life returned.

"Love helps us when we are down. Love guides us when we are lost. Love relieves our pain. Love comforts us when we are alone. Love gives us strength to keep going when all hope seems lost," Tsoria said.

A small green bud grew from the roots connecting Relvin to Tsoria. She turned to watch as the bud bloomed into a purple and white flower. A second bud emerged further down and opened to a deep red bloom. The connection between them was soon covered in beautiful flowers of all colors. Tsoria's heart skipped a beat as Relvin's heart restarted. She gasped for breath as his lungs filled with air again. Tears flowed down Tsoria's face as she watched Relvin open his eyes and sit up from where his body had fallen.

"Welcome back, my love," Tsoria said to Relvin as she smiled.

Tsoria turned her head to Myrkar but didn't look up.

"And love...gives life. Can you feel it?" Tsoria said.

"Love? Hahahaha...You call this strength?" Myrkar asked, confident he still had the upper hand.

Tsoria lifted her head to look at the tree in pity. "Can you feel it?" Tsoria asked again.

"I can feel your life dra..."

"Do you feel it now, Myrkar?" Tsoria asked, feeling his confidence crack as he realized what Tsoria was doing.

"How could you have learned that already?" Myrkar asked. "It took Voletia decades to learn how to do that."

"And she passed her knowledge to me."

"She's alive?"

"I took her life in the process of learning how to defeat you. I buried her a little over a week ago in the mountains where she lived."

"*Now, you are corrupted like Voletia,*" Myrkar said. Tsoria could feel his smugness growing. "*What will you do with all the years you are taking?*"

"*You still don't get it. The skill I learned from Voletia isn't the same ability you taught her,*" Tsoria said. "*If you hadn't been so blinded by your selfish pursuit of power, you might have realized why I told my sister to stay back. My pain—the one thing you didn't block—was the signal she was waiting for. Your enjoyment of our suffering distracted you long enough for the crystal roots from Voletia's ring my sister dropped into the sea to break through the barrier and link me to the forest.*" Tsoria felt a brief twinge of panic from Myrkar that turned to overwhelming rage. "*I'm not keeping your life. I'm returning it to the world for the ones I love!*"

The crystal roots from Voletia's ring strengthened their connection. The trickle drain on Myrkar's life increased to a river. Myrkar stopped pretending to be the benevolent protector of the twisted trees and bled their life in a last-ditch attempt to replace what he was losing. The palpable feeling of suffering on the island multiplied. Tsoria and Relvin's connection to the forest around them was flooded with the dying screams of the twisted trees. Blocking out the immense pain from the corrupted forest was as futile as Myrkar's attempt to stay alive. Tsoria and Relvin couldn't prevent the torrential flow of tears as each tree's heartwood broke and emitted intense snapping sounds as the last of its life was pulled from it. They cried out in anguish as they felt a sharp stab in the heart with each tree's death until Myrkar was the only one remaining.

"*Rest, dear Tsorianya and Relvin,*" Mykel said as his warm and familiar presence embraced them and provided welcome relief from their suffering. "*Your struggle is over. You have done well. I'll take it from here because you won't survive the experience of Myrkar's death.*"

The roots from Relvin's ring and Myrkar retreated from Tsoria, and she collapsed to her hands and knees as her wounds healed. Their armor turned back into their regular clothes. Relvin scrambled over to Tsoria and wrapped his arms around her.

"How are you?" Relvin asked.

"Exhausted, relieved, loved, like I rehearsed our child's birth," Tsoria said.

Relvin pushed back from his wife and looked at her quizzically. Tsoria pulled her husband's hand to her stomach and smiled at him.

"I think Willow is a nice name for her," Tsoria said. "How about you?"

"We're going to be parents!" Relvin said with a smile before kissing Tsoria. "Willow...I like it."

Tsoria smiled as she rested a hand on Relvin's cheek and kissed him. She studied his face when their lips parted drinking in every detail as if she hadn't seen him in years.

"When you were...I..." Tsoria's voice faltered as tears began to fall.

No amount of words could express more than each tear that fell as they clung to each other, not wanting to let go.

Jestin walked with Farouq under the shade of the palms in the late afternoon of the oasis. The year's harvest was nearing completion as the last date pedicels were removed and stripped of their fruits. Jestin's parents had returned to the Wispryn Weald after a long stay with their son and his new family.

"Jestin, my son," Farouq said. "How are you adjusting to life in the desert?"

"It's hotter than Mukward, but regardless of location or temperature, friends and family make it livable."

"True. My wife and I felt barren as the sands around us when our daughters were taken, but it feels like an oasis has sprung up in our hearts with their return. To also gain a son in the process...makes the heartache worth it."

"Those who seek to avoid pain, forfeit the joy on the other side." Jestin turned to see why Farouq had stopped walking. Farouq's eyes were wide and mouth ajar. "Malikan, are—"

"I'm fine. I remembered something from when I was a boy," Farouq said, shaking his head. "The Kalumat will need a Malikan like you to lead them."

"I'm not wise enough to be Malikan," Jestin said.

"Only a fool thinks they are wise enough to lead. I'm glad you aren't a fool."

A scout on horseback rode up to them with two horses in tow.

"Malikan, you need to see this," the scout said.

Farouq and Jestin each mounted a horse and followed the scout up a high ridge that overlooked the oasis and surrounding desert landscape. The reason the scout sent for them was plain to see. The vast yellow sea of sand was becoming one large oasis as vegetation took over.

"I understand now, Jahd, it's beautiful," Farouq said.

They took in the view for several minutes before Farouq broke the silence.

"My Jahd—or grandfather as you would say—told me he saw this day in a vision, but I didn't believe him. I was surprised earlier because the words you spoke about pain and joy were the last words he said to me before he died."

Back on Dragonhead Island, Mykel was making one last attempt to save Myrkar.

"*Myrkar, my brother, I'm sorry that it has come to this, but Tsorianya has chosen this world's fate,*" Mykel said.

"*I never had a chance because you hobbled my power,*" Myrkar said.

"*Didn't you notice that my powers were also limited?*" Mykel asked. "*You showed them your way, and I showed mine. They chose their path; I did not choose for them.*"

"*You didn't give me a chance to learn everything.*"

"*You had thousands of unhindered years to learn from me but ignored my lessons. Nothing would have remained of this world if I had let you continue your selfish pursuits.*"

"*You wanted the power to yourself. You couldn't stand watching me surpass you.*"

"*Myrkar, you would have had a world to shape for yourself had you listened to me,*" Mykel said.

"*Because I didn't follow your rules, I don't get a chance to prove myself?*" Myrkar asked.

"*The laws that govern this universe were established long before you or I existed. I'm bound by them as well.*"

"*That's the difference between us, Mykel. I don't want to be hobbled by limitations.*"

"*Then there is nothing more I can do. Goodbye, brother,*" Mykel said with sadness in his voice.

Myrkar screamed curses at Mykel until the last of his life was siphoned away.

Tsoria and Relvin huddled in each other's arms with their eyes closed as the ground rumbled and groaned. The earth jumped beneath them as if uncoordinated giants were dancing. They heard great splashes from the waters around them as if there was a competition over which giant could throw a boulder the farthest. For several minutes, the rumbling continued before it subsided into peaceful silence.

"*Rise, my children. It is finished,*" Mykel said.

Tsoria and Relvin stood and opened their eyes to see the newly transformed island. The surrounding mountains had sunk into the sea along with the pillars marking the boundary of the dead zone. The twisted forest had disappeared, replaced by fruiting plants and trees of all varieties. The clearing around Myrkar was a grassy field surrounded by Pyratsori Astranya plants in full bloom. Sunlight shined through the now crystal clear leaves and trunk of Myrkar, creating dancing rainbows upon the ground around them. Despite the beauty, Tsoria and Relvin felt a quiet solemnness because, at Myrkar's core, there was an insatiable blackness, devouring all light.

"*What happens now?*" Tsoria asked.

"*The world heals. Even without Myrkar's influence, the corruption could take generations to be undone but that is up to the people. They must choose the path they wish to follow. I want to give them time to learn a better way,*" Mykel said.

"*How will we know when the corruption is undone?*" Relvin asked.

"*When Myrkar's dark core disappears,*" Mykel said.

A root pod rose from the earth and unraveled, leaving Eviara in the grassy field with Tsoria and Relvin.

"I was worried about you," Eviara said, throwing her arms around them. "I'm happy you are both well. I wanted to do more but—"

"My dear sister," Tsoria said as she withdrew from Eviara's embrace and crouched before her, "You are the reason Relvin and I are standing here. There was nothing more you could've done. I knew I could depend on you..." Tsoria stood and embraced Relvin and Eviara again. "...on both of you."

Eviara's stomach grumbled followed by Relvin and Tsoria's joining in agreement, causing them to chuckle. A miniature crystal tree grew nearby with three chairs surrounding it.

"*Sit and rest while I create a banquet for you,*" Mykel said.

Tsoria, Relvin, and Eviara felt how deprived of energy their bodies were as they took a seat. Three buds grew from the miniature crystal tree and bloomed into opalescent flowers.

"*You will be the first to taste crystal fruit. Contained within the fruit is a specific gift for each of you,*" Mykel said. "*Tsorianya, as the queen who had endured more pain than any woman birthing a new future for this world, you will be the first to experience no pain during childbirth.*"

"Thank you," Tsoria said as the center of each flower swelled into a small round dark green fruit.

"*Relvin, you gave your life without expecting to receive it back. You will be the first and only King of the Vol'aerai with every power of the forest Tsoria has and hasn't yet discovered.*"

"Thank you," Relvin said as each fruit grew larger and turned paler green.

"*Eviara, Priter Elorai's little captain,*" Mykel said with amusement. "*You have always been eager to learn, make new friends, try new things, and explore unknown places. You and the Priter Elorai will always know where to find new adventures.*"

"Thank you," Eviara said as the fruits stopped growing and turned pearl white.

"*Tsoria and Relvin, you will be the last monarchs of the Vol'aerai. I have another gift for you when you are older...*" The crystal fruits turned milky transparent with rainbows dancing inside as if made of opal as they ripened. "*...but the time has come for you to eat.*"

They each reached for a fruit that felt smooth and firm but gave way to pressure like a plum. The fruits dripped juice like liquid diamonds as they took a bite and experienced a taste that could only be described as pure joy. One bite was all it took to satisfy their hunger, quench their thirst, and replenish their energy, but subsequent bites were no less pleasurable than the first as they finished the fruit. They stayed up all night talking with Mykel and each other without sleep.

EPILOGUE

AKIMA AND HER DAUGHTER LEAFA were camped in the north where Jaxier province and the Wispryn Weald now met. It had been nearly ten years since Myrkar's removal and few knew what Tsoria, Relvin, Eviara, and the Priter Elorai had done, but they all felt the after-effects. The chaos in most minds had ceased as if everyone had woken from a nightmare. The deeds were done, the wounds were scars, and the memories remained, but the world began to heal.

"Leafa, you must understand that a queen doesn't show up for everyone who calls," Akima said trying to prepare her eight-year-old daughter for disappointment after two days of waiting.

"I know, but she will visit. I know she will," Leafa said. "Please, can we stay one more day?"

Akima looked at her daughter and couldn't help smiling at the one person she had difficulty saying no to, especially when she showed the cute expression she had perfected to get her way.

"Using that face is not fair. You know I have a hard time saying no," Akima said and laughed. "One more day."

"Thank you, Mother, you are the best!" Leafa said as she hugged her mother.

Akima was about to gather wood for the fire and start the evening meal when the trees parted, and she watched two riders emerge from the forest. When they stopped at the edge of the camp, Queen Tsorianya's daughter dismounted while some steps grew beside the queen's horse so she could dismount without disturbing her sleeping baby nestled against her chest. The horses trotted into the forest after receiving a pat on the neck. Tsoria and her daughter approached the campers.

"I apologize for making you both wait," Tsoria said, "but I had to slow down for my son, who is still nursing."

"I told you she would come, Mother," Leafa said.

"Queen Tsorianya, I'm Akima." The mother curtsied and prompted her daughter to do the same. "This is my daughter Leafa. She insisted on coming to speak with you."

"Pleased to meet you both. I brought Willow, my eldest, to help me with her baby brother, Asher. I have two more children, but they are with my husband."

Tsoria grew a bassinet a short distance from the campfire and lay Asher inside to finish his nap.

"Akima, if you are willing, I would like to speak to Leafa while Willow helps you prepare a meal. We won't walk far."

Akima nodded.

"Mind your manners, Leafa," Akima said as Tsoria and Leafa started walking through the grassy field.

"I will," Leafa said.

Tsoria asked a few questions to get to know Leafa before the queen inquired about her visit's purpose.

"How long will you punish my father for his mistakes?" Leafa asked.

"What punishment are you referring to?" Tsoria asked.

"He has markings of chains here," Leafa said as she showed the location of the marks on her arms.

"I see. Has he told you the reason for them?"

"Yes. When I was six, I asked about the marks, and he told me what he did to get them."

"And you understand why I marked the men?"

"Yes. I was mad at him for days after he told me and wouldn't speak to him. One night, my mother sat on my bed beside me and told me her story."

"Please, go on."

"Years before you became queen, my mother married a man named Teivel."

"I know him," Tsoria said, telling Leafa how she knew him.

"Teivel was a mean, drunk, and angry man whenever home. He never found anything good in my mother. She had hoped he would like her better if she bore him a child, but in an angry fit, he attacked her, and she lost the baby."

"That's tragic."

"My father, Garret, saw how he treated her and began to do little things to make her smile. It led to them having an affair behind Teivel's back. I know it's wrong, but I'm happy it happened. He's good to my mother. They eloped after Teivel left."

Leafa looked at her mother for long enough that Tsoria noticed.

"Are you worried he will return?" Tsoria asked.

"Yes, even after all these years," Leafa said.

"He won't. The Kalumat Malikan had Teivel killed in the Heblana desert."

"Oh, I'm glad he won't return to hurt my mother."

"Me too."

Leafa stopped walking and turned to Tsoria.

"Please, will you remove the markings from my father? He has worked hard to be a better man."

"Why isn't your father asking?"

"He says that bearing the marks for a lifetime is the least he deserves and won't ask for forgiveness he doesn't deserve. I had to beg my mother to let me plead on his behalf."

"Why are you asking for his punishment to be lifted?"

"Because...I love him. I know he lost his way for a while, but I'll ensure he stays on the right path."

Tsoria chuckled. "I don't doubt that. Come, my son will wake soon to be fed. Let's walk back to camp."

Tsoria talked about her children as they returned to camp and answered several questions Leafa had about the animals in the forest.

"I enjoyed the conversation with your daughter, Akima. Bring your husband, Garret, next time," Tsoria said.

"Will you remove his punishment if he visits?" Leafa asked.

"No, dear child—"

"Why not?" Leafa asked, stomping her foot almost in tears.

Tsoria smiled as she crouched before Leafa and looked her in the face.

"You didn't let me finish. I've known what you wished to ask before you traveled to see me. I've seen how each of the remaining enslavers has changed, and their markings were removed when you reached the border two days ago."

Leafa's face beamed, and her eyes sparkled as she threw her arms around Tsoria's neck.

"Thank you!" Leafa said.

"You're welcome. I wanted to hear your story before telling you."

Tsoria parted with Leafa before standing to hug Akima and whisper in her ear. Leafa saw her mother's shoulders relax and a calm smile spread across her face as she rested her head on the queen's shoulder. Leafa didn't hear what was said but smiled when she saw the sparkle in her mother's eyes before they closed.

Asher stirred in the bassinet and cried for attention. Tsoria let go of Akima, removed her son, sat in a chair grown for her, and nursed him while the evening meal was readied. The mothers bonded over stories of their children and life. Their girls played together or with the animals when not fawning over the baby. A true era of peace and understanding had begun...

…and Myrkar's black core gradually diminished.

CHARACTER LIST

MAIN CHARACTERS

Relvin Moriss (26): Islatrian. Well-built, wavy chocolate brown hair, hazel-eyed, ruggedly handsome, six-foot tall. Parents are Gregory and Daisie. He grew up in Khuraja with two brothers (unnamed) and two sisters (Fayla and Varial). When he was twelve, Relvin was sent as tribute to King Dhar's army during hard times. His favored weapons are duel daggers though he is proficient with many weapons. After the Suraddin Uprising, his view of his future with the army changes after what is left of his platoon goes rogue.

Tsorianya or Tsoria (21): Vol'aerai. Petit, red-haired, green-eyed, woman with freckles. She was stolen by enslavers from the Wispryn Weald when she was nine and sold to Lord Darrick in Wardrich to be used as a sex slave. She is raised by the other enslaved women of the "Flower Garden" and becomes especially close to Cecelia, who is like a second mother to her. Her name means "balm of grace."

ISLATRIAN CHARACTERS

Lord Darrick Tersan (63): Stout, Lord of Wardrich Castle near the border of the Wispryn Weald. He grew up with King Dhar and is a champion boxer. He was badly beaten in the last boxing match he participated in by someone seeking revenge for the death of their brother from a tournament years prior, and Darrick is never the same again.

Cecelia Hobber (50s): The pleasantly plump head of the Flower Garden in Wardrich. Sold to Lord Darrick along with her sister (who was one of many women who was killed by Darrick or killed themselves after.) She is like a mother or grandmother to the women of the Flower Garden. She doesn't let her situation dampen her spirits. She cares deeply for her ladies and is always searching for any opportunity to save any of them from a terrible life.

King Dhar Taurille (64): King of Islatria. His queen is Isida. He is a proud man who has outlasted several coup attempts including the most recent Suraddin Uprising. His family is responsible for bringing the eight provinces together and forming the Islatrian Kingdom.

Queen Isida Taurille (60): Queen of Islatria. She is married to Dhar. She and Dhar were a good match but had been at odds for many years until the treaty with the Vol'aerai.

General Rashe: One of King Dhar's most trusted Generals. He trained Relvin in advanced combat skills and recommended him as a courier guard. His wife is Daleah. Has two sons and twin daughters.

Generals Torridol, Fasid, Norrik: King Dhar's three other most trusted generals.

Commander Burmad: Burmad leads a hunting party into the Wispryn Weald, searching for Tsoria and Relvin. He is the only survivor of that hunt.

Captain Brent Harkis (50s): Captain of the Magnus Releon, King Dhar's best ship. He teaches Eviara about sailing on the way to the Tashtari Islands.

Fasik (40s): Leader of the enslavers.

Teivel (40s): Enslaver who kidnapped Tsoria. He is a mean drunk who was married to Akima and caused her to have a miscarriage.

Leidon, Lyrkin, Jorvel, Dormin, Nezara: Other enslavers.

Garret (30s): An enslaver. He has an affair with Teivel's wife and they have a daughter named Leafa. He is an enslaver who turns their life around after being marked by Tsorianya.

Karah (20s): A young woman living on the streets of Islatria after the death of her husband Kaden because her in-laws kicked her out after thinking she was cursed. She does whatever she needs to to survive and care for her crippled son. She leads her son, Shadir, on a journey out of Islatria after a street encounter when she mistakes Relvin for her dead husband.

Shadir (6): Karah's son. One of his legs was injured in an accident and it never healed well, forcing him to limp along with a makeshift crutch. His favorite fruit is apples.

Myrna Werner (24): Grew up in Drianfir. Myrna was waylaid by four members of Relvin's platoon and raped by one of them before Relvin showed up allowing Myrna to escape. She met her husband Harlan on the bridge leading out of Drianfir which prevented her from going through with killing herself. Relvin's parents became like family to Myrna and Harlan when they moved to Kharaja.

Harlan Werner (27): Husband of Myrna. His presence on the bridge leading to Drianfir kept Myrna from jumping off and killing herself. Harlan's parents shunned him because he married Myrna.

Kelin Werner (2): Son of Harlan and Myrna Warner.

Colston: The messenger Dhar sent to Wardrich under the protection of Relvin and Tsorianya to announce the treaty with the Vol'aerai.

Gregory Moriss: Relvin's father.

Daisie Moriss: Relvin's Mother.

Fayla Moriss: Daughter of Gregory and Daisie Moriss. Relvin is older brother.

Varial Moriss: Daughter of Gregory and Daisie Moriss. Relvin is older brother.

Daleah: Wife of General Rashe. Has two sons and twin daughters.

Sargon: King Dhar's most trusted scribe.

Captain Erdon: Captain of the courier guards.

Morgon: A cantankerous old courier who doesn't like Relvin or the open road, and prefers city comforts.

Sarai: A young woman of the Flower Garden with brown curly hair who helps Cecelia assess Relvin's qualities and helps Tsoria escape.

Josier: A guard in Wardrich who makes the mistake of slapping Cecelia during a search for Tsoria.

Raven: A young woman of the Flower Garden, killed by Dhar four days after Tsoria escapes.

Duke Viktor Suraddin: Duke of Ekbahn Province until he led an army against King Dhar in what would become known as the Suraddin Uprising. He, his wife, and only male heir are executed, and his daughters are sold into slavery.

Jerwin and Marlin: Only survivors of the explorers who stepped foot on Dragonhead Island.

Captain Frennik: One of the leaders of an expedition who was killed by Myrkar on Dragonhead Island.

Dorin: First mate of Captain Frennik. Became the captain after Frennik's death.

Akima (30s): She married Teivel but had an affair with Garret. She eloped with Garret and bore him a daughter named Leafa.

Leafa (8): Daughter of Akima and Garret.

VOL'AERAI CHARACTERS

Eviara (10.5): Red hair and green eyes like her sister, Tsorianya. She meets her sister for the first time when Tsorianya and Relvin save her from enslavers. She is the Priter Elorai's captain. She befriends the Tashtari princess, Tikka.

Lellia: Elder of the village north of Wardrich where Relvin and Tsoria end up after escaping.

Grryffan: Male Alpha grey wolf of the Prime pack in the Wispryn Weald. Frrynner is his mate.

Frrynner: Female Alpha grey wolf of the Prime pack in the Wispryn Weald. Grryffan is her mate.

Elders Oren, Nemica, Yarah, Torin, Vellios, Pearla, Kaled: Several elders of the Vol'aerai villages.

Mykel: The crystal tree most Vol'aerai know about, residing in the Wispryn Weald.

Myrkar: The corrupted crystal tree on Dragonhead Island.

Priter Elorai: A trio of hollarck trees formed into the first Vol'aerai boat. They select Eviara to be captain.

Gafre (50s): Vol'aerai plant specialist tasked with creating a new type of tree to be used as boats.

Terril (15): Gafre's apprentice.

Corin (23): One of the children kidnapped from the Wispryn Weald along with Tsorianya. He is sold to a Duke in Bruen Province and put to work in a mine. He escapes on a Tashtari ship named Aurora and marries the daughter of its captain.

Jeki (22): One of the children kidnapped from the Wispryn Weald along with Tsorianya. He is sold to Duke Westin in the Oundar Province. He is a healer and saves the Duke's daughter's life. He became instrumental in transforming the Oundar Province's slave labor practices before Tsorianya signed a treaty with King Dhar.

Jestin (19): One of the children kidnapped from the Wispryn Weald along with Tsorianya. He gets sold to Lord Damian Carvell in Mukward where he works with clay. He befriends Erza, Tahira, and Sadon, Kalumat children taken from the Heblana Desert.

Briel (20): One of the children kidnapped from the Wispryn Weald along with Tsorianya.

Aleya (20): One of the children kidnapped from the Wispryn Weald along with Tsorianya.

Voletia (??): Long white hair, quite old. Founder and first queen of the Vol'aerai. Wife of Lorca. She is thought to be long dead, but due to a mistake she made, her life is extended well beyond normal years and she goes into exile in the mountains. She passes her knowledge on to and trains Tsoria.

Lorca: Husband of Voletia. Was killed by Myrkar on Dragonhead Island.

Willow (9): First of four children of Relvin and Tsorianya daughter of Relvin and Tsorianya.

Asher (<1): Youngest son of Relvin and Tsorianya.

ᴋALUMAT ᴄHARACTERS

Farouq Majidd (40s): Malikan (leader) of the Kalumat in the Heblana desert. Father of Erza and Tahira who were taken to be slaves in Mukward.

Erza Majidd (17): Kalumat. Older sister of Tahira. She marries Jestin.

Tahira Majidd (14): Kalumat. Younger sister of Erza.

Sadon (17): Kalumat. Friend of Erza, Tahira, and Jestin.

ᴛASHTARI ᴄHARACTERS

King Arion Marín (40): King of the Tashtari Islands.

Queen Zaria Marín (30s): Queen of The Tashtari Islands.

Princess Tikka Marín (11): Long black hair. Daughter of Arion and Zaria. She hates being a princess and doesn't want to inherit the throne. She wants a brother since male heirs inherit the throne even if they are younger.

Captain Diego Monito (40s): Captain the Tashtari ship, Aurora. Competitive but is a good sport. He is married to Lucía. He has a daughter Adeline who marries Corin.

Lucía Monito (40): Wife of Captain Diego Monito.

Adeline or Adie (20): She is the daughter of Diego and Lucía Monito, and is married to Corin.

Lucas: An official of King Arion.

Safia: Lady-in-waiting to Princess Tikka.

Mina (11): A friend of Princess Tikka.

Author's Note

If you have made it this far, then you have read through my first novel. Or perhaps you decided to flip to the end of the book to see how it ends, but there are no spoilers here—you will have to flip a few more pages for that, cheater.

I hope you enjoyed the story. It's been a fun project occupying nearly all my after-work hours and weekends for almost two years. Though to be honest, there were many nights of doubts, writer's block, and wondering if I would ever satisfy the questions and suggestions of my editor, but the struggle has improved my writing, though I know there is room for growth. The process has been quite an eye-opening journey.

Thank you to my English teacher for reading my first draft and bringing up some great points for me to ponder, my workmates for encouraging me, a certain cafe owner and his employees who listened to me talk about how things were developing, a friend for critiquing my layout design, my editor for helping me make the story clearer and catching the things I failed to see, and all the readers for taking a chance on a first-time author.

To everyone: I hope you find your lighthouse in the storm—if you haven't found it yet.

—Seth Myhre

www.ingramcontent.com/pod-product-compliance
Lightning Source LLC
Chambersburg PA
CBHW020226260626
47156CB00002B/565